"What have we got?" he asked.

Speedle pulled a UV alternate light source case from the floor of the Hummer. "Well, H—we've got a mess."

Not a good omen when a criminalist described a crime scene as a "mess."

"Chauffeur, Felipe Ortega according to his license," Speedle explained. "Dead in the trunk of his limo, trussed up with duct tape."

"Dead how?"

"Looks like he asphyxiated on his own vomit."

"Somebody really had it in for this guy," Delko said. "Bad way to go."

"Evidence tell you that?"

Delko winced, shook his head.

"Work the evidence, Eric. Not your feelings?"

"Right, H."

The cell phone in Caine's pocket chirped and he withdrew it and tapped a button. "Horatio Caine."

The voice was sultry and pleasant. "You're a hard man to track down, Lieutenant Caine."

"Well, Catherine—you're a detective. I wouldn't expect less of you."

"Horatio—you recognize my voice . . . I'm flattered."

"CSI Willows from Las Vegas—you do make an impression." Caine wasted no time. "What can I do for you?"

CSI: miami™

FLORIDA GETAWAY

a novel

Max Allan Collins

Based on the hit CBS series
"CSI: Miami" produced by
ALLIANCE ATLANTIS in association with CBS
Productions and Jerry Bruckheimer Television.
Executive Producer: Jerry Bruckheimer;
Carol Mendelsohn, Ann Donohue, Anthony E. Zuiker,
Jonathan Littman
Co Executive Producer: Danny Cannon
Series created by Anthony E. Zuiker; Ann Donohue; and
Carol Mendelsohn

POCKET STAR BOOKS
New York   London   Toronto   Sydney   Singapore

This book is a work of fiction. Names, characters, places and incidents are products of the author's imagination or are used fictitiously. Any resemblance to actual events or locales or persons, living or dead, is entirely coincidental.

An Original Publication of POCKET BOOKS

A Pocket Star Book published by
POCKET BOOKS, a division of Simon & Schuster, Inc.
1230 Avenue of the Americas, New York, NY 10020

CSI: MIAMI and related marks are trademarks of CBS Worldwide Inc.

ISBN: 0-7434-8055-4

First Pocket Books printing August 2003

10 9 8 7 6 5 4 3 2 1

POCKET STAR BOOKS and colophon are registered trademarks of Simon & Schuster, Inc.

Front cover illustration by Patrick Kang

Printed in the U.S.A.

For information regarding special discounts for bulk purchases, please contact Simon & Schuster Special Sales at 1-800-456-6798 or business@simonandschuster.com

For Karl Largent—
who has made his
share of FLA getaways. . . .

M.A.C. and M.V.C.

"Gone are all my hours of pleasure,
Vanished with my vanished treasure;
for a deathly shadow fell. . . ."

—HORATIO ALGER

"Every day we meet people on
the worst day of their lives."

—GIL GRISSOM

CSI: miami™

FLORIDA GETAWAY

Prologue

Lessor Evil

THE WIND WHISTLING down from the mountains, like a mournful conscience, carried with it a solemn chill. As the sun set on Las Vegas, bringing night to a city that refused to sleep, an unusual crispness was in the air, a knife edge that keened the senses. Streaks of purple and magenta disrupted the salmon-colored sky, threatening to deliver a night as dark, if not as foul, as Gil Grissom's mood.

The supervisor of the Las Vegas Metro Police Department's criminalistics graveyard shift abandoned his black Tahoe in the white zone, flashing his ID at a protesting security guard and marching toward the entrance of the McCarran International Airport terminal, his white-knuckled fists at his sides. There he paused to search out his prey—Thomas Lessor, vice president of operations for Boyle Hotels, Inc., sauntering away from his stretch limo as a skycap struggled to keep up.

Tall, blond, and decked out in a suit that cost about half again as much as Grissom's monthly condo bill, Lessor strode the sidewalk with the confidence of a killer who was getting away with murder. Terminal doors opened before him, much as the court system had, not so long ago. Grissom quietly seethed, following Lessor as the man swaggered toward the security gate, the skycap peeling off to check the killer's bags.

The cell phone in Grissom's jacket pocket felt heavy. He willed it to ring, but the cell ignored him. Catherine Willows, his second in command, would call him any moment now, to tell him they had the new evidence needed to hold Lessor . . . or else Grissom would have to stand by and watch as a murderer caught a first-class flight to Florida.

Grissom's team had worked hard tracking down the killer of Erica Hardy. The young woman in question was a singer who'd built a devoted local following and a growing reputation that had just started to attract some national coverage and the much-needed tourists who were the town's life's blood. Her regular gig had been fronting a small jazz combo in the lounge at the Oasis, one of Vegas's new swank, high-end, high-concept hotel-casinos, this one recalling the Rat Pack cool of the sixties.

Then Erica Hardy's nude body had been found in her apartment on her bathroom floor. The singer had been beaten, strangled, and sexually attacked. Detective Barney Evans had theorized that the murder was just another senseless, brutal sex crime.

Following the sparse but telling evidence—the lack of any fingerprints but the victim's on the tub indicated gloves on the part of the perpetrator—Grissom and his team had interpreted the crime scene a different way.

Erica Hardy's beating had been so severe, her face so pulverized, that she had to be identified by her fingerprints. Grissom prided himself on a reserved, even remote response to even the most sobering crime scene evidence, but he had felt a shudder of sympathy for the dead woman when he heard the autopsy report from Doc Robbins.

"She was beaten with the proverbial blunt object," Robbins said as they stood over the mutilated body that lay on the cold metal table between them. "My educated guess is an aluminum baseball bat."

"I'm not much for guesses," Grissom said.

"I'm well aware—but we've had several gang-related killings that involved that specific instrument of choice."

"Baseball bat."

"Yeah—interestingly, the beating was post mortem."

"Not the cause of death?"

"No—manual asphyxiation."

Grissom frowned. "Semen?"

"No," Robbins said with a regretful shake of the head. "You'll have to find your DNA elsewhere."

"But she was raped?"

"Yes—vaginal bruising and the presence of a common condom lubricant and spermicide."

Grissom just stared at Robbins. "This guy came to the party with a baseball bat, latex gloves and a condom?"

"I would say so."

Grissom looked down at the ugly thing that had been a beautiful woman. "This victim was not random, Doc—the killer has a motive for this murder."

Though the CSIs never found the murder weapon, they did have other strong evidence. Erica had put up quite a struggle against her attacker and they got their DNA from under her fingernails—the killer's skin.

Tracing the singer's activities, the team's resident computer whiz, Sara Sidle, ferreted out a key piece of the puzzle: Erica was the mistress of the man Grissom was now following through the airport, one Thomas Lessor, the Boyle Hotels executive who had first booked the singer into the lounge. The couple had been trading intimate e-mails for months. All had been deleted. All had been retrieved.

Boyle Hotels, Inc., a family business, consisted of two high-rise resorts—the stately and respected Conquistador in Miami Beach and the brand-new, opulent Oasis here in Vegas. With the opening of this new palace, the company's CEO, Lessor's wife, Deborah—widow of the company's third-generation owner, Phillip Boyle—had moved the corporate headquarters to their new home in Sin City . . . and her current husband had moved into his cushy new VP's office just down the hall.

Lessor's job was to book talent into the lounges and showrooms of the two hotels and his duties called for him to bounce back and forth between Vegas and Miami. Sara Sidle's digging had uncovered that Lessor appeared to be bouncing Erica Hardy as well.

When Grissom had first met Lessor, barely forty hours after the murder, the man's face bore several long, ugly scratches. Lessor claimed the cuts came from a scrap with his wife's angry cat, but a DNA test proved it had indeed been the hotel VP's skin lurking under the fingernails of Erica Hardy. Lessor had been arrested immediately, an apparent quick CSI victory . . .

. . . only since that early triumph, the case had gone seriously south.

The concourse buzzed with traffic and activity and Lessor didn't immediately notice when Grissom pulled even with him. They went only a short distance before Grissom said, "Cuts seem to be healing nicely, I see, Mr. Lessor."

Lessor stopped and turned slowly, his ice blue eyes hard, his expression unworried, his smile slight and condescending. "Mr. Grissom. Thank you for your concern. . . . Taking a much-needed vacation, I hope? So you can bring a sharper focus to your work, and not victimize the innocent?"

People behind them almost piled into the pair, who now stood calmly eyeing each other in the middle of traffic.

"No," Grissom said. "I'm just seeing off a friend."

"And who would that be?"

"Why, Mr. Lessor . . . you. I've come to feel I know you very well."

Lessor sighed and shook his head. "How disappointing. Your behavior, I mean. I really thought you were a professional."

"Maybe we should walk and talk." Grissom nodded ahead. "You wouldn't want to miss your flight."

But Lessor didn't budge. "How sad to see a man of your caliber lowering himself to such . . . harassment."

People were moving around them now, hostile.

Grissom merely smiled. "This isn't harassment, Mr. Lessor—I'm just trying to do you a service."

"And what would that be?"

"To advise you not to leave Nevada."

The slightest furrow of concern touched the man's brow. "Why? Do you have a warrant for my arrest?"

"No . . . but I will shortly. And I'd hate to see you go to the trouble of flying all the way to Miami only to have to get on a plane and fly right back."

"I see. Just trying to save me bother. And expense."

"That's right."

"I think you should run this concept past Mr. Peters. Don't you?"

Harrison Peters—Lessor's flamboyant, thousand-dollar-an-hour defense attorney—had gotten his client off by persuading a judge to throw out the DNA evidence against his client. For a criminalist of Grissom's standing, and a crime lab of their stature, having such routine, easily processed evidence disallowed was, frankly, humiliating. If Grissom hadn't had to rely on one of the dayshift lab techs to do the comparison, Lessor would still be in jail awaiting trial.

"This was a courtesy on my part, Mr. Lessor," Grissom said with dry, unhidden sarcasm. "No need to call your attorney . . ."

Lessor smiled, his straight white teeth glinting.

". . . until," Grissom completed, "I do have that warrant."

The smile vanished, Lessor's face tightened, and he removed his cell phone from a pocket like a western gunfighter drawing a side arm.

Grissom wished he felt the bravado he was displaying to Lessor; but in truth, he was stalling. Catherine Willows—the best and most experienced CSI on his shift—was no doubt at this moment hovering over the shoulder of Grissom's trusted DNA lab rat Greg Sanders, as he processed their new evidence.

Lessor's lip twisted into what might be mistaken for a good-natured grin as he punched the speed dial button of his cell phone. "You see," he said cheerfully, "I'm not sure whether I'm to sue you or the department or both."

If it had been Sanders who'd processed the original evidence, they wouldn't be in this bad place. But even Greg got a vacation every now and then, and that was why the DNA evidence found its way into the hands of a dayshift counterpart, one of Conrad Ecklie's techs, a certain Dennis Spencer.

It turned out that Spencer had once been suspected of dealing cocaine from the evidence locker. Harrison Peters made sure every case Spencer ever worked on became suspect; the media howled, and Internal Affairs got back involved, quickly finding two instances of broken chain of evidence under Spencer's watch, one of which tainted the Thomas Lessor DNA sample. Peters had his client out of jail and the evidence thrown out of court before the ink was dry on his motion.

Staring at Grissom with those icy blue eyes, Lessor said into the phone, "Put me through to Harrison— Tom Lessor." After pausing to listen, he added, "I can only hold for a few seconds, dear—I have a plane to catch."

Grissom summoned an angelic smile to cast upon the killer. Though he had no doubt that they had the right man, Grissom had been forced to watch from the sidelines as Lessor strolled out of jail, the press swarming him, buzzing like the bastard had just kicked the winning field goal in the Super Bowl.

Peters must have pulled some kind of strings because when Lessor walked out of the jail, instead of exiting unshaven and unkempt, he might have been departing some fashionable spa. The tailored Armani suit—this one the bleached tan of the desert—gave him the appearance more of a movie star than a suspected killer being led out of lockup (not that those two categories were exclusive these days).

The reporters had all cried for a comment from the released murder suspect, and he had been happy to oblige.

"I don't blame the LVMPD," Lessor said, benevolently, his tone one of pity not censure. "This is just another sad example of what cuts in governmental spending can bring—if they weren't understaffed and overburdened, surely the LVMPD would not have arrested the wrong man, nor would they have turned a blind eye to the presence of a suspected drug dealer in their own midst."

It was a pretty long-winded sound bite, but a good one, and it got all the way to CNN, who later interviewed Lessor at the Oasis against a showgirl backdrop in the lounge where the girl he murdered had once sung.

And it didn't even give Grissom pleasure to see Sheriff Brian Mobley suspend the dayshift supervisor for three days with no pay. Whatever their rivalries might be, however Ecklie might deserve this comeuppance, the bottom line was unmistakable: a killer they had nabbed, cold, was about to stroll onto a plane and fly away to some Florida beach . . .

. . . and there wasn't a damn thing Grissom could do to stop him.

"Harrison," Lessor said crisply, when his attorney finally came on the line, "I hate to bother either of us with this . . . but that would-be crime scene 'expert' is here at the airport harassing me."

He listened for a few moments.

"No, not Ecklie—the other one . . ."

In grim silence, Grissom watched the killer's face, but it gave away nothing as the man listened to his lawyer, other than perhaps (feigned?) amusement. Finally, Lessor held the phone out to Grissom. "He'd like a word."

Though the CSI supervisor had hoped for a phone call while here at the airport, this was not the one he'd longed for. On the other hand, anything to prolong this departure, or better yet to delay it, was a positive thing. He looked at the phone curiously, as if it were an object he'd never seen before.

Lessor arched an eyebrow and thrust the thing into Grissom's face. "If you don't mind—Mr. Peters bills by the millisecond."

Grissom took the phone and identified himself.

Peters's voice was the roar of a jet engine. "What in the hell are you doing harassing my client?"

"I'm in no way harassing your client," Grissom said, his voice cool, calm.

"What in God's name would you call it then?"

"I explained to your client."

"Explain it to me."

"We are developing new evidence in the Erica Hardy case and I would hate to see Mr. Lessor using up his frequent flyer miles, not if he's going to be needed back here, more or less immediately."

The silence lasted only a few seconds. "What kind of evidence?"

"When we have it," Grissom said lightly, "you'll be among the first to know." Without waiting for a response, Grissom handed the phone back to Lessor.

Lessor turned away and spoke to his lawyer.

Grissom turned and walked off a few feet, giving the lawyer and client some privacy . . . and getting some for himself. The CSI supervisor pulled out his own cell phone and punched his speed dial.

The familiar musical voice said: "Catherine Willows."

Still watching the killer, Grissom said, "Where are we?"

There was a sigh in Catherine's words as she said, "Greg's working as fast as he can, but it takes time to replicate the DNA into a sample big enough to test."

"How long?"

"A couple of hours, at best."

"At worst?"

"Come on, Gil—you know the drill. At worst . . . tomorrow."

"He'll be gone by then."

"Someone once told me, science jumps through hoops for no one."

Grissom frowned. "I told you that."

"Riiiight. Gil, I want the SOB as bad as you do, but we can only do what we can do."

"And if he jumps from Florida to some South American country?"

"So he's a flight risk." Catherine's tone attempted to minimize the situation. "We have friends in Miami. We can cover that."

"We'll need to." He hesitated. " 'Bye."

" 'Bye."

Grissom punched the END button. He had known this delay was possible, even probable. And he blamed himself—though he was lucky even to have further evidence to examine.

Police photos of Lessor when he was arrested showed not only the deep scratches on his face but a nasty gouge in his upper chest, just below the throat. Originally classified as one of the scratches inflicted by Erica's fingernails, the cut on Lessor's chest—when Grissom took a second, harder look—seemed wider than a fingernail, even a thumbnail, might leave. With his original DNA sample disallowed, Grissom embraced the possibility that the cut on Lessor's chest might have come from something else.

Only after they had gone through the struggles of getting a court order, exhuming the Hardy woman's body, and taking it back to the autopsy table was Grissom's theory confirmed: Doc Robbins discovered a sliver of tissue under Erica's left big toenail.

The sample had been taken immediately to Greg Sanders, who started replicating the DNA in order to get a large enough sample. In an ideal world it would take only minutes to develop and match DNA evidence, but in Grissom's world the process just didn't move that fast.

Lessor broke his connection, slipped his cell phone into his pocket, and cast a pitying smile at Grissom.

"Don't take it personally, Mr. Grissom—you were always working at a disadvantage."

Grissom returned the smile, his just as cold as the killer's. "Don't make the mistake of confusing luck with intelligence, Mr. Lessor."

"I make my own luck, Grissom."

The polite "Mr." had suddenly vanished, a wolf-like gleam glimmering in the cold eyes.

Grissom tipped his head in a barely perceptible shrug. "Well, this time the luck you made was bad."

Lessor strode over to Grissom and, not at all smiling, asked, "How so?"

Grissom gestured gently toward the man's neck. "I know now how you got the scratch on your chest. . . . Erica really struggled, didn't she? Not just scratching but kicking."

Lessor said nothing; he was as still as a statue.

Grissom went on: "The evidence demonstrating that wasn't discovered until recently. It will stand up in court . . . and so will you—when the judge changes your address to death row."

Lessor paled, his skin turning nearly as white as his suit. Then he blustered a laugh. "Melodrama coming from you, Grissom, I thought were a scientist."

"Science is dramatic. The strides we've made in recent years boggle the imagination. Why, ten years ago, you'd have gotten away with this."

"I didn't get away with anything. I didn't kill Erica."

Grissom smiled gently, like a sympathetic priest. "I wouldn't get too comfortable in Florida, Mr. Lessor, if

I were you. I think we'll be seeing you back in Nevada, very soon."

The killer's eyes tightened, but he offered no rejoinder.

Grissom nodded to his prey. "Have a pleasant trip, Mr. Lessor—even if it does prove to be truncated." The CSI assumed a wistful expression. "But, in a way, your travels have just begun—why, there's the trip back here . . . then the one you'll be taking up the river. Melodramatic enough for you?"

Lessor grunted a non-laugh, turned, and hurried through the security gate. Safely on the other side, he wheeled to find Grissom still staring at him. Grissom watched while Lessor went through the latest security dance, and then, finally, the murderer disappeared from view.

Back at HQ, Grissom pushed through the double glass doors into the DNA lab. Immediately to his left, in front of the polarized light microscope, Catherine Willows sat on an office chair, turning from watching Greg Sanders as Grissom came in.

Typically, her attire was understatedly chic and her blonde-tinged red hair framed her high-cheekboned face. The slacker-ish Sanders sat across the room, hovering over his worktable next to the Thermocycler. As he sat on his chair bent over his work his whole body seemed to vibrate.

"You see our friend off?" Catherine asked.

Grissom ignored the question. "Progress?"

She turned back to Sanders. "Greg?"

Sanders looked over at them, shrugged, then returned his attention to the slide on his table. "Somebody told me once, science keeps its own timetable."

Grissom frowned. "Are you quoting me, Greg? To me?"

Greg looked up from the slide. "Uh . . . yes?"

"Do you think that's a good idea?"

"Uh . . . no."

Catherine—who had earlier thrown words of Grissom back at him—seemed to be simultaneously trying to swallow her smile and disappear into her chair.

Unamused, Grissom said, "I'll be in my office," and went out.

Hours later, his regular shift had begun and the CSI supervisor was in his office, catching up on the logjam of paperwork piled precariously on his desk, when a beaming Catherine walked in, Sanders on her heels like a happy puppy.

"Nailed him," Sanders said, squeezing past Catherine, waving a file folder in his hand, giddy as a lottery winner. "Actually, *toe*nailed him."

"It's a match, then," Grissom said.

"That was his DNA under her toenail," Greg said.

Grissom consulted his watch, did some quick math, and said, "Lessor will have landed by now."

"Time to get our Miami friends on the job," Catherine said.

Hating that it was out of his hands, Grissom said, "Warrick has good things to say about the Miami people."

"As do I," she said. "Shall I call Caine?"

Grissom nodded. "See if he can give us a hand and pick up Lessor."

Catherine checked her own watch, now. "Might be kind of hard at this hour. He's dayshift, and I don't have a home number for him . . . but I'll track him down."

"Hope we do better with the Miami dayshift," Grissom said grimly, "than we did our own."

And Catherine went off to make her call, Sanders headed for his lab, and Grissom went back to work. There was no shortage of other murders in Las Vegas, unfortunately; and for the time being, Lessor was in Miami's hands.

1

Goin' Back to Miami

LIKE ALL BIG CITIES, Miami throbs and moves.

Not with the business bustle of New York, or the big-shouldered muscle of Chicago, or even the breezy hustle of Los Angeles, though it does share the latter's sun-bleached sprawl.

No.

Miami is a city of dance.

The Latin rhythms of salsa and merengue are heard everywhere, to fuel the two million souls who call South Florida their home. Miami's blood races, charging the city with an exotic vibrance—sexy, passionate, and . . . occasionally . . . dangerous.

For some, Miami was thought of primarily as a beachfront retirement community, the place where America went to die. But for the crime scene investigators of the Miami-Dade PD, Miami is also a place where on each and every sunny day, citizens and visitors, young and old alike, unexpectedly find new and unusual ways to accomplish that fatal task. . . .

* * *

Just this one last fare, Felipe Ortega thought as he wheeled the limo through the light late evening traffic, heading west on the Dolphin Expressway toward Miami International. Then he could go to see Carolina Hernandez, his latest girlfriend. Salsa music pulsed through the limo's powerful sound system—tuned to 95.7 El Sol, *"Salsa y Merengue, todo el tiempo,"* as their ad promised.

The vehicle's monster sound system was a perk Felipe relished . . . although he figured his pickup, "Thomas Lessor," would probably prefer easy listening, or maybe that baby boomer "classic rock." But in between clients, Felipe could give the stereo a real workout, playing real music.

The pleasant evening inspired Felipe to put the front windows down—why breathe recycled air when the outside world was cooperating so nicely? But the loudness of the music did get him an occasional dirty look, particularly at stoplights, before he got on the expressway. He would ignore these looks-to-kill and just focus on the strait-and-narrow, the heel of his hand keeping rhythm on the steering wheel.

Twenty-four, and slight of build for his six feet one, Felipe gave off an easygoing vibe that assured the world—and his clients—that he was harmless, even sensitive. Although this gentleness had been often misread growing up just off the famous Calle Ocho in Little Havana, Felipe had learned early in his young manhood that women appreciated his vulnerability.

As one who'd been bullied as a boy, Felipe surprisingly now found himself the subject of envy among other men. Hombres much bigger, some better-looking, most with more money, tried their luck with the same ladies; but in the end, Felipe was usually the one that won those feminine hearts.

For a decade now he had traveled the path of a Don Juan, but this new girl, Carolina, she had Felipe thinking about settling down, about retiring his Lothario lifestyle and being with just one woman forever. She was smart, she was funny, and would make as wonderful a wife as a lover, as wonderful a mother as a wife. Never before had thoughts of settling down stayed with him like this . . . it had been weeks.

Checking his watch, Felipe knew Carolina would already be home from her hostess job at the Leslie, one of the Art Deco hotels on Miami Beach. Carolina had worked there for the last year and made pretty decent money. The tall beauty, her straight raven hair flowing to the middle of her back, was to lure tourists off the Ocean Drive sidewalk and into the sidewalk café of the hotel. With her looks, it wouldn't have mattered if she had the personality of a potted plant; but she was in fact a charismatic, friendly, flirty girl blessed with a smile that could light up all of South Beach.

Thinking about her, he let the limo drift across two lanes and drew an angry honk and an obscene gesture from the pissed-off driver of a passing Geo Storm. Out of respect for the elderly, Felipe declined to return the gesture. Just then he caught sight of an overhead sign and jerked the wheel to the right, gliding the limo across two lanes just in time to catch his exit.

Following the ramp around, spiraling down through the pools of yellow spilled by mercury vapor lights, Felipe cruised through a stop sign, crossed a street, and rolled into the parking garage of Miami International Airport, the salsa music still blasting as it reverberated off the parking ramp's concrete walls.

He braked to take the printed ticket from the machine, then moved ahead. As the car rolled slowly onto the second level, Felipe reached over and shut off the radio. He made sure to turn the volume down and change the setting to some dull-as-dishwater station before even thinking about parking the car.

But even with the radio off, Felipe's fingers tapped out a rhythm on the steering wheel as he eased through the concrete maze toward the livery spots. Though much of the airport traffic evaporated at night, the limos still moved in and out at a fairly regular clip. Many of the celebrities and VIPs landed their private jets here late at night to avoid the paparazzi.

Pulling into a space, Felipe saw that tonight was a slack traffic evening. Mondays usually were, the jet set who came in for the weekend mostly long gone or on their way home by now.

Two spaces over, puffing casually on a cigarette, a white-bearded old man wearing a chauffeur's uniform leaned against a black Cadillac; Felipe didn't recognize him—a sub, maybe—but nonetheless bestowed the man a brotherly nod, and the codger waved with his smoke. Even older than Felipe's Tio Acelino, the driver looked sixty if he was a minute, and Felipe wondered idly if he'd still be renting out his car to pay the bills when he was this viejo's age.

Driving for the rich and famous was generally a young man's job, but Felipe was well acquainted with the idea that you had to do what you had to do to keep the wolf from the door. Even as lucky as he'd been in his life—and Felipe knew he had been lucky— he had to wrestle that wolf from time to time himself. Despite his natural attractiveness to women, he still had to spend some money to impress, sometimes more than he would have liked.

Married life would change all that. He and the beautiful Carolina would be partners. Who could say what wonderful vistas lay ahead, what opportunities for both of them. The excitement of such prospects, the new life ahead of him, put Felipe in a particularly up-tempo mood.

He plucked the microphone from the dashboard and keyed the button. "Dispatch—you there, Carmon?"

"What do you want, Felipe?" came a crackling voice from the speaker.

"I'm at the airport. Tell Tio Acelino."

"This your last trip for the night?"

Felipe glanced at the clock on the dash and thought about Carolina waiting. "*Si*. This last drop-off, and then I head home."

"Fine. Just let me know when you get him where he's going."

"Will do."

Grabbing the handwritten placard bearing the

client's name—LESSOR—Felipe locked up the limo, easily made his way across the lanes of light traffic, and strolled into the airport.

Between eighty-five and a hundred thousand souls passed through Miami International every day, depending on which day of the week it was, but most of those were long gone by the time Felipe entered, only a skeleton crew of the thirty-three thousand MIA employees still here at this hour. He passed a businessman towing a carry-on, a pair of women in floral dresses, and a drunk couple that looked like they'd hooked up in the airport bar and were off to a motel to do something about it. *Ah, romance,* he thought. Holding up his placard, the chauffeur stood just outside the baggage claim area and waited.

Barely five minutes later, a tall, good-looking yuma with girlish blond hair and a sharp suit pointed at the placard, then curled his finger as if scratching the air, in a condescending "come here" gesture.

Patronizing or not, the possibility of a good tip from the client caused Felipe to jump forward. A redcap was coming their way, pulling a cart with Lessor's luggage. As the businessman tipped the redcap—a ten!— Felipe took over pulling the cart and gestured to his fare, heading for the car. Lessor quickly caught up, then established a faster pace.

"Hablas ingles?" Lessor asked, striding briskly for the exit.

Practically running as he dragged the cart and willing himself not to sound annoyed, Felipe said, "Yes, sir—I'm a Miami native."

"I would have said Cubano," the man said, nothing positive or negative in his voice, just a fact.

"My grandparents on both sides fled from Castro," Felipe said conversationally, still managing to keep up as he hauled the cart. "My parents were just kids. We've been here ever since."

"Really," Lessor said, his voice cold, a signal that their chat was over.

Lessor went out the automatic doors and then Felipe finally got out in front, leading the man across to the parking ramp and then the limo. They went down the passenger side of the sleek black vehicle, Felipe knowing the man would want to sit inside, maybe pour himself a drink while the chauffeur loaded bags in the trunk. He beeped the alarm and heard the locks pop, then deposited the cart at the rear of the car, leaving Lessor by the back door.

Returning to the client, he opened the door for him and Lessor climbed in; but before Felipe could do anything else, the older chauffeur from before appeared again out of nowhere.

"Got a light, kid?" the old man asked.

Felipe shook his head. "Sorry, Viejo, I don't smoke."

The old man shook his head. "Nasty habit," he said, and a gun materialized in his hand.

The weapon was small and shiny and, for just a moment, Felipe thought it was one of those trick lighters—pull the trigger and a flame pops up. Then he looked closer and realized the viejo's beard was fake, which somehow said the gun was real, and a chill coursed through him.

"Driver!" Lessor called, sounding a little pissed. "What is the holdup?"

Holdup was right. . . .

Two more men, both wearing rubber masks, came around on either side of the car, from wherever they'd been hiding. One, on the driver's side, wore a rubber Bill Clinton mask and the other, who'd come up behind Felipe, was in a Richard Nixon mask.

Nixon eased the chauffeur out of the way and swung into the car with Lessor, a small silver pistol in his right hand as well. Felipe had been carjacked one other time and knew enough to keep his mouth shut and not look any of the men in the eye for too long. These things scared the shit out of you, but if a guy kept his head, he could survive.

Felipe heard Lessor say, "What the hell . . . ?"

Then silence. Lessor had probably seen the pistol in Nixon's hand. His client's arrogant attitude would be held in check now. But the silence spoke volumes, about Lessor's fear, and the lack of any commands from the intruder—no sounds of a robbery. Maybe all they wanted was the car. . . .

On the driver's side, Clinton kept a watch on the parking garage, his gun-in-hand out of sight, but not out of Felipe's mind.

The fake-bearded viejo—was he really an old man, or was that just more makeup?—waved Felipe toward the back of the car.

"You just relax, Fidel," the old man said. "Ain't nothin' goin' to happen to you, you behave. *Comprendo?*"

The old man dragged out the last word, making it sound like *comb-pren-doe*.

"Comprendo," Felipe said, putting the syllables back together, and nodding.

Felipe made the short walk around back, to the trunk, the old man's lack of menace somehow reassuring.

Clinton joined them in back of the car. His voice muffled through the mask, he pointed to the trunk and said, "Open it."

Felipe used his remote and did as he was told, but doubt crept into his fear now. If these *pendejos* wanted the car, why take him and Lessor along? That made it kidnapping, even if they dumped the pair alive and well along a roadside. . . .

"Give me your hands," Clinton said.

A bad, sick feeling began to crawl through his belly, but Felipe stuck out his hands.

"Behind you," Clinton growled.

Turning his back to Clinton, Felipe put his hands behind him, and then could feel the man removing the remote from his grasp, and duct-taping his wrists. For the first time, Felipe wondered if he and the client were going to get through this night alive.

"I'll do what you want," Felipe said. "You don't have to tie me up."

Finished binding Felipe's hands, Clinton spun the driver around and slapped a piece of duct tape over his mouth.

"Get in the trunk," Clinton said.

Felipe froze.

"We want the passenger, kid—not you," the viejo

said reassuringly. "Let somebody else do the drivin' for a change."

Clinton added: "Just shut the fuck up and don't raise a fuss, and you'll live through this shit no problem."

Then they helped him into the trunk and shut the lid on him. He heard the beep of his own remote click the lock.

The inside was blacker than anything Felipe could imagine, and stuffy. He could see nothing and he couldn't move much. He wasn't afraid of the dark—he never had been, not even as a child—but he certainly was scared now.

He heard them dump Lessor's bags into the backseat with their owner, or so he hoped. Next, he heard the driver's door close and a moment later the engine throbbed to life. His stomach churning, Felipe did his best to remain calm . . .

. . . but it wasn't easy. From up front, he could hear the yuma businessman's strained voice, as the man begged for his life. Though the words were garbled through the padding of the seat, that the man was pitifully pleading was unmistakable.

Occasional words could be made out. "Please," Felipe heard, the voice high-pitched, whiny. Then there would be a whole sentence where he couldn't understand a syllable, then suddenly that mournful "Please," at the end again, like an urgent "Amen" at the close of a prayer.

Then the radio came on—loud—and the audio blur of scanning for channels provided an unnerving if brief soundtrack to Felipe's discomfort. A station was settled upon and, caught in midsong, suddenly Frank Sinatra was singing, "It Was a Very Good Year."

The car stopped for a few seconds—they were paying the parking attendant, so the masks would be off. But that meant Lessor was in the backseat with a gun pressed into him, seeing their real faces. Men like this didn't leave witnesses, did they?

On the other hand, the man in the trunk told himself, that was bad for Lessor, but not for Felipe—he had seen only those rubbery presidents' faces and that fake beard. They had no reason to kill him. None. He felt panic rising in his throat.

Stay calm, he told himself, *stay calm.*

The call had come in early in the morning, a limo illegally parked across three spaces in the metered public parking lot just north of the Eden Roc.

The uniforms were about to have the car towed when one of them noticed the smell. The cop with the twitchy nose made the tow truck wait while he called in the Crime Scene team.

And now, with the sun rising and the heat of the day building, Lieutenant Horatio Caine stepped down from his silver Miami-Dade Hummer and closed the door with a snick that might have been a round fired from a silenced automatic.

Pasty white, Horatio Caine never seemed to tan, no matter how much time he spent in the Florida sun. The upside was he never got white circles around his eyes or little lines on his temples from his ever present shades, either. His red hair and freckles and that fairer-than-fair flesh bespoke an Irish heritage, and what appeared to be a constant scowl gave him the appearance of a man forever pissed off. But Caine's CSI team knew the serious expression only bespoke a natural intensity—he wasn't irritated, just focused on the work.

His vehicle sat only a few feet behind its twin, which had arrived earlier. Caine walked to the back of the Hummer and opened the rear doors.

Coming around the passenger side of the vehicle, Tim Speedle and Eric Delko strode into view. Caine started toward the limo. It sat horizontally across three spaces, rather than being pulled in nose-first. Whoever left it here wanted it to be found, this much he knew. His gut told him that the reason the perp wanted it found was not going to be a pleasant one.

"What have we got?" he asked.

Speedle pulled a UV alternate light source case from the floor of the Hummer. "Well, H—we've got a mess."

Not a good omen when a criminalist described a crime scene as a "mess."

"Chauffeur, Felipe Ortega, according to his license," Speedle explained. "Dead in the trunk of his limo, trussed up with duct tape."

"Dead how?"

"Looks like he asphyxiated on his own vomit." Speedle shrugged, made a face. "It's a little rank, H. He made a number three."

By which Speed meant the victim had evacuated both his bowels and his bladder upon dying, a common occurrence.

Delko trailed along behind the pair as they moved toward the car; a perimeter had been established by draping and tying crime scene tape around parking meters. Several uniforms stood fifteen to twenty feet away, respecting the crime scene—and avoiding the stench.

Ducking under the tape, Caine entered the perimeter and glanced down into the trunk. The sickly sweet smell of death mixed with vomit forced Caine to breathe more shallowly and through his mouth in order to keep his own breakfast down.

The body lay on its right side in an S-shape, the knees bent, the man's hands bound just as Speedle had said. Bits of vomit that had run out the man's nose clung to the duct tape gag and the man's cheek, and a small sample had puddled on the floor of the trunk. The victim appeared young, mid-twenties and Hispanic.

"Somebody really had it in for this guy," Delko said. "Bad way to go."

Caine looked up at the younger man, his expression sharp but his tone soft. "Evidence tell you that?"

Delko winced, shook his head.

Caine twitched a smile. "Work the evidence, Eric. Not your feelings?"

"Right, H."

The cell phone in Caine's pocket chirped and he withdrew it and tapped a button. "Horatio Caine."

The voice was sultry and pleasant. "You're a hard man to track down, Lieutenant Caine."

He allowed a tiny smile to find its away across his

face. "Well, Catherine—you're a detective. I wouldn't expect less of you."

"Horatio—you recognize my voice . . . I'm flattered."

"You do make an impression." Caine wasted no time. "I'm assuming this isn't a social call. What can I do for you?"

The voice on the cell phone explained the case in question, quickly and efficiently, ending with the new DNA evidence recently uncovered. Caine had heard of Lessor, and the Boyle family into which he'd married, but had never encountered Lessor or any of the Boyles, professionally or otherwise. He knew of the case vaguely because it had been covered in the local media, due to the family's connection to Miami.

"So," Caine said, "you'd like me to arrange a pickup on Thomas Lessor for you?"

"If you could handle it yourself, that would be reassuring."

He turned and surveyed the limo; this crime scene could be processed without his supervision easily enough. "Do you know where Mr. Lessor will be staying?"

"Most likely he's at his wife's hotel—the Conquistador. There's a family home, but he apparently prefers to stay at a suite there. To be near the business office."

Caine glanced north on Collins Avenue, his gaze moving toward the Westin and, just before that, the Conquistador. "I think I can manage that," he said, finally.

"Thanks, Lieutenant."

"Now, Catherine—it's Horatio."

"I'll owe you, Horatio."

He smiled half a smile. "I'll call when we've got him. What's your number?"

She told him, and he entered it into his cell phone's speed dial.

"And I'll fax the paperwork to you straightaway," Catherine said.

"Good. I'll collect Mr. Lessor and get back to you."

Caine pressed END, slipped the phone away, and turned back to his two CSIs. "You two work the scene. I've got to do a favor for a friend."

The two younger men exchanged a look of surprise.

Caine ignored them. "Who was the driver's last client?"

Delko shrugged. "Driver's sheet is gone. The limo's listed to a"—he checked his notebook—"Acelino's All-American Livery. They've got an office on Flagler in Little Havana."

"And what did they have to say?"

Another shrug. "Can't get ahold of them—they must hit the office about the crack of noon."

"But you left a message."

"I did."

"And you'll keep trying."

"I will."

"Good." Caine motioned toward the limo. "Work the scene. Call me if you get anything."

"Anything," Delko said, "or anything interesting?"

For an endless several seconds, Caine looked at

Delko with his sunglasses-obscured eyes. Then he said, "Eric, I think I'm gonna leave that judgment call up to you."

And Horatio Caine went to do his favor for Catherine Willows, never imagining that the man he was planning to arrest had been Felipe Ortega's last pickup.

2

Vanishing Act

SITTING TOWARD THE NORTH end of Collins Avenue, the Conquistador was part of a high-rise lineup that included the Westin Miami Beach, the Conquistador, then the Eden Roc, the Fontainebleau and the Four Points. Horatio Caine had been here several times over the years, in his role as crime scene investigator; but that said nothing negative about the hotel. The place had a good reputation; any resort like this would have its share of heart attacks, accidents, and the like. The Conquistador had always been a class act, and the Boyle family—particularly the late Phillip Boyle—had a classy rep to go with it.

Two uniformed officers trailing him at a respectful distance, Caine entered the air-conditioned lobby, slipping off his sunglasses, taking in the well-maintained fifties-style ambiance. It was easy to imagine Frank and Dino and maybe Jerry (with or without Dino, depending on the year) moving through this lobby with a fawning entourage, inciting wide eyes and pointing fingers and oohs and ahhs from the tourists.

Matching suits of armor stood sentinel on either side of the generously wide glass front doors, the carpeted path to the front desk red, making a bridge over the expanse of white marble floor. Rich tapestries and paintings adorned the walls, and massive windows overlooked the swimming pool and the beach beyond, with the shimmer of the Atlantic Ocean. Two elderly women sat sipping iced tea and watching the activity of younger generations outside.

Caine crossed to the desk, the cops trailing dutifully, silently, and waited for the only visible clerk to get off the phone. When the phone call ended, the clerk gave Caine a sincere smile. "Terribly sorry for the wait, sir. How may I be of assistance?"

Caine discreetly showed the clerk his badge-in-wallet ID. "I'm looking for one of your guests—Thomas Lessor."

The man's smile remained but his eyes tightened. "Mr. Lessor isn't technically a guest," the clerk said. "He's vice president. He keeps a suite here, although sometimes he can be found at the family home."

"Is he here or isn't he?" Caine asked.

The clerk seemed suddenly confused.

"It's not a trick question," Caine said. "This is official police business and I need to speak to Mr. Lessor."

"You can't," the clerk said, frowning now.

"Actually, I can. That's one of the privileges of carrying a badge."

"What I mean to say is, he's not here."

"Okay," Caine said. "We've finally established that. Would he be at the family home?"

"No."

"You're sure of that?"

"Yes. He was expected here. We were told to make his suite ready for him."

"Expected here? He hasn't arrived?"

"No. And, uh, frankly, Mr. Boyle is a bit concerned."

"Which Boyle would that be?"

"Daniel Boyle. Our manager." The clerk's eyes darted around, as if this important man might appear in a puff of smoke at the mention of his name. "Son of Mrs. Lessor, Deborah Lessor, owner of the hotel."

Caine leaned an elbow on the counter. "Father was Phillip?"

"Yes, sir. He's the son of the late Mr. Boyle."

Caine considered all of this, momentarily. "Have you checked with the airport?"

"I did that myself, sir, personally. Mr. Lessor's plane landed right on time, and he was on it—the airport confirmed that this morning."

"All right. Then where can I find Daniel Boyle?"

The clerk gestured toward a hallway beyond the chairs to Caine's left. "He's in the lounge now—working with the talent."

Caine thanked the clerk and started off toward and down that hallway, the two uniformed cops falling in silently behind him like a pair of burly, obedient attack dogs. Old-fashioned, glittery homemade signs along the way touted the Explorer Lounge and the nightly attraction, singer Maria Chacon.

An 8 by 10 black-and-white photo, in a sparkly starburst, revealed the singer to be a strikingly attractive dark-skinned woman, with big black hair, large dark eyes, and a self-confident, sultry half-smile; she had plenty of personality and even more cleavage. Caine kept walking, but the cops openly gawked. Somehow Caine just knew that Maria Chacon would be the "talent" Daniel Boyle was working with.

As they neared the double doors to the Explorer Lounge, the thumping bass of the band rolled out to meet them and he could feel it in the pit of his stomach and even in the bottoms of his feet. When he pulled open one of the doors, the volume increased to just below ear-bleed level and the bass now pounded against Caine's chest, like an external heartbeat.

The tiered room had banquettes arranged in ever-widening C-shapes with aisles down either side, stadium-style seating, the middle one aimed at the barely raised stage. The banquettes' open side faced the entertainment and Caine guessed the place probably seated about five hundred. The floor bore that same red carpeting with the coats of arms—the Conquistador consistently rolled out the red carpet for its guests. The lounge was empty but for a fourteen-piece Latin band onstage, fronted by Maria Chacon, and one man down front in the center banquette—presumably, Daniel Boyle.

On the stage, the woman looked even more beautiful than she had in the photo—in the same skimpy sparkly dress—and she seemed electrically charged as she danced around the stage.

That dress looked to be constructed entirely of silver sequins, what there was of it, cut low and high at the same time—low on top and high on the bottom. The pastel-colored lights favored her dark skin and black hair, making for an even more high-voltage performance, as the sequins reflected like countless tiny mirrors. Behind her, the band pounded away. Caine counted bass, two guitars, keyboard, drummer and two other percussionists, four horn players, and two backup singers, encouraging the vocalist with their choruses of "Shake your bon bon, baby." Maria Chacon, doing as instructed, brought the count to fourteen, as she flounced across the stage.

Immersed in his work as he was, Horatio Caine often felt bewildered by the gaiety he encountered in Miami. Didn't these people know that murders were happening out there? What was there, exactly, to sing and dance about?

As the song wound down, Caine led his little posse up the center aisle. Just as the music ended with a flourish, the man Caine assumed to be Boyle rose and walked to the foot of the stage, where he talked quietly with Maria Chacon. Caine could see that she'd noticed his presence, flicking her eyes toward him occasionally as she spoke to her oblivious boss; but she said nothing as the three officers came up behind him.

". . . and don't be shy about shaking that moneymaker a little more during that last chorus," Boyle said—his voice was like good whiskey, smooth but with a bite. "Hey, it's not like you're going to break it."

Maria rolled her eyes. Up close and in person, she was even more beautiful than the starburst 8 by 10 indicated. Her eyes were dark but flashed under the stage lights. "Jesus, Danny! I'm a singer—not a stripper!"

"Hey, honey," he said, raising his voice just a little. "You sing great—but they'll think you sing really great if—"

Before he could finish, Caine stepped forward. "Sorry to interrupt—Daniel Boyle?"

"I'm Daniel Boyle and this is a closed dress rehearsal," the man said as he turned, before seeing the uniformed cops.

Boyishly handsome, the thirtyish Boyle had high, wide cheekbones, close-cropped dark hair that was starting to recede a little, springing out in unruly cowlicks here and there. His slender frame was encased in an expensive black cashmere sweater, gray slacks, and black Bruno Magli's. His clothes said "money," and his attitude did too.

Caine flashed his badge. "Miami-Dade Police, Mr. Boyle. We understand you're concerned about Mr. Lessor not showing up here at the hotel."

Boyle frowned. "I didn't call anything in. Anyway, isn't it twenty-four hours before you can report a missing person?"

"That's a myth, sir. But do you consider him missing?"

"Well, he's not here. What would you call it?"

Boyle's gray eyes were sharp and intelligent, but carried a hint of weariness; the presence of Caine and the two cops wasn't the only thing in this life that didn't impress him much.

"We're looking for Mr. Lessor ourselves," Caine said. "I was hoping maybe you could help us."

Boyle looked impatient, but he said nothing to Caine. Instead, he turned back to the singer and the musicians. "That's all for now! Maria? . . . We'll talk later."

The singer gave him a blank look that nonetheless

struck Caine as most expressive; then she took a few discreet steps away and accepted a white hotel towel from one of the backup singers. As she moved off, Boyle turned back to Caine again, but remained silent.

It occurred to Caine that Maria Chacon could probably still hear them, as she dabbed at her sweaty hair; he didn't particularly care, but wondered if she were purposely positioning herself to eavesdrop.

Caine said, "Thomas Lessor is, I believe, your stepfather."

"Yes he is," Boyle said noncommittally. "What does that have to do with him being missing?"

On stage, the band was beating a hasty, murmuring retreat into the wings. In the end, only Maria Chacon remained.

Caine pressed on with this mildly hostile witness. "Wasn't your stepfather supposed to come to the hotel after his plane landed last night?"

Shrugging, Boyle scratched absently at one of the cowlicks. "That was the plan, but he doesn't always come straight here."

"Where else would he go?"

"He's a grown-up, Mr. Crane. He goes where he pleases."

"It's Caine. He isn't staying in your family home?"

"That's where I live. He'd be welcome, of course, but Tom prefers a suite here at the hotel. What's this about, anyway?"

Keeping his cards close, Caine said, "We need to talk to him about an ongoing investigation."

"What the hell 'ongoing investigation' could there

be? Tom hasn't even been in Miami in . . ." Boyle's
voice trailed off. "This is about that supposed murder
in Vegas, isn't it? They're not still trying to pin that
Hardy thing on him, are they? Jesus!"

"I'm not at liberty to say."

The hotel manager gestured dismissively. "The
judge threw that pile of lies out of court."

"When was the last time you saw your stepfather?"

Boyle eyed him as if deciding how far he was going
to let this go. "Two weeks ago. I spent the weekend
with him and my mother at our new resort hotel.
Why in God's name are you still hassling him after the
judge threw the case out?"

Ignoring the question, Caine asked, "How did you
feel when your mother moved out to Vegas with
him?"

That drew a nasty grin from Boyle. "You're fishing
now, Detective Caine."

"Actually, it's Lieutenant."

"Lieutenant. Just out of civic-spiritedness—I'll tell
you anyway. I had no reason to be angry when my
mother and Tom moved to Las Vegas. I was glad that
she found happiness again, and when they left, this
whole hotel fell right into my lap. Why exactly would
I be *un*happy?"

Caine said nothing, but something just didn't seem
right.

"The truth is, Lieutenant Caine, I like my stepfather
very much. Great guy. I'd even say, we're very close."

"He's a little near your age to be a father figure,
isn't he?"

"We're more like brothers."

Except one of the brothers is sleeping with Mom, Caine thought. Nodding, the CSI said, "You just don't know where he went after his plane landed last night?"

"No, and you're right, I have been worried. My people called the airport and were told Tom's plane landed around twelve-thirty, midnight and I have no idea where he went after that."

"Where might he have gone?"

Boyle shrugged. "Tom's been doing business down here for a long time—he has a lot of friends at the other hotels. Could have stayed at any one of a half dozen of 'em last night."

"But why would he do that?"

"You'll have to ask Tom."

"And he didn't call and tell you of a change of plans?"

"No. Isn't that obvious?"

Caine shrugged. "It's just, you'd think he'd call you—close as you are—to keep you from worrying."

"Well, he didn't, and I don't know that I'd have done differently in his place."

Eyes narrowed, Caine said, "You were concerned enough to have the airport called."

Boyle's eyes widened in exasperation. "Try curious! Look, he landed safely in Miami, but he's free to do what he wants. If he wanted to spend the night somewhere else, that's his decision."

Caine cast another line into the water. "Even if he spent it with a woman who wasn't your mother?"

Boyle's upper lip curled. "Tom worships my mother. He would never do that kind of thing."

"It's been well established that the woman he was accused of murdering, Mr. Boyle, was his mistress."

"'Mistress'?" Boyle snorted a laugh. "What an antiquated, moralistic word . . . but coming from a throwback like you, Lieutenant Caine, I'm not surprised." He thrust an arm, pointing toward the lobby. "You've worn out your welcome, Officer—get out of my hotel. Now."

For several long moments, Caine kept his eyes on Boyle. Finally, he said, "All right, Mr. Boyle. I'll leave your premises—that's your call—until I come back with a search warrant."

Boyle's eyes and nostrils flared. "Jesus Christ! *Tom is not here!*"

Calmly, Caine said, "Your stepfather is wanted for murder, Mr. Boyle. Harboring him could be a serious criminal offense."

"God damn!"

"And we're going to have officers watching this facility—if we see any sign of Mr. Lessor, they'll move in." From the corner of his eye, Caine saw the singer disappear into the wings. "So you might wish to spare yourself the embarrassment, and—"

"Get the hell out," Boyle said, tugging a cell phone from his pocket. "I've got a business to run. I don't have the luxury of hanging around on the taxpayer's dollar."

Caine flinched a non-smile. "Thank you for your help, sir."

Leaving the seething hotel manager to make his call—to his stepfather? to a lawyer?—Caine and the two cops headed back up the aisle and into the hall that led back to the lobby.

They hadn't gone far when a door on the right opened and a lushly black-maned head popped out—the singer, Maria Chacon.

The uniformed cop to Caine's right was startled, but the CSI held out a calming hand.

The woman stepped out and glanced quickly up and down the hall, apparently to make sure they were alone. "I need to talk to you, Lieutenant." Lieutenant—not "Officer" or "Detective"; she *had* been eavesdropping.

"Go right ahead, Ms. Chacon," Caine said, planting himself, folding his arms.

"Ssshhh!" she said. "Not here—not now. Mr. Boyle could come out at any moment and see us!"

"All right," Caine said. "How about the coffee shop at the Eden Roc, next door? In one hour?"

The dark-haired beauty considered that for a moment, then nodded. "One hour. . . . Just you. Not the blue boys."

She meant the uniformed cops.

"Not the blue boys," Caine said, quietly amused.

The two cops were exchanging glances—one confused, the other a little hurt.

"All right," she said. "Be there—it'll be worth your time, Lieutenant."

"I won't stand you up," Caine said.

She smiled, just a little. "No man ever has."

"I believe that."

And then she was back inside the lounge.

As the three cops walked into the lobby, Caine already had his cell phone out, dialing Judge Balin to get a search warrant. Caine had called Balin, a long-time law-and-order jurist who believed in dispensing justice swiftly, because he could get fast service. If Lessor was on the premises, they would find him.

His second call was to dispatch, to arrange for officers to cover the entrances, and he was told, as usual, to make do with the group he had. No way could the three of them cover all the exits, but they would have to do the best they could. One went around back to the boardwalk that stretched most of the length of Miami Beach, while the other one kept his eyes on the front door. As for Caine, he waited impatiently for the warrant that would allow him to find out if Lessor was here.

A patrolman rolled up to Caine in the U-shaped driveway of the Conquistador in less than an hour. The officer came out of his car waving the document, then hustled over. The CSI supervisor had the officer radio the cop around back as Caine ordered the one out front to remain there while he and the patrolman went inside.

After Caine handed him the warrant, the desk clerk phoned Daniel Boyle and the manager appeared from somewhere down the hall, shaking his head as he walked up to the desk.

"What now?" he asked.

The clerk handed over the warrant.

"That's my passkey to your hotel," Caine said.

Bristling, Boyle said, "I don't like your attitude."

With a shrug, Caine said, "I get that, from time to time—don't you?"

Boyle looked the warrant over. "This limits you to my stepfather's suite."

Caine nodded. "Would you like to accompany us?"

Reaching for his cell phone again, Boyle said, "Manuel, you go with the officer—I'll watch the desk."

Manuel's face showed that he didn't like the order much, but he said nothing and came around the counter with a key. "This way, sir."

Leaving Officer Jacobs on watch in the lobby, Caine followed the desk clerk onto the elevator, standing silently while the clerk fidgeted nervously as they rode up the twenty floors to the penthouse.

"Your name is Manuel?" Caine asked conversationally.

"Yes, sir."

"Ever see a TV show called *Fawlty Towers?*"

"No, sir."

"Probably just as well."

When the double doors opened, they came out into a short foyer with a large mahogany door in front of them. The CSI supervisor pulled on a pair of latex gloves.

Most of the rooms in the hotel used an electronic Ving key, but this one had a Yale lock. The desk clerk slipped his key in and swung the door open and got out of Caine's way as the CSI entered, shutting the door behind him, leaving his host in the hall.

As Caine expected, this was not your typical hotel room—no functional carpeting, rather a hardwood floor accented by two area rugs, one in the middle of the living room and a long narrow one that disappeared down a hall to the left. To Caine's right, a white sofa piled with cushions hugged the wall, facing a coffee table and two highback chairs that matched the sofa. A big-screen TV sat at an angle to the right of the sofa, in front of floor-to-ceiling windows—curtains open—overlooking Atlantic beachfront twenty floors below. The wall to Caine's left was dominated by a fireplace, the mantel arrayed with photos of Thomas and, presumably, Deborah Lessor, as well as one of a blonde Deborah and a younger Daniel Boyle. A doorway on that wall led to the kitchen.

Despite the breathtaking view, the expensive furnishings, even the family photographs, the suite had a sterile, unlived-in, showroom feel. Not only was there no sign that Lessor was here now, it was hard to imagine that he or anyone other than cleaning staff ever had been.

Still, Caine had a job to do.

He began in the living room, finding not so much as a fingerprint. His next stop was the high-tech kitchen, where a stainless-steel refrigerator, stove, and dishwasher were interspersed between sections of black countertop. A black table with service for six sat in the middle of the oversized room. He opened the refrigerator and found several untouched oversized bottles of Evian, two bottles of wine, and a six-pack of imported beer, but no real food.

The bathroom was next, and although it had larger-size toiletries than a normal hotel bathroom, the soap, shampoo, and other products were untouched. The only toothbrush in the medicine chest was still in its blister pack.

Shaking his head, Caine moved on to the bedroom. The king-size bed sat immediately to his right, the same floor-to-ceiling windows as the living room beyond that. The mattress was hard—he could have bounced a quarter off it—and although he found clothes in some of the drawers of the large armoire on the north wall, they all looked brand new, the socks still on those little plastic hangers, the handkerchiefs next to them still in their packaging.

Nothing in this apartment gave Caine any sense of the man—no magazines, no books, nothing significant about the decoration; his wife stayed here, too, from time to time, but no evidence indicated a female's presence—not even clothes or toiletries.

Caine had the distinct feeling that this suite was a fraud—that not only had Lessor spent no time here in the past twenty-four hours, but the man perhaps kept some other, secret quarters in town.

Another thought was nagging Caine. Had Lessor simply landed in one plane and caught another for some country with no extradition agreement with the United States? While they would be combing Southern Florida looking for him, Lessor would be combing some beach in Rio. Caine considered calling Catherine in Vegas and sharing these thoughts, then decided to instead wait until after he met with Maria Chacon.

The search warrant coming up empty would have disappointed him a lot more if he'd actually expected to find something here. Of course, he was pretty sure it hadn't been a completely wasted trip. He'd confirmed to his satisfaction that Thomas Lessor hadn't set foot within this apartment within the last twenty-four hours. Hell, the last six months.

But Thomas Lessor had to be somewhere, and Caine was sure this place could be taken off the list of

Miami possibilities. He needed more information to come up with any other options. He checked his watch.

In about ten minutes, Maria Chacon would be at the Eden Roc, and he didn't want to keep the singer waiting. She had something on her mind, something to share about Daniel Boyle and perhaps Thomas Lessor.

And whatever she had to give him, it was more than he had right now.

3

Lessor Is More

THE HIGH SUN ricocheted off Horatio Caine's sunglasses as he walked from the Conquistador, south on Collins Avenue. He glanced across the six lanes of traffic, past the yachts in Indian Creek, to the far side and the expensive homes that lined the bank.

Lots of money over there on the island.

A gated community of luxurious homes, only the richest of the rich gained entry. Passing Indian Beach Park and nearing the parking lot that was their crime scene, he wondered if the late chauffeur had picked up someone from that side of the creek. At the edge of the lot, he paused, then shook his head—no point overthinking it. Let the evidence tell him the story.

Most likely this killing wasn't anything more than a carjacking gone bad. There'd been quite a few of those lately, if not in quite so high profile a neighborhood. The closest had been in the park just off Rickenbacker Parkway headed into Key Biscayne. Maybe the carjackers were moving up in the world.

Caine glanced over at Speedle and Delko processing
the limo—hard at work, doing fine; though tempted,
he decided not to bother them. Better to leave the
process to them while he went on to interview the
Conquistador's eager-to-talk lounge singer.

As he entered the lobby of the Eden Roc, Caine's
sunglasses came off again and he draped them around
his neck. The differences between here and the
Conquistador, just up the street, were subtle but important.

Where the Conquistador tried hard to present itself as elegant, the Eden Roc managed to accomplish
that with little effort. The rich brown carpet was
deeper, more plush, the paneling classy, distinctive
and well maintained, and the six wooden columns
that were the lobby's centerpiece gave off an air of
Old World craftsmanship. Where the Conquistador
struggled with swank, the Eden Roc provided easy
opulence.

Crossing the lobby, Caine figured Maria Chacon
would be waiting for him in the Aquatica, the fashionable glass-enclosed restaurant that overlooked both
the pool area and the beach. Harry's Grille, the hotel's
other restaurant, was a more austere, formal dining
room and Caine doubted that the place was even open
at this hour.

So, he passed that and strode into the Aquatica.
Near the back, in the smoking section, Maria Chacon
sat in a corner booth, nervously working on a cigarette. He told the hostess that he'd just be having coffee and found his own way over.

Maria Chacon was no longer wearing the silver-sequined mini-dress—even in Miami, that would've attracted attention. Instead, she wore sleek black shorts and a zebra-printed silk tank top, her mane of black hair in a loose ponytail under a black Florida Marlins baseball cap. When she saw him approaching, she stubbed out the cigarette and began to rise.

Caine waved for Maria to keep her seat, which she did, immediately fishing another cigarette out of a pack of Doral Menthol 100's. She already had her coffee, and a waitress magically provided Caine with his before he'd barely sat down.

Maria had her back to the east wall windows; past her, Caine could see the roughhewn wood of the boardwalk and its rails, the green scrub beyond and the white beach past that, and finally—stretching just past infinity—the Atlantic Ocean. Outside the southern windows to his right, a few tourists lounged around the Olympic-sized pool. One couple had even braved the chilly water, but most wouldn't tackle it till afternoon, this time of year.

When he looked back at Maria Chacon, she seemed a lot less confident than she had on stage. Most of the makeup was washed away and eyes that had seemed radiant had dimmed considerably.

"Hope you haven't been waiting long," Caine said. "I'm in the middle of processing a crime scene."

Just to remind her he was a cop.

She glanced down at the cup of coffee in front of her, thought about something a moment, then raised her eyes back to his. His gaze met hers and then she looked away, smoking anxiously, eyes moving in thought.

Suddenly she didn't seem so eager to talk. He would have to prime the pump.

"Something I've never understood," Caine said.

She frowned up at him, exhaling smoke.

He shrugged a little. "Always surprised me how many singers smoke."

She returned his shrug with a more elaborate one. "Most of us are trying not to. . . . It's the nature of the life. Stress. Uncertainty. It's a habit I really don't make a, uh . . ."

"Habit of?" he said with a smile.

She flashed a dazzling white smile. "When I'm nervous, I do burn through my share."

"Now what would a successful, talented performer like you have to be nervous about?"

"Nothing, really. I guess it's really more . . . frustration. Agitation?"

"And you're agitated now? Frustrated?"

Just when he thought he'd finally got her talking, she began to concentrate on her smoking, her eyes moving with thought again.

"I don't mean to be rude, Ms. Chacon," Caine said, with a flinch of a smile. "But I'm on the clock. If you don't have anything for me, then—"

"He lied," she blurted.

Caine raised an eyebrow. "Who did?"

Maria's eyes darted around the restaurant, to confirm no one was watching them. Then she leaned forward: "Daniel—Mr. Boyle. He lied through his teeth, and you're the police."

"I'm well aware I'm the police. Which part was a lie? All of it, or—"

"No. I really don't think he knows where Mr. Lessor is. People have been bustling around, wondering where Tom is, all day. I mean, Daniel lied regarding his, you know . . ."

"No, I don't know."

". . . relationship with his stepfather."

Caine twitched a tiny smile. "I thought you were listening in on our conversation."

She didn't even look embarrassed; smoke dragoned out her flared nostrils. "Cops talking to the guy that pays my check? Of course I did."

"What makes you think he was lying about his relationship with his stepfather?"

"I don't think he lied."

"You said—"

"I *know* he lied. Oh, if you asked around the hotel, people would probably confirm his story. I mean, he brownnoses his stepfather. To the average eye, the two might seem close."

"And why is yours not the average eye, Ms. Chacon?"

She blew a little smoke in his direction—not in his face, not that direct a comment. Then she said, "I work for them both. And I just know, okay? Daniel hates his stepfather."

"This is an instinct? An observation—?"

"Daniel told me so."

Caine shifted in his chair. "Ms. Chacon, I observed the two of you, rehearsing. I was not getting a . . . warm and fuzzy vibe off either of you."

She smirked, tapping ash off her cigarette into her empty coffee cup. "You're a detective."

"Why would Daniel Boyle tell you that he hated his stepfather when he was generally trying to indicate otherwise to the world at large?"

She sighed smoke. "To let me know where I stood with him."

Caine frowned. "Which was where?"

"Daniel Boyle doesn't give a rat's ass about me. He's never even hit on me. He's just interested in the lounge making money. He's made it clear that it's my job to make sure the coffers kept on filling up."

"What makes the lounge's profit margin your concern?"

She gestured at herself—specifically, at her chest. "Let's just say Daniel made it clear to me which of my talents he thought would bring in the patrons."

"And he didn't mean your voice."

"He didn't mean my voice."

"For what it's worth, I don't happen to agree with him. But how do you derive his hating his stepfather?"

"It was Tom who booked me into the lounge."

"Thomas Lessor."

"Yeah. Tom's all right. Anyway, right after my first rehearsal, Daniel comes back to tell me he doesn't think I've got the greatest voice in the world, but that I had other . . . assets. The implication was that I wasn't really up to the standards of the venue. And he was wondering if I 'did' his stepfather to get the gig."

Caine frowned. "He asked you that?"

"Point fuckin' blank."

Caine just looked at her.

She glared at him, then answered the unasked

question: "No, I didn't do Tom Lessor! You think I need to do that kind of thing to get a job?"

"Of course not. I heard you sing, and I was impressed."

Her glare faded. "Thank you," she said crisply.

"And from this you've extrapolated that Daniel hates his stepfather . . . ?"

"I . . . got that feeling, yes. And then . . . Daniel spent a lot of time working with me, on the act—some of it was more useful than what you saw today. One evening, we sat and talked and drank, and he loosened up, you know, about how he felt about his stepfather. Really felt."

"Asking you if you'd slept with Lessor was a way of getting something on his stepfather, you think?"

She nodded, smoke trailing out her nostrils again. "Oh, yeah—big time! Deborah Lessor could never believe he'd ever fool around on her."

"But Daniel could."

She nodded forcefully. "Daniel hired a detective to follow Tom—both here and out in Vegas—to see if he was cheating on Daniel's mother."

"But came up with nothing?"

"Nothing that I know of. But I'm on the sidelines of this, remember."

Caine frowned in thought. "Why is Daniel Boyle so eager to bring down his stepfather?"

Maria rubbed her fingers against her thumb. "Money money money. . . . If his mama dies now, there's someone between Daniel and two hotels worth of inheritance."

"No prenup?"

"Not from the way Daniel acts, doesn't look like it. Seems to me, he'd like to get Tom out of the way, which'd put Danny boy right back at the top of the list, should Mama meet misfortune."

Caine took another sip of his coffee, but he was also ingesting, and digesting, this information. After a moment he asked, "Why seek me out like this? Why tell me, a cop?"

She made an open-palmed gesture. "I don't know. Tom's a decent enough guy, I guess."

Some people might give her an argument, Caine thought, but he said only, "And you prefer Tom to Daniel."

Her lovely face wrinkled up as if she'd smelled something foul. "Well, it pisses me off that Daniel, silver spoon and all, is such a two-faced little weasel."

"I see."

"Plus, when you see blue uniforms, and a detective like you is asking missing-persons-type questions, well . . . you start having weird thoughts."

"So, you think Daniel would be capable of something . . . more than just a lousy attitude?"

"If there's foul play involved?"

"That's the way cops put it. Little surprised to hear it come from you."

"Whatever. I can't say that Daniel is or isn't capable of something, I don't know—bad, really bad. Is Tom missing?"

"Not officially. I'm just looking to connect with him. For a friend."

"Not police business?"

Caine stood, ignoring the question. "Thank you for sharing this information, Ms. Chacon."

"Funny, him going missing right when you need to look him up," Maria said.

"Hilarious," Caine answered dryly. He paid for both coffees, and walked Maria Chacon out through the lobby, chatting with her about her work schedule, how many shows a night, just conversation growing out of a detective's innate nosiness. Then they went their separate ways, she catching a cab, he slipping on his sunglasses and walking back up the street to the parking lot and his crime scene.

Thomas Lessor would have to go on the back burner until they were further along with the chauffeur in the trunk. He made a mental note to call Vegas and bring Catherine up to speed on what little he'd learned, in his thus far unsuccessful attempt to arrest Lessor.

Crime scene tape was a flame that drew moths, but the small crowd that had been milling around earlier had pretty much dissipated by the time Caine returned, no doubt disappointed by the surface tedium of crime scene activity. The trunk lid was open, the EMTs having just removed the body and placed it on a gurney. Caine watched as they loaded it into the ambulance for the unhurried, siren-off ride to the morgue.

Eric Delko was kneeling next to the open rear driver's-side door, the young CSI using the UV light to look for something in the carpeting. Tim Speedle stood off to one side talking with Detective Adele Sevilla and jotting in a small notebook.

Barely over the Miami-Dade PD height minimum, Sevilla wore her black hair long, over her shoulders, and let it blow free much of the time. Her skin was a rich caramel, but a narrow, high-cheekboned face conspired with dark eyes to make her appear somber even when she was happy. She looked more like a business exec than a plainclothes detective, as she spoke quietly but intensely to the vaguely disheveled Speedle.

The young man looked up now, saw Caine, and nodded a businesslike hello. He turned back and said something to Sevilla, then broke off that conversation and headed over to talk to his boss, slapping the notebook against his blue-jeaned thigh.

"Hey, H."

"Hey, Speed. Find out anything about Mr. Ortega?"

"Yeah," Speedle said. "Worked for his uncle— Acelino's All-American Livery."

"Eric told me that. Did you arrange for a detective to go over and deliver the bad news?"

Looking sheepish, Speedle said, "We didn't know they were family at the time, and so I sort of . . . told 'em on the phone. . . ." Speedle made a grimace of a smile—oops.

"How did that happen?"

"They had different last names, who knew? It caught them by surprise. Hit them pretty hard."

"I guess," Caine said, both eyebrows up.

Speedle sped on. "But the owner, Acelino Lopez, said they were worried when Felipe was gone all night. That was when we found out they were uncle and nephew."

"Damn," Caine said, shaking his head, hands on his hips. "This sucks. Really truly sucks."

Speedle, stunned by his boss's uncharacteristic if quiet outburst of profanity, nervously added, "Anyway, I called Calleigh, and she went over to do a more thorough interview."

Caine sighed. "Good save, Speed," he said, meaning it.

Calleigh Duquesne was a woman of many virtues, among them speaking fluent Spanish. She would hopefully present a nonthreatening presence to the Lopez-Ortega family, her easygoing people skills counteracting the mistake of the phone call.

"So," Caine said, "what have you found out?"

Consulting his notebook, Speedle said, "Felipe Ortega—twenty-four, limo driver with six years of experience—seemed to be having a pretty normal night. On time for work at four P.M., after which he had two clients that he delivered on time. Took him about three and a half hours before his lunch break."

"Out of town trips?"

Speedle shook his head. "Lots of stops, though . . . and Ortega checked in at each one."

"Go on."

"Short dinner break. He was on a roll—four more customers between eight and midnight."

"And everything was cool."

"Cool as could be. Then he was scheduled to pick up one last client at MIA at around twelve-thirty."

Caine's eyes tightened. "When?"

Speedle double-checked his notes. "Twelve-thirty

midnight, H. Then he called into dispatch that he'd arrived at the airport, and no one heard another word from him."

"So this happened either at the airport or after he left the airport. Rest of the night seems accounted for."

"Roger that."

"So. Did he meet the client? Did he make a pickup and then a delivery?"

Speedle shrugged. "That we don't know for sure yet."

"Did you get the name of the client?"

"Yeah." The notebook came up but Caine knew.

"Thomas Lessor," he said.

"What are you, psychic now, H?"

Caine shook his head. "Pieces just fit together, that's all. I have a missing guy who was supposed to be picked up at the airport. And we have a hijacked limo scheduled for the same time as my missing guy's pickup."

"Missing guy?"

As they moved closer to the limo, Caine explained what he knew about Thomas Lessor. Delko crawled out of the limo and joined the pair.

"Got some hair," he said, holding up a small plastic bag.

Caine quickly shared the story with him as well.

"Do we have a kidnapping?" Eric asked. "Or a murder?"

"Yes," Caine said.

"How do you want to play this?" Speedle asked.

Looking toward the big black Cadillac, Caine said, "Eric, stick with the car. Any little thing will be Christmas, okay?"

"On it, H."

"Speed, we're going to rent some videos and we're not going to Blockbuster."

Speedle was nodding. "Airport security tapes."

"Bingo. Then find Felipe Ortega on those tapes and see if he made the Thomas Lessor pickup or not."

"You got it," Speedle said, turning to walk away.

"Speed! The parking garage tapes, too."

"All over it, H."

As Speed took off, Caine's hand slipped into his pocket and came out with his cell phone. This was not going to be a pleasant call.

She picked up on the second ring. "Catherine Willows."

"It's Miami, Catherine."

"Tell me you have him."

". . . I wish I could."

"Damn. Has he slipped from the country? Lessor's made several trips to Brazil in the past couple of—"

"Catherine, I don't think this is a flight situation. We don't have him and what we do have is a dead limo driver—who was supposed to be picking your man up at the airport."

He filled her in and she did not interrupt.

When he'd finished, she said, "Lessor could be using this as a cover to head south—very south."

"Could be."

"You're about to look at airport security tapes, and parking garage tapes, right?"

"Great minds think alike, Catherine."

"And if you see Lessor being abducted, what will you do?"

"We'll check both theories, Catherine, but we won't know either answer, for a while. Have you entered Lessor into CODIS?"

CODIS—combined DNA index system, the national computer database for DNA.

"Long since done," she said.

The weariness in her voice saddened Caine, who didn't like being the bearer of bad tidings to a fellow cop; but there were not a lot of other avenues open to him at this moment.

"Catherine, we're working the car. We'll see what we come up with."

"Keep me apprised?"

"You know I will. First you'll know, then God."

"I like the way you think, Horatio," she said, and was gone.

The rest of the day the crew spent on their various assignments. Calleigh interviewed the various members of the livery service and Ortega's family. Delko worked the car and the scene immediately around it while Speedle and Caine split the videotapes from the airport and searched for their victim in the footage. At the end of the shift, they met in the layout room.

The room was dominated by a lit-from-below, Lexan-covered, billiards-size table. Right now, the table held very little: the strips of duct tape used to bind Ortega's hands and feet; photos of some tire tracks Delko had taken at the crime scene; and several stills rendered from the videotapes that he and

Speedle had been working on. Nothing else in the way of evidence.

"Calleigh," Caine said, "you first."

She looked over at Speedle. "First of all, Tim," she said, in her soothing near drawl, "they weren't really upset with you contactin' them by phone. They'd been mad with worry and didn't know what to think 'til you called."

Speedle just shook his head, still embarrassed.

Calleigh went on, now directing her words to the whole assembly. "Felipe's Uncle Acelino told me basically what I assume he told Tim about Felipe's evening in the car."

"Just another routine night," Caine said.

"Except for the getting abducted and choking to death on your own vomit part," Speedle said.

The remark did not make Calleigh flinch; she had a cast-iron stomach and a steely attitude they all might envy. She only nodded.

"His cousin, Elena Lopez," she said, "told me that Felipe never did drugs, didn't run with a gang, that the only thing he ever did that you might consider—and she used the word 'naughty,' which I have to say I found charmin'—was chase girls."

"Does that move the motive onto Felipe?" Caine asked. "Did he anger someone's boyfriend?"

"I don't really think so," she said thoughtfully. "Accordin' to Elena, Felipe was in love. For a month or so, he'd been a one-woman man."

"A whole month," Speedle said.

Calleigh ignored that. "Felipe had a new girl—Carolina Hernandez."

Caine's brow furrowed. "Did we talk to her?"

"Yes," Calleigh said, and her eyes tightened just a little. "Afraid she took the news hard. She worked until eleven at the Leslie, where she's a hostess, then she drove home to her apartment in Little Havana."

Caine turned to Delko. "Amaze me, Eric."

The demand did not faze the CSI, who said, "The hair I retrieved from the limo was blond, same color as this Thomas Lessor who's disappeared, and when I ran the skin tab through CODIS, H, I got a match with the sample of Lessor's DNA your CSI contact in Vegas put in."

"Thomas Lessor was in that car last night," Caine said. "And where is our missing hotel magnate now?"

Delko shook his head. "No idea. And no other sign of him in the car—certainly not blood."

"How about luggage?"

"None in the backseat, and you saw the trunk, H."

Almost to himself, Caine said, "Catherine Willows, the Las Vegas CSI, said there was luggage."

"Then the killer or killers took it," Delko said. "Even took the driver's log. Somebody wasn't taking any chances."

"Fingerprints?"

"Wiped clean."

"Trunk lid too?"

"Dusted the trunk lid too. Wiped clean."

"Good work, Eric," Caine said. "What about tires?"

"I got plenty, but—"

"It's a parking lot," Caine said with a shrug.

"It's a parking lot. And as for any tracks that can help us, too early to say."

"Well, Speed and I have been watching television," Caine told them. "And we had some luck."

Speedle stepped forward and gestured toward the TV on the cart. "We got this from the airport security cameras. One frustrating thing: no camera at the exit, the tollbooth? Maybe we'll get lucky and the attendant'll remember 'em. Anyway, I made a dub splicing together everything that we thought was germane."

The quartet quietly watched the silent movie unfold before them.

The first shot was Ortega's limo passing into the parking garage. From a camera mounted high in a corner, they saw Felipe pull into a parking place and, after a moment, climb out of the car carrying a cardboard sign.

The next shot was inside the airport and showed Ortega coming through the door. A later shot captured him in the concourse and yet another had him walking next to a blond man toward baggage claim. They were caught one last time inside the terminal, Ortega pulling a cart with Lessor's luggage; then the shot changed again to the fisheye ceiling cam and the parking garage.

The picture was grainy and the angle terrible, but the team saw a man come up to Ortega, then two more men, after which Lessor and one of the men got into the limo, Ortega ended up in the trunk, one of the men drove the limo, and the third one—the one who'd approached Ortega—walked away, out of the shot.

"So it was a kidnapping," Calleigh said, but there was the lilt of a question in it.

Delko said, "Where did the third guy go? Was he bearded?"

Calleigh asked, "Do we have any enhancements yet?"

"Or other angles?" Delko asked.

"Slow down, troops. It does look like a kidnapping, but with the quality of these tapes it could be Jehovah's Witnesses passing out *The Watchtower*, for all we know."

Nods all around.

"And," the CSI supervisor continued, "we can't rule out the possibility that the whole thing was staged. Lessor is, after all, a fugitive from a Nevada murder charge and he might be looking for a way to disappear."

"And to distract the cops," Speedle said.

"We're the cops," Delko pointed out.

Speedle just looked at him.

"So, we have two crimes," Calleigh said, as if savoring the words. "Felipe Ortega's murder, and either a kidnapping . . . or an escape."

"One at a time," Caine said. "Let's start with going after Felipe's killer. If we get evidence that has to do with Lessor, bring that to me, and we'll sort that out as we go."

Back in his office, he called Las Vegas and told Catherine Willows about what he had seen on the videotape.

"You think it's legit?" she asked.

"Too early to tell. I'll keep you posted. You want my gut on this?"

"That would be refreshing," she said. "I work with a guy who thinks opinions are a contagious disease."

"I think it's a real kidnapping," he said.

4

Beach Party

SOUTH BEACH—the lower half of the city of Miami Beach, home to the fabled Art Deco hotels of the area—included, not surprisingly, the south beach.

And that beach could be chilly on a spring night, which of course didn't stop Jim Miller and Julie Daly. The two teens were determined to find a place where they could be alone, and the lack of pedestrian traffic on the beach made that a relatively easy task.

Julie was the most amazing girl Jim had ever met; she was smart and funny—they spent so much time laughing. Imagine a girl who liked Adam Sandler movies! And the Three Stooges! He could not believe his luck. Plus, she was right out of a Britney Spears video—not Britney, but like one of those other girls who were almost-but-not-quite as cute.

At home, Jim shared a room with his little brother, and at Julie's, her mom was always home, as were two little sisters, so they never got any time alone. When they watched TV together, there were always family members around, whichever house they chose. Only when they went out to a movie did they have any privacy. But tonight, they had skipped the movie they had told their folks they were going out to see, and had driven here to South Beach instead.

Jim had parked his mother's BMW at Collins Park and the couple crossed Miami Beach Drive hand in hand, headed for the beach. By the time they found a nice secluded spot—where the beach curved slightly, bordered by scrub brush, and they could be alone—they were almost two blocks east up from the southern end of the boardwalk that ran all the way up to the Fontainebleau.

Julie helped him spread the blanket. Then they sat on it and talked for a while, about silly things at school that day, and dumb things their respective siblings had done . . . finally, some privacy!

Maybe fifteen minutes had passed when the scent of the ocean rode the breeze and brought a chill to the air that threatened to overcome the mood and the moment.

Although they had planned on coming here, neither of them had brought a jacket. Next to him, Julie shivered, and Jim slipped an arm around her. She looked up at him then, her face shining in the moonlight, her blue eyes taking on a silver cast, her full lips only inches from his.

He kissed her.

It was tentative at first, only their lips meeting; then he felt her lips part and his tongue seemed to act of its own volition. The chill he had felt only a moment ago was gone, and he was flushed with excitement.

Her willingness banished all shyness from him, and his hands moved on their own now, too. His embrace shifted and she moaned. He'd never heard anyone make a sound like that, except maybe on Cinemax; and then a phone rang.

They both paused.

"Do you need to get that?" he asked, thinking it was her mom or something.

She was sitting up now. "It's not mine. . . . Isn't it yours?"

He sat up too. "No. I didn't bring mine."

She dug in her jeans and held up her tiny cell, which was silent, even as the phantom phone rang on. "See—it's not mine."

The phone trilled on, sounding strangely muffled.

Whoever it was, making this unwanted call, the mood was broken.

"Where's it coming from?" she asked, the ringing continuing.

They both stood, the blanket at their feet, and glanced around the moon-swept beach.

"Somebody must've dropped their phone," Jim said. "You know, by accident."

"Nobody drops their phone on purpose," she said.

He glanced at her—she seemed suddenly a little cross for some reason.

"Find it," she said, "and make it shut up."

Dutifully, Jim started crawling around on his hands and knees, while Julie straightened her shirt. The ringing seemed to be coming from just this side of the scrub brush that formed a border to the boardwalk.

With the phone still ringing, Jim started feeling

around the edge of the brush when he realized the chirping phone was behind him—he'd overshot it somehow. If he ever found the damned thing, he was going to give whoever was on the end a good cussing-out for screwing up his chances tonight.

Julie was next to him now, on her hands and knees as well, digging in the sand, like they were looking for buried treasure. "I think it's down here somewhere," she said.

She looked so cute in the moonlight. Angrily, he pitched in and started digging in the spot where Julie was frantically hauling out handfuls of sand.

"Who would bury a cell phone?" he asked.

She didn't answer—it was sort of a rhetorical question, after all—and just kept digging.

Then Jim touched something that didn't feel like sand. "I've got something!"

Stopping, Julie sat back and watched as he started excavating more carefully. Clawing at the sand, he soon realized they had uncovered a black garbage bag, inside of which the phone tittered one last time, then fell silent, as if all the cell had wanted was to be found.

This pissed Jim off even more. Now the phone had finally stopped its annoying interruption of his potential ecstasy; but they were too far into digging out the bag to quit. He knew Julie wasn't likely to say, "Oh well," and grab his hand and lead him over to the blanket and go straight for his zipper.

Finally, Jim cleared enough sand away that he could tug on a corner of the bag, but . . .

"Ick!" he said, pulling his hand away.

"What?" she asked, wide-eyed.

"It's . . . sticky."

"You think this is just somebody's garbage they buried on the beach? After a picnic, maybe?"

There was a little picnic area with tables just beyond the scrub brush.

"I don't know," Jim said. "Maybe. And their cell phone fell in or something?"

She started digging again. "Let's get the cell phone out, anyway."

"Why bother?"

"You want it to start ringing again?"

This hint of a promise that they might be able to resume their petting—however unlikely—propelled Jim back into action. He pulled hard, harder, and the bag shifted, starting to pull free from the sucking sand.

As the bag broke free, the plastic ripped, and the abrupt shift sent Jim tumbling backward, and when he came up, that sticky wetness was on his hands, arms, and chest. The sticky stuff, whatever it was, looked black in the moonlight. He looked over at Julie, holding up his damp gooey hands, and saw the girl staring into the hole, her eyes so wide the white was showing all 'round, and her face was white, too, and it wasn't from the moonlight.

She took a deep breath, then another, like someone preparing to start a race . . .

. . . and then she screamed.

Still on his knees, Jim leaned forward to look into the hole himself, to see what she had seen.

Jim felt all the air being sucked out of him and his

stomach jumped into his chest and his heart leapt into his throat.

Looking up at him, its hair matted and stiff, eyes open and staring, was a man's face. The face was attached to a head, but the head wasn't attached to anything at all.

Next to one cheek, almost as if the bodiless head were leaning against it, was a left hand, hacked off at the wrist, and just outside the hole, where it had flopped in the sand, was the right hand, similarly hacked, the cell phone lying near the stiff-fingered palm.

Julie turned to him, in shock, and grabbed at him for support. Then—apparently feeling the sticky goo he'd gotten on him and now her—pulled back and screamed again, even louder. She got to her feet and sprinted toward the surf, screaming as she went. The sound got fainter even as it echoed across the night.

Only then did Jim realize that the black all over him was black just in the moonlight. If there had been any other kind of light, the goo dripping off him would have been a wet scarlet smear of blood.

His dinner tried to make a break for it, and Jim forced it down, as he instinctively pushed away from the hole; then he scrambled toward the scrub brush and there was no stopping it. He hurled, lurching with spasms that were also, somehow, sobs. When his stomach finally emptied, Jim looked toward the ocean where he saw Julie in the surf.

She was naked and she was frantically scrubbing blood off herself.

Following her example, he tore off his shirt, dropped his jeans, and dashed toward the water in socks and tightie whities. In his wildest dreams he had never imagined they would get naked together on the beach.

And it didn't feel good at all.

Shortly after 5:00 A.M., the sky like a purple bruise the rising sun was miraculously healing, Horatio Caine was driving in almost nonexistent traffic across Tamiani Trail when his cell phone rang. He took it off his belt and punched a button. "Horatio."

"Actually," Catherine Willows's voice said apologetically, "I thought I'd get your machine. It's mid-shift, here. Did I wake you?"

"No. I'm heading in early. Don't like to let trails grow cold."

"Well," she said, "I was just going to leave you some information I thought might help."

"By all means."

"Lessor made four trips to Brazil in the last twelve months. Ostensibly to look for talent, but he's also purchased a beach house. Appears he may have been setting up a new life."

Caine picked up the thread. "Then he hired the three guys to 'kidnap' him so he could disappear."

"Yes. It's a viable theory—at least, one that fits the facts, such as we have at this stage."

"Maybe Boyle Hotels is contemplating a Rio hotel. Guy obviously likes to have living quarters handy when he's going to be doing prolonged business in a place."

"I can check into that."

"Would you, please?"

"Sure. . . . Do you have any evidence I don't know about?"

"Not really. When we spoke, it was near end of shift, yesterday. But we're hitting this hard, and early, today." The phone made its "call waiting" signal in his ear. "One second, Catherine," he said.

"No problem."

Caine clicked over to the other line. "Horatio."

"Rise and shine, H." It was Speedle.

"What's up, Speed?"

"Remember we talked about coming in early today, gettin' a head start?"

"I'm in my car now, heading in."

"Well, don't. Come to me. I got something you're gonna want to see."

"Where are you?"

"Miami Beach, south end of the boardwalk. It's Lessor."

"You found him? Dead or alive?"

"The part we found is dead. Some kids dug up a garbage bag on the beach—somebody threw away Thomas Lessor's head and his hands."

"I'll be there in fifteen," the CSI said. As he clicked back over to the other line, Caine hit the button that turned on the flashers and the siren.

Practically yelling to be heard over the siren, he said, "If Lessor's kidnapping is a hoax, Catherine, it's a pretty damn convincing one."

"Is that your siren?"

"It is. I've just been told we found our missing man's head and hands in Miami Beach."

Astonishment in her voice, the Vegas CSI asked, "Where in Miami Beach?"

"Like I said, Catherine. In it."

He assured her he'd be back in touch and roared down the mostly empty roadway.

Head start indeed.

5

According to Boyle

A PAL ON NIGHTSHIFT had called Tim Speedle in. Caine had circulated throughout the department the Vegas booking photo of Thomas Lessor, and the nightshift guy had recognized the victim. So the ball had been passed to Speedle, who'd intended coming in early, anyway.

As soon as Speedle saw the head, draped in a garbage bag, in a hole in the sand, the young CSI knew that Thomas Lessor hadn't fled the country to avoid facing murder charges in Nevada.

Farther up the beach, Eric Delko searched the area around a circle of four picnic tables while Calleigh Duquesne worked the sand with ground-penetrating radar—probably a futile gesture on a sandy beach, but maybe she'd get lucky. The GPR worked well with soil, but sand made it practically worthless.

Lessor's body had to be somewhere, though, and Speedle figured the chances were fifty-fifty that the killer would bury the body somewhere near the head. After all, who wanted to be driving around the city with a headless, handless corpse in the trunk?

Speedle continued to document the scene with his camera. Photographing took a long time, but the pictures were important. He stayed with it, working as fast as possible, not wanting to leave the head and hands under the rising sun any longer than necessary. Nonetheless, he was thorough, shooting the scene from the place where the two kids had said they were necking, then grabbing a 360 from the grave itself and then another using the nearest of the Art Deco lifeguard huts as a centerpiece.

The latter happened to be yellow with lavender trim. *Laker colors*, Speedle thought. After finishing the second 360, he took more photos from the boardwalk looking out toward the beach. You just never knew what might be important later, or what part of the scene you might have to testify about in court. Juries always liked to have photos as references and Speed was happy to oblige.

He was shooting the last of his pictures when Caine strolled up, dressed in his usual black suit and sunglasses. "You're sure it's Lessor?" he asked.

"Take a look," Speedle said and pointed toward the hole in the sand.

Caine walked and, lifting his sunglasses, peered down. "That would be a yes," he said.

"His wallet was in the garbage bag, too—all his ID."

"How did this happen to get unearthed?"

"Two kids fooling around on the beach," Speedle said, gesturing vaguely. "They heard Lessor's cell phone ringing and dug it up from under the sand."

"Where are they now?"

"Home with their respective parents. This happened around eleven—the MDPD didn't get to this till near dawn."

"Why not?"

Speedle shrugged. "The kids were scared. They freaked out. Went home. Called each other on the phone and hashed it over. Finally, the girl told her parents."

"Probably didn't want to get in trouble for not being where they were supposed to be," Caine said.

"Which wasn't on the beach, making out."

"One can assume. What detective caught this?"

"Bernstein."

Bernstein was devoted to the job and a hard worker, which Speedle appreciated. He had a no-nonsense attitude that, intimidating or not, made him one of the most popular detectives with the CSIs.

"What else have we got?" Caine asked.

"Two in the back of the head."

"Execution?"

Speedle nodded. "Looks like a pro hit, .22, maybe. Mob style."

"Any other evidence?"

Speedle gave his boss a one-shoulder shrug. "We're looking, only the sand runs from here to Myrtle Beach and there's no guarantee that the killers buried anything here other than what we found."

Caine sighed, surveyed the endless beach. "We won't find the rest of the body, but we have to keep looking. Who knows what else we'll turn up."

"You don't think the rest is buried here?"

"No. The head and hands, the ID, deliberately disposed of separately from the body. It won't be around. What I don't understand is . . . why here?"

"Why not?"

Caine gestured out to the ocean. "A short boat ride, and Lessor's identity would be so much chum. Why would professionals bury this crucial evidence in a foot of sand on a well-traveled beach?"

"So—we stop looking for the body?"

Caine arched an eyebrow.

"I know—we still go over every square inch. If there's anything, H, we'll find it."

His boss allowed a brief smile to escape. "This is a double murder now, Speed—let's stay alert. We may not have a stellar citizen in the late Thomas Lessor, but he still deserves our best . . . as does Felipe Ortega."

"Right, H."

After helping the EMTs bag the body parts and collecting the cell phone and wallet as evidence, Speedle went up the beach to check on his co-workers. Calleigh, her blue eyes hidden behind dark glasses, her long hair tied back in a ponytail, wore tan slacks and a brown-striped white short-sleeve blouse. As Speedle approached, she stopped and wiped her forehead with a damp rag.

"And what's your story?" she asked.

"Just finishing up. The body—what there is of it—is on its way to the morgue. How's your luck?"

She shook her head and sunlight glanced off her ice blonde hair. "It was a long shot to begin with."

"H says, stay at it."

Eyebrows lifted. "What a shock," she said coolly.

"Hey, guys!" Delko called. "Over here."

The pair went to Delko, whose black shirt and gray slacks were touched with sand, his field kit opened on the beach near him.

"Find anything fun?" Calleigh asked.

"Oh yeah. Somebody was partying, all right." Delko pointed at a dark spot on the side of one of the planks that made up the top of one of the four picnic tables in the circle he was working. The little area was bordered on either side by scrub brush.

Calleigh leaned in close and stared. "Dried blood?"

Delko nodded. "Looks like it. Testing it now." He held up a cotton swab that was a bright pink . . .

. . . meaning that Delko had just run a presumptive blood test using phenolphthalein, indicating that the dark spot on the picnic table was, in fact, blood.

"Looks like a photo op," Speedle said.

In her breezy drawl, Calleigh said, "I'll call for a truck to take all these tables back to HQ."

Delko said, "I'll check the sand again and see if I missed something under the table."

They all went about their various duties, and then Delko called out to them again.

"Calleigh! You got a photo marker handy?"

"I can make that happen." She reached down into her field kit and walked over to Delko with the plastic A-frame, on which the number "1" was etched. "Got a bullet for me?"

Delko smiled a little. "Is that all you think about?"

"No. I think about guns, too."

He shook his head, laughing a little. "Well, this is a battery, small one. Watch battery, maybe."

"Or maybe somebody's hard of hearing."

Delko took the marker and set it on the sand next to a small metal object. "Could be. . . . Let's hope whoever it is doesn't hear us coming."

Delko bagged the battery, and they kept at it.

Horatio Caine stood in the morgue's elevated observation room, a cubicle with an eagle's-eye view of the main one below, where Medical Examiner Alexx Woods had Lessor's head and hands arrayed on the central metal table, positioned where they would be if the rest of the body had been present. It was as if the ME were examining an invisible man who'd only partly materialized.

"You been through it, haven't you, sugar?" she asked Lessor's face, her voice soothing. She often spoke to her patients, and they would speak to her—not in words, but in the evidence they and their killers had left behind.

Caine wondered if her habit of talking to the dead was a method of distancing herself from the tragedies that regularly appeared on her silver table; or was it just the opposite, a method of personalizing the victims? He had never asked. Probably he never would.

Both Caine and Alexx wore headsets that allowed them to hear everything the other said. Upstairs, watching the autopsy through a computer monitor, Caine said, "Magnify four times, please."

The image on the monitor grew by four as the computer carried out the voice command.

There were ongoing political squabbles over funding the crime lab in so elaborate a manner; but Caine's arrest and conviction record was just what Miami needed in a day and age when their once idyllic city had become unfortunately identified with crime. Those who considered Caine's "toys" an indulgence didn't understand the realities of criminal investigation in the twenty-first century. To Caine, any "toy" that made it easier for his team to serve justice was worth its price.

Right now he was studying the entrance wounds at the back of the skull at the same time as Alexx, down in the main room.

"Double tap," he said.

"Small caliber," she added. "Could be a mob hit."

"I had the same thought."

"Head and hands removed to make ID of the body difficult to impossible."

"Yes," Caine said, "but buried on the beach not far from the picnic table where the dismemberment apparently took place."

Alexx did not offer an opinion on why that might be; this was outside of her purview. She asked, "Did the victim have a history with organized crime?"

"Not that we know of, but he was in the hotel industry both here and in Vegas. The thought isn't beyond the pale. Any luck with the bullets?"

She was having a closer look. "There's no exit wound, so they should still be in there. If it's a .22, which is what the entrance wound looks like, it could have pinballed around. . . . If the little devils're in there, I'll find them."

"I know you will," Caine said, his voice as soothing as hers had been to the corpse. "What about the points where he was dismembered?"

She held up the hands, looking at the fairly smooth amputation cuts. "Sharp," she said. "Wide blade."

"Magnify two times," Caine said to the monitor, and took a closer look himself.

The cut looked very smooth—no interruptions, no serrations, nothing to make it appear that it took the killer more than one blow with whatever tool he used to dismember the body.

He asked, "Any ideas, Alexx?"

She shrugged. "Could be a machete. You know the Columbians and the Haitians are both partial to them—Cubans, too."

The crime unspooled in Caine's mind's eye. . . .

Lessor gets off the plane, and his driver Felipe Ortega is waiting for him, holding up a name placard. The two meet, gather Lessor's luggage, and head for the door. In the parking garage, the three men are waiting. They load Lessor and his bags in the back, bind Ortega, and stuff him in the trunk.

This much Caine has seen on the airport security videotapes, lousy though they were. The difference was, now he knew it wasn't staged.

The killers drive the limousine to the parking lot on Collins Avenue, force Lessor outside onto the beach, and put two in his head, leaving the limo unstained by blood.

Lessor's body is transported to the picnic area—deserted on a cold night, hidden from view of the boardwalk by scrub brush—and the head and hands are cut off. The rest of the body is cut into pieces, too, possibly put in several bags, and disposed of elsewhere. The head and hands and the victim's personal effects are buried on the nearby beach. . . .

Had they been interrupted? What caused them to

hurriedly bury the most readily identifiable body parts?

The car is moved into a spot where it will be easily found, so that the chauffeur will be recovered alive. This is a hit— only Lessor targeted, and the masks have kept the chauffeur from being a viable witness; no need to kill him . . .

. . . only something goes wrong—Ortega gets sick and when he can't open his mouth, he asphyxiates on his own vomit.

"What can you tell me about Ortega?" Caine asked.

Alexx moved to the late chauffeur's lanky corpse on another metal table and looked up toward Caine, in the observation perch. "I think he was scared to death, Horatio."

"Who wouldn't be under those circumstances?"

"No," she said, an uncharacteristic edge in her tone. "I mean literally scared to death. He may have been clinically claustrophobic, reacting to the small space; or he heard the gunshots and figured he was next. Fear is not just a mental state, Horatio."

"It's physical," he said, with her now.

"Yes," she said. "His epinephrine level went through the roof—blood glucose, blood glycerol, and blood fatty acid levels were all raised from sympathetic impulses sent by the hypothalamus."

"Panic attack," Caine said.

"Panic attack," she nodded. "Which led to his vomiting, and the duct tape kept him from being able to expel."

"And he asphyxiated."

"He had no other choice."

This confirmed Caine's own view. He said, "Okay, let's get the testing done on Lessor—start with finding those bullets, get them to Calleigh, and both of you keep me posted."

"Heading somewhere?"

"I'm going to inform Lessor's stepson of this death in the family."

"I don't envy you."

"Actually, it's going to be interesting. Lessor's stepson hated him."

"By the time I get them," she said, nodding toward the bodiless head on the adjacent table, "the hatred's out of them. It's the other residue that helps us find the killers."

"Isn't it, though."

"I'll take care of it." Then she turned back to the body parts on the table and almost cooed, "Don't you worry, sugar—we'll find out who did this nasty thing to you."

As he exited the observation room, Caine got on his cell and phoned Detective Sevilla to ask her to accompany him to see Daniel Boyle.

"Meet you at the car," Sevilla said.

Instead of taking the big, obvious Hummer, Sevilla drove her unmarked Taurus. Caine called ahead to the Conquistador and learned that Boyle was not there, rather at the family home, a large two-story stucco near mansion on Key Biscayne. When Sevilla pulled up in front of the place, she let out a low, appreciative whistle.

"I guess if you run hotels," she said, "you get to live in one."

"Sometimes you have to check out, anyway," Caine said.

"Oh?"

"Just ask Thomas Lessor."

The lushly well-manicured lawn was slightly smaller than a football field, and—like most South Florida homes—Boyle's castle had no screen doors, just massive double oak slabs.

Caine rang the bell.

Soon the door swung open and he found himself standing before a beautiful, very pale woman in a perfectly cut white pants suit; she was tall—her eyes met his—and her dark hair was bobbed, her eyes large and light blue. She had an Audrey Hepburn neck rising out of the turned-up collar of her jacket, with a single strand of pearls tight around her throat.

"You'd be the police," she said, her voice deep and rich, but a slight tremor betrayed emotions beneath the carefully controlled surface.

Her assumption about their official status was no wild deduction: both Caine and Sevilla wore their badges, Caine's on his breast pocket, Sevilla's on her belt.

Sevilla affirmed, "Miami-Dade Police. Is Daniel here?"

Before the elegant woman could answer, a voice Caine instantly recognized as Boyle's came from inside the house. "Who is it, Mother?"

This confirmed Caine's suspicion that the door had been answered by Deborah Lessor, Thomas's wife; presumably she had flown here from Vegas out of concern for her missing husband.

"Mrs. Lessor," Caine said with a nod. "I'm Horatio Caine, with the crime lab. This is Detective Sevilla."

"You're the people who've been looking for my husband. Have you found him?"

He ducked the question. "May we come in? We'd like to talk to you and Daniel."

She stepped aside and Sevilla entered, Caine just behind her; they were barely in when Daniel Boyle appeared.

Today, the handsome if pug-nosed hotel manager wore a black cashmere pullover, black slacks, and (again) Bruno Magli loafers. Seeing Caine, Boyle's voice turned cold and hard. "If you have something to report, call first."

His mother took Boyle's arm. "Daniel—please be civil. These people are trying to help."

Caine said, "Listen to your mother."

Boyle frowned and seemed about to take things up a notch, when Sevilla got between the two men, heading off a confrontation. "Is there somewhere we can sit down and talk?"

"Certainly," Mrs. Lessor said.

To the left, a door opened on a home office and a hall that led toward the back of the house; to the right, a doorway led to the dining room and, beyond that, the living room.

Still glaring at Caine, Boyle made an open-palmed gesture toward the living room.

They all went in, Mrs. Lessor taking a seat at one end of the huge black leather sofa that dominated the far wall. The near wall was home to an entertainment center and large-screen plasma TV that seemed to Caine at least as sophisticated as his much-vaunted equipment back at headquarters.

Boyle flopped sullenly into one of two matching leather chairs that sat angled on either side of the sofa.

A low, black metal table sat in the middle of the group, matching end tables at either end of the sofa between the chairs, all the pieces seeming to hold each other at arm's length. On the left wall rested a wheeled silver cart with several liquor bottles, an ice bucket and a pitcher of water. The walls were white stucco and bare but for the occasional modern art litho. With the air-conditioning turned up at least one notch too far, the room had all the charm of a meat locker. Sevilla sat at the other end of the sofa from Mrs. Lessor and Caine perched on the edge of the leather chair to her left.

"What's this about?" Boyle asked. "Have you found him or not?"

Ignoring the man, Caine looked at his mother, and could not help being struck by her wide blue eyes. "Mrs. Lessor, I'm sorry; but we have bad news."

Mrs. Lessor turned from Caine to her frowning son, then back. "Then you haven't found Thomas?"

Caine shook his head. "I'm afraid we have. Mrs. Lessor, your husband died last night."

The woman's pale features managed somehow to fade even more, her eyes closing, her chin drooping to her chest; twin tears trailed down her cheeks.

"I . . . I knew just looking at you . . ." Her voice choked off as a sob clogged her throat.

Finally, the son rose and went to his mother, kneeling in front of her, letting her lean into his arms, hugging her as she wept, all the time repeating, "I'm sorry, I'm so sorry, Mother," his voice low, intended only for her. Boyle seemed genuinely sorry, too—but the compassion, Caine sensed, was for his mother . . . not his late stepfather.

Sevilla pulled a tissue from her pocket and leaned in, offering it to Mrs. Lessor. "We know this is difficult, but if you think you're at all up to it . . . we need to ask you some questions."

Mrs. Lessor pulled away from her son, graciously, giving herself room to sit up straight. She took the tissue from the detective, touched it to her eyes and face; then she took in a deep breath, held it a moment, and let it out in an audible rush. Boyle remained at his mother's knee, her right hand holding his left, the tissue wadded in her left hand.

"Then this is still a police matter," she said, dignified.

"It is," Sevilla said.

"Then the circumstances . . . must involve . . ."

Mrs. Lessor began to cry again. Another tissue, more sympathy from her son; but soon she steeled herself. "I want you to tell me what happened to my husband. How did he die?"

Sevilla said, "Mrs. Lessor, the circumstances were not pleasant. I must ask you to prepare yourself, as best you can."

"Go ahead, Detective." Her voice was shaky, but her face held a determination that Caine respected.

"I'm going to have Lieutenant Caine, from Criminalistics, give you the details."

"Please."

Caine said, "Mr. Lessor was kidnapped at the airport and taken to a secluded place where he was shot and killed."

"Oh dear God . . ."

"While the kidnapping was undoubtedly a terrible

experience for him, Mrs. Lessor, he died instantly. He did not suffer."

"Shot . . . shot, you say . . . ?"

"Yes. I'm sorry."

"Who did it?" Boyle asked through his teeth.

Caine tilted his head. He drained any hostility he might feel for Boyle from his voice, which came out soft, reasonable. "That's why we're here, bothering you when we would prefer not to. We are going to find the people who did this."

Mrs. Lessor touched her son's hand—a signal. Like an obedient dog, he climbed on the sofa next to her. She asked, "When can I see my husband's body?"

Sevilla glanced at Caine, who said, "In a case like this, the remains are physical evidence. We do not need an identification from a family member in a—"

"Lieutenant, I want to see my husband's body. Is there a reason why that's a problem?"

Sevilla and Caine exchanged another glance, then Caine said, "We did not recover your husband's body." There was no dancing around it. "Not in its entirety."

Fingers holding the tissue moved to the woman's mouth.

"What . . . what . . . ?"

Sevilla spat it out: "Whoever killed your husband also dismembered him."

The pale woman went gray and Boyle jumped up and ran over to the drink cart. He poured a glass of water and returned, handing the glass to his mother, who seemed to not even notice, her eyes flitting around the room as if trying to decide where to land.

"Dismembered?" Boyle asked tactlessly, sitting beside his mother, his eyes large and intensely focused on Caine.

"Yes. As for the rest of his body—"

"You will try to recover it," Boyle's mother said urgently.

"Of course, Mrs. Lessor. We're doing everything we can."

She finally seemed to notice the glass in her hand. She took a sip, then set the glass on the end table next to her. "Where did you find . . . him?"

Caine could tell that the woman would not let up until they had given her all the details; and she had a right to them.

So he said, "The body parts had been placed in a garbage bag and buried on the beach, South Beach." He explained about the two kids and the cell phone, then added, "Which brings me to my first question—did either of you call Mr. Lessor last night?"

Mrs. Lessor nodded. "I was worried when I hadn't heard from him. Daniel called and told me the police were looking for Thomas. I just wanted to hear the sound of his voice."

Sevilla picked up the questioning. "Was it common for your husband not to call for such a long period?"

She sighed. "It never used to be, but we had so much trouble with the cell phones when he made his trips to Brazil that he kind of got out of the habit, you know . . . of calling all the time. He was very busy, after all."

Caine asked, "Why did he make those trips to Brazil?"

"Business. He was always looking for new acts for

the hotels. He had an eye for talent." She mentioned several prominent recording artists who had first performed at one of the two Boyle hotels.

"Had he made any discoveries on these South American trips?" Caine asked. "That have been booked into either hotel?"

Boyle answered this one. "We were in negotiations with several acts from down there. Tom was a real starmaker, no question."

"I see." As casually as possible, Caine asked, "Was Erica Hardy on a path to stardom, you think?"

The name of the woman Lessor had killed—or in the view of his family, had been accused of killing—hung a moment in the air.

Mrs. Lessor's color returned. "I would appreciate it, Lieutenant, if you would not mention that name in my presence."

"I apologize for bringing up a sensitive subject," Caine said, "and at a time like this. But the situation with your husband in Las Vegas may be pertinent."

"That woman was a liar and an extortionist," Mrs. Lessor said, cold fury in her tone. "Bad things happen to bad people."

Like somebody cuts off their heads, Caine thought.

"The Las Vegas authorities believe your husband murdered the young woman," Caine said.

"Well, they are mistaken."

She was shredding the tissue in her hands now, an unconscious gesture Caine found interesting.

"Thomas," she was saying, "was a loving and faithful husband. Erica Hardy was an ambitious climber, who tried to blackmail Thomas into giving her more money and hyping her to record producers and other venues. The truth was she was a minimally talented singer, but she did have a local following, and Thomas continued to book her into the lounge for purely business reasons."

About halfway through his mother's obviously sincere speech, Boyle began to slowly shake his head.

"You don't agree?" Caine asked.

Boyle looked from his mother to the two detectives. "As much as it pains me to say so . . . I'm afraid my stepfather wasn't as faithful as my mother believes."

Mrs. Lessor's eyes widened, her nostrils flaring, as she recoiled from her son. "Daniel! How dare you?"

"Mother, it's the truth."

"It's the truth as you see it, Daniel, but you have no right to share these family thoughts in public."

Caine said, "Mrs. Lessor, we're not the public. And what you share with us stays with us."

"Unless it gets into court," she snapped.

"Unless it gets into court," he admitted.

She glared at her son. "You have the gall to attack Thomas after he's dead? *Moments* after we learn of his death? I'm ashamed of you. Ashamed."

"Mother . . ."

Sitting forward, Caine said, "Mr. Boyle, at the hotel, you professed to be close to your stepfather."

Stiffly came Boyle's lame response: "We were friendly."

Caine twitched a small smile. "I'm not convinced."

Boyle drew a deep breath; let it out. "I had suspicions. Strong ones. I shared them with Mother. But Thomas and I, we were cordial. We had joint business interests, obviously, and we got along . . . as far as it went."

"You felt your stepfather was . . . not faithful to your mother?"

Boyle nodded forcefully. "But Mother is right: I have no proof."

Now Mrs. Lessor sat forward; the conflict had beaten back her grief and she was again in complete control of herself. "You'll have to forgive my son, Detectives," she said. "Daniel has always been jealous of my relationship with Thomas."

She turned her gaze upon her son now, who again wore a puppy dog mien. "You never did find proof of these alleged affairs—did you, Daniel?"

"No, Mother."

Mrs. Lessor said to Caine, rather haughtily, "Which I think only further shows that Thomas was, indeed, faithful to me."

"I'm not trying to cast any aspersions on your late husband," Caine said. "He was murdered. I'm looking for motives, for enemies."

Mrs. Lessor, slightly embarrassed, said, "I . . . I understand. Forgive me, Lieutenant."

"Yours is a natural reaction. Please understand that my role here is to find your husband's murderer. We are on the same side—whether your husband was a saint or Satan makes no difference to me whatsoever, other than to examine the reasons someone might have to want to harm him."

She considered that. "I can't think of anyone. He was a charming man. People liked him."

Out of his mother's line of sight, Boyle rolled his eyes.

Caine changed tactics, wheeling toward the son. "Where were you two nights ago, Daniel?"

Mrs. Lessor's eyes flared again; she was apparently about to jump to her son's defense, but—surprisingly—Daniel put a calming hand on his mother's arm.

"It's all right, Mother," he said with a bitter little smile. "After what I said, I suppose I'm the most likely suspect now, aren't I?"

Caine neither confirmed or denied this, merely saying, "You didn't like your stepfather. There's no crime in that. What concerns me, Mr. Boyle, is that you lied to me about it, when we first met."

Boyle slipped back into his chair so he was on even ground with Caine; he did not sound at all argumentative when he replied.

"The reason I lied about how I felt about Tom," Boyle said, "is that I've always kept my real feelings from anyone—other than Mother. And, anyway, there was no reason to drag Tom's name through the mud."

"Until you had proof, you mean," Caine said.

"Until I had proof," Boyle admitted.

"So you—if you don't mind my saying—ingratiated yourself with your stepfather."

"That's right. I admit it—I brownnosed the son of a bitch."

"Daniel!" his mother said, horrified.

Boyle pressed on. "I didn't want to tip my hand. I wanted to catch the bastard cheating, so I could prove it—so I could convince you, Mother, of how wrong you were about him."

She shook her head, folding her arms, looking away from her son, eyes glistening.

Caine said to Boyle, "And when you couldn't convince her?"

Boyle shrugged. "I'm a patient man."

"Do you believe he killed Erica Hardy?"

Mrs. Lessor looked at her son with hard, accusing eyes.

"I don't know," Boyle said. "I do find that a little hard to buy. . . . Mother, I never said he was a killer. I said he was a no-good, cheating SOB." He looked back at Caine. "And sooner or later, I would have caught him. . . . Only . . . now it's over. No reason to worry about it. Or fight about it. Right, Mother?"

She said nothing.

Caine said, "If we could get back to my initial question. Where were you two nights ago?"

Boyle shrugged. "The hotel. Ask the staff. Check the security video, if you want. You don't need a warrant—I'll sign off on it. Look at the tapes and you'll see me all over 'em, until after midnight."

"Then?"

Another shrug. "I came home."

"Any proof of that?"

Boyle thought for a moment. "My driver, Ron Plummer, can confirm it."

"Anything else?"

Another moment of thought. "Yes! The security code on my house. The security company will tell you that I reset the alarm system sometime between one and one-fifteen. Only two people know that security code—myself and my mother, who was in Las Vegas at the time."

Caine glanced over at Sevilla, who'd been taking

copious notes. She said, "We'll check that out, Mr. Boyle. Thanks for cooperating."

"No problem." His demeanor arrogant now that he had the apparent upper hand, Boyle said, "I'll send my driver over with the tapes—then you can question him too."

Caine returned his attention to Deborah Lessor. "My apologies, but I have to ask. Is there anyone in Las Vegas who can verify that you were there?"

She nodded; she seemed rather distant now. "Anybody and everybody in the Oasis Hotel. I was staying in the suite that Thomas and I keep there. I had room service for dinner and didn't go out until breakfast the next morning."

Rising slowly, Caine smiled and said, "Thank you for your time, Mrs. Lessor, Mr. Boyle. This has been difficult for you, and uncomfortable for us."

Sevilla said to Mrs. Lessor, "We're sorry for your loss."

"Thank you," she said.

Neither Mrs. Lessor nor Boyle rose; they both were settling into a kind of shell-shocked state after the unexpected interrogation.

In the car on the ride back, behind the wheel, Sevilla asked, "So—how big a blip is Boyle on your radar?"

"Just because he's on a videotape inside his own hotel," Caine said, "doesn't mean he didn't hire this out. Lessor's death was execution style—a mob hit or a contract killing. Having an alibi is a long ways from being innocent."

Sevilla tossed off a smile. "I don't like him, either."

Caine smiled back. "Adele, you know me better

than that. It doesn't matter whether I like this guy or not. The evidence will tell us whether he's a murderer."

"Or just an asshole?" she asked lightly.

"Or just an asshole," Caine said.

Sevilla said nothing for a while, driving, thinking, then shared those thoughts: "There's a lot of money at stake here, Horatio—at least for Daniel Boyle. Maybe between the money and his hatred for his stepfather, Boyle decided that the only way to deal with Lessor was to kill him."

"You don't buy this as a mob hit, then? It's just supposed to look like one?"

She looked over at him. "What do you think?"

Caine shrugged. "Double tap, small caliber, head-and-hands removed—you have to admit, it does sound familiar."

"Is there a mob motive, though? We don't have any evidence, no indication, in that direction, do we?"

"Only the nature of the killing itself. We'll take a closer look at Lessor's life, and if there were mob ties we don't know about, we'll find them."

"What about Ortega, our dead chauffeur?" Sevilla asked. "Any way this was about him, and Lessor's just a coincidence?"

Shaking his head, Caine said, "Kid was clean. I don't think he was even supposed to die."

"How can we be sure of that?"

He slipped off his sunglasses and showed her his eyes. "They cut up Lessor's body and buried it. A sloppy job, I grant you, but they didn't want him found. Then they turn around and leave the limo in plain sight—which you don't do unless you want it found."

Sevilla half-smirked. "They found Jimmy Hoffa's car."

"Unless I missed it on the news, they haven't located Hoffa yet. Okay, Adele, try this. If you double-tap Lessor and cut him up, why not do the same to the chauffeur? Why leave the guy trussed up in the trunk?"

"If his death was an accident, maybe . . ."

". . . or maybe," Caine said, "he meant nothing to you and you left him to be found alive."

Sevilla nodded, seeing it now, but her jaw remained set. "Only the kid died an accidental death. But we're in Felonyville, so it's still murder."

"It's two murders," Caine said, making a peace sign. "It's just too damn bad that the death of a prick like Lessor had to lead to an innocent kid like Felipe buying it, too."

And they drove on in somber silence.

6

Deuces Wild

DISGUSTED WITH HERSELF, Calleigh Duquesne shook her head over her microscope, her ponytail swinging back and forth like a platinum pendulum.

The CSI wasn't often wrong when estimating the caliber of a bullet from an entrance wound; but she had missed Thomas Lessor's. Just by a titch, granted . . . but a miss was a miss. She had figured on a .22 and the culprit had turned out to be a .25. To most, the difference would have been impossible to see, let alone recognize; Calleigh chastised herself all the same. "Bullet Girl" just didn't make ballistics mistakes.

She sat looking at a side-by-side of the two slugs retrieved from Thomas Lessor's skull. Each had tiny lines carved in it from the rifling of the barrel through which it had been fired. A deep gouge in the one on the left was surrounded by tinier scratches flying down either side of it, like tailing streamers. The bullet on the right, though, seemed to have only the stream-

ers. Slowly, Calleigh rotated it, the deep gouge showing up on the other side . . .

. . . the two bullets a match.

Lessor had been shot by one gun, most likely—
one shooter . . . *pop! pop!* and it was over, the bullets
bouncing around inside his skull like a demented
game of puddleball. She wished she had the casings as well, but—so far, anyway—that was wish-
ful thinking. Though they were pretty sure Lessor
had been cut up at the beach, on a picnic table, no
proof had surfaced indicating he'd been shot there,
too.

That didn't mean he hadn't.

The killer could have picked up the casings or
kicked sand over them . . . and it wasn't like the CSIs
hadn't looked. After Calleigh had finally given up
with the ground-penetrating radar, she'd gone back
over the area with a metal detector, in hopes of finding the elusive casings, only she'd struck out with
that, too.

The next step was NIBIN—the National Integrated
Ballistics Information Network. Developed about six
years ago by the boys and girls at Alcohol, Tobacco
and Firearms, NIBIN worked on the same basic theory
as AFIS and CODIS. The only real difference was the
subject for each: fingerprints for AFIS; DNA for
CODIS; bullets for NIBIN.

The NRA had fought the database tooth and nail,
but law enforcement was slowly winning the fight for
wider use. NIBIN would search for matching bullets
used in the commission of crimes both in Miami-Dade
and nationwide. The ATF's expansion plan had sup-

plied over two hundred sites nationwide with the IBIS (Integrated Bullet Identification System) equipment necessary to run NIBIN.

Calleigh had used NIBIN several times to match bullets from unsolved crimes within the county—and even a couple of times with crimes committed upstate—but she'd never had any luck beyond that. Still, it was a good tool, and worth the time.

Since the ATF and its partners had started using NIBIN, over 5,300 hits had been logged. So, a double tap like this one—a classic but by no means routine MO—the bullets might just show up in another hit somewhere around the area. She was lucky she had .25s. If she'd been right about the bullets being .22s, NIBIN would have been worthless without casings.

Jurisdictions didn't even bother loading .22s into NIBIN. The bullets were so soft that they were unmatchable in most cases. The casings, on the other hand, could be matched up easily. With only the bullets in the Lessor case, however, Calleigh felt like she'd caught a real break, having a killer who'd used the slightly larger caliber.

While she waited for NIBIN to do its thing, Calleigh began filling out the paperwork to send the bullets to the FBI for a neutron activation analysis (NAA). When she and the rest of the CSIs finally narrowed in on a suspect in the case—and if they found a box of bullets in said suspect's house—she wanted to be able to prove in court that her bullets, the bullets removed from Lessor, came from the same box that the killer had at home.

The NAA would do just that. It was one of those things, though, that was just too expensive to do locally or even on a statewide basis. She was only about halfway through the process when NIBIN matched her bullets.

Calleigh was blown away. Getting a match like this was like winning the ballistics lottery. But . . . New Jersey? Having never gotten a hit from out of state before, she feared a false positive—that the computer had come up only with a near match.

And a near match, like a "near hit," was, after all, a miss.

The match had come from Trenton, where the CSI of record was a firearms expert named Irv Brady. This was a helpful coincidence—Calleigh had met Brady at a ballistics convention in Dunedin, Florida, a little over a year ago; he'd been one of the featured speakers and was a well-respected expert in the field. She fumbled through her Rolodex—he wouldn't have made it into her PalmPilot—and came up with the business card he had given her at the convention.

Calleigh punched Brady's number into her cell phone.

It took only one ring. "Brady."

"Irv? That is, Mr. Brady? This is Calleigh Duquesne, Miami-Dade Police. I don't know if you remember me . . . ?"

"Nickname 'Bullet Girl'?" he said good-naturedly. "With a charming southern accent? . . . Now, I just might. How are ya?"

"Irv, I'm fine, only I'm on a case that could stand to

catch a break. And I think maybe we just did . . . in your backyard."

"Yeah?" His voice was deep and rich, like that of a really first-rate department store Santa. She hoped he had a real nice gift for her, too.

"I got a hit from NIBIN that matches a case number from Trenton."

"No kidding? I love it when the technology actually works. What have you got?"

"It's a .25—matches an unsolved homicide of yours back in '87."

"You got the case number?"

"Sure," she said, and read it to him.

Not missing a beat, Brady said, "Mob hit."

Calleigh blinked. "You remember it just from the case number? Irv, you *are* good."

"Not that good. This is just one that, well . . . it pissed me off. Moke named Johnny 'The Rat' Guzzoli went and got himself whacked in a dark alley in the Burg."

She smiled again. "You fellas out east . . . you have such colorful names for your bad guys."

"Oh yeah? This coming from a gal who works in the city that gave the world Juan 'El Patan' Padillo?"

Johnny the Slouch.

He had a point.

Her smile turned wry. "I retract the remark. So, this gun was used to kill Johnny The Rat?"

"Yeah . . . and we thought we even had a good candidate for it. A slick scumbag named Vinnie Ciccolini."

"You didn't nail him?"

"Naw. Tell ya, Calleigh, the system around here was bent as hell back then. We presented our evidence, but the judge was in some goombah's pocket, and it all got thrown out. Ciccolini walked without so much as an indictment."

"And the gun?"

"We never had it. Ciccolini hid it, or maybe got rid of it, before we got to him."

"Where is he now?"

"I don't know—dead maybe. He's gotta be, like, a hundred by now."

"Really?"

"Well. Seventy-five, eighty . . . if he's still above ground. Who knows?"

"You have a jacket on this guy?"

"Yeah, it's—I don't think it got onto the computers, but—yeah, I could round it up and shoot it your way. What's your fax number?"

She told him, adding, "Thank you, Irv. You're a doll."

"Look who's talkin'. Only, next convention you're buyin' the drinks."

She laughed. "Fair enough."

Calleigh rolled her head on the column of her neck, and rose, stretching. Then she got back to work. No point sitting on her hands, waiting—plenty to get done before Irv Brady got that file to her.

Horatio Caine dropped into his chair behind his desk. He didn't even bother to take off the black sports coat he wore—he didn't figure he'd be staying that long.

The office had all the cheer of a Holiday Inn room

housekeeping hadn't gotten around to. A green sofa (dating to the Carter administration) squatted against a blue wall. Above the couch loomed a big frame displaying painted blue spheres on a green background. Around that were crowded dozens of framed citations Caine had earned in his fifteen-plus years on the force. Against another wall stood a black chair that might have been acquired on a crackhouse raid, though frankly Caine didn't recall its actual history. Truth was, he didn't much care. The office was a place to receive information or decide where he was going next, not a room to be occupied for long periods of time. So it didn't bother him that his office seemed to be the place in the building where old furniture went to die.

He had just started sifting through the mountain of paperwork on his desk when Delko strolled in, a sheaf of papers in hand, and sat on the edge of the desk. "Lessor was dismembered on that picnic table, H."

Caine looked up. "We know this because?"

"Scraped a bloodstain from between the planks of the top. Matched Lessor's blood."

"Good. But I just know there's more."

"Found some cuts in the wood, probably where whatever they carved him up with went through. Speed's trying to figure out what made them."

Caine considered that, then said, "Try a machete."

Delko gave him a sideways look. "Why a machete? I would think a portable chain saw, maybe . . ."

"Did you find any wood dust or shavings to indicate that?"

"Well, no."

"Our ME says the wrists look as though they'd been severed with one blow—she thought it might be something like a machete."

"Well, it's a popular tool in this part of the world. I'll tell Speed."

"Please. Any other blood on the table?"

Small shrug. "A few drops on both benches—also Lessor's, but nothing else on the table. I figure the killer spread out a sheet of plastic or garbage bags and did his butcher-shop bit."

"Makes sense."

"The benches got dripped on by the runoff. The spot on the top probably came when the killer punctured the plastic while cutting Lessor up."

Caine nodded. "Any sign of the torso?"

"We're still searching, but not having much luck and it is a big beach."

"It's probably elsewhere."

"My thought, too. Are we wasting our time?"

"We follow every lead. Stay on it."

"No prob."

Delko was heading out when Caine asked, "Any luck turning up a mob connection with the hotels? I know you've been busy."

The young CSI shook his head. "I only took a quick look, H, but so far everything looks legit. Soon as I finish the picnic tables, I'll get back on it."

"Good." Caine's cell phone chirped. "Good-bye, Eric."

"Uh, 'bye, H," Delko said and walked out.

Caine picked up the phone on the third ring. "Horatio."

"It's Alexx."

"Make me happy."

"That's kind of a tall order, Horatio."

"Give it a try."

"Okay. I rushed the tox screen. There wasn't much blood left, but enough."

"And?"

"Alcohol level was .075. Lessor was tipsy, but not drunk, at least by state law. Probably just taking advantage of flying first class and having a few cocktails."

"Any other drugs in his system?"

"Not so much as an antacid or an aspirin."

"All right, Alexx. Thanks."

"Are you happy now, Horatio?"

"Ecstatic." He said good-bye and clicked off.

Half a moment later, Detective Adele Sevilla knocked on the doorjamb and Caine waved her in as he laid the cell phone on his desk. His office—the one place in this building he didn't care to be—was turning into Pro Player Stadium. At a Dolphins home game. On Sunday.

"Adele. Are we making progress?"

"Some. Starting with, I did some checking on Daniel Boyle."

"Did you find out something wonderful?"

"Moderately wonderful. Thomas Lessor's stepson knows a few mob guys—Gino Forlani and the Cappelletti brothers."

"Knows?"

Sevilla shrugged. "Gladhands with them in the lounge, seen playing golf with them once."

Caine saw where she was going. "But he's got no real ties to them."

"Not anything really solid . . . but that doesn't mean Boyle didn't get them to do him a favor."

"No, it doesn't." Caine shifted in his seat. "This town has had a mob presence since the 1920s; a guy in the hotel and entertainment business knowing mob guys 'a little' is hardly a stop-the-presses event."

Sevilla's eyes tightened. "But he does know them."

"It's not evidence."

From the door a soft but businesslike female voice said, "This might be."

Caine smiled wearily. "Come in, Calleigh. As a great detective once said, make my day."

Calleigh walked briskly in, a stack of papers held tightly in hand.

"You hold those like they're precious," Caine said.

"They are," she said, with a tiny satisfied smile. "They're the case file for a murder committed by the same gun that killed Thomas Lessor."

He sat forward now, waving her nearer the desk. "Where and when?"

"Trenton, 1987."

Sevilla did a double-take. "Trenton? New Jersey?"

Caine said, slowly, "1987?"

Calleigh nodded. "NIBIN made the match and I talked to the firearms expert who worked the case—Irv Brady?"

"Heard of him," Caine said with a nod.

"He faxed me the file on the case that our bullets match."

"And what does the file have to say?"

"Irv never found the gun, but bullets matching ours were used in a hit on a wiseguy named Johnny 'The Rat' Guzzoli."

"In 1987," Sevilla said, frowning.

"Yes," Calleigh said.

Caine asked, "Conviction?"

"No. Not even an arrest."

Sevilla's eyebrows went up. "That's not a lot of help."

"This might be," Calleigh said, holding up a page from the file. "Brady had a guy he liked for the hit— Vincent Ciccolini."

Sevilla, frowning again, said, "I thought you said no arrests?"

Calleigh's eyes widened, just a little. "Brady says a connected DA ignored the evidence—called it too circumstantial to justify going to court. Anyway, this Ciccolini—he hung out with a couple of other guys, Abraham Lipnick and Anthony Rosselli. Trenton cops thought they had their own little independent Murder, Incorporated."

"Amplify," Caine said.

"They supposedly were doing freelance hits for various mob families all over the East Coast, and sometimes in the Midwest and even in California. They had no known affiliation with any family. Again—strictly freelance."

"Any of them ever busted?" Caine asked.

Shaking her head, Calleigh said, "Closest call these boys ever had was Brady going after Ciccolini. Other than that, none of them ever did so much as a night in the tank."

"Is it worth going up to Jersey to talk to them?" Sevilla asked, finally seeming interested.

The question was posed as much to Caine as Calleigh, though it was the latter who answered.

"We don't have to—they all retired and moved . . . right here in Miami."

Half a smile dug a hole in one of Sevilla's cheeks. "Retired? How the hell old are they?"

Calleigh smiled a little. "Ciccolini and Rosselli are in their mid-seventies; Lipnick'll turn eighty later this year."

Sevilla's eyes were wide. "An assassination squad in their seventies? I don't think so. That's just a gun that's got around—passed from one dirty hand to another, over a lot of years."

Caine shook his head. "It's too big a coincidence not to look into."

Calleigh said, "Back in their heyday, they were suspected of a couple dozen different crime-related hits—and not just for the mob. They allegedly popped drug dealers, pimps, and even the odd lawyer here and there. Anybody who met the price could have whoever they chose meet their maker."

Sevilla was shaking her head. "A geriatric hit team?"

Caine was not so skeptical; and certain stray facts were forming a bigger picture in his mind. He asked Sevilla, "What happened to 'El Patan' Padillo?"

The detective shrugged. "Disappeared. The way bad guys who get on other bad guys' bad side do."

"Who had a motive to get rid of him?"

"Haitians, Jamaicans—they both hated his Cuban ass."

Caine was nodding; a faintly mocking smile was starting to form. "What about that pimp, Jimmy Martin?"

"Gone, and who cares where? The Cubans hated him for trying to recruit in Little Havana." Again Sevilla shrugged. "Everybody wanted Jimmy out of here—including us."

"How much time have we spent looking into it?"

"None. Nobody reported either of those stellar citizens missing. We had no crime scene to hand you and your team to process. . . . Why?"

"As in . . . as long as they only kill each other, what do we care?"

"Now, Horatio, I didn't say that."

"Or I should say, as long as they only kill each other discreetly, what do we care?"

"You may have a point. Don't quote me."

Caine said, "I'm seeing a pattern."

Calleigh jumped in. "I saw it too . . . and I checked. There's been a total of five crime-related disappearances in the last nine months, with no serious evidence of foul play."

This information hung in the air for several seconds while everyone contemplated it.

Then Caine asked, "How long have the Trenton boys been here?"

"Fifteen years."

Sevilla gave them both a sideways look. "They've been here for fifteen years . . . and now you think they've suddenly gone back into business?"

"What if," Caine said, twitching little smiles, "—and this is only 'what if'—a retired team of hit men got bored with retirement and resumed their business practices, taking on occasional freelance hits? Meds are expensive, after all."

"Guns and walkers?" Sevilla asked.

"Don't stereotype, Adele," Caine said, raising a gently lecturing forefinger. "Besides, you ever see any of these old boys play shuffleboard? Stay out of their way, when it's their turn."

Sevilla was shaking her head. "How can you even think it? It's absurd."

Caine shrugged. "I don't think anything . . . but the bullets from our murder match the bullets to a murder allegedly committed by someone now living in Miami. Adele—are we not going to look into it?"

"Of course we will," she said, cracking a smile. "We have local addresses for these guys?"

Calleigh referred to her notes. "Ciccolini and Lipnick live together. House on Granada Boulevard in Coral Gables."

"Nice digs," Sevilla said, rolling her eyes. "And Rosselli?"

"He and his wife, whose name is"—Calleigh checked the notes—"Rebecca, live around the corner on Palermo."

"Not far from the Biltmore," Caine noted.

Sevilla half-smiled. "You suppose they go over there every day—play golf and talk about the good old bad old days?"

They all knew that the Biltmore Hotel—built in the

twenties, with two hundred eighty rooms—had served America's elite, including the Roosevelts, Vanderbilts, and dozens of entertainers; but it had also been Al Capone's favorite hotel.

"I wonder if reminiscing is all they've been doing," Caine said.

Sevilla stood. "Let's find out."

Caine tilted his head. "Sure, Adele—it's your lead, after all."

The detective smirked. "Don't be a smart-ass, Horatio. Doesn't become you."

He turned to Calleigh. "What do you have on your plate?"

"Right now," she said, "just Lessor."

"Come along. You're the one most familiar with the file."

Founded by George Merrick during the Florida land boom of the twenties, Coral Gables was still known as "The City Beautiful." Merrick had envisioned an affluent, mostly residential city with gardens and wide boulevards; he founded the University of Miami and partnered with hotel tycoon John McEntee Bowman to build the nearby Biltmore. His dream remained realized on the Miami scene in the form of upscale houses, banyan-shaded streets, and whitestone street signs that huddled on each corner instead of unsightly metal poles. The business district was now served by over one hundred fifty multinational companies, the community still thriving.

Turning off the Dixie Highway and driving past the modern facilities of the University of Miami, Caine might have been fooled into thinking he was entering a high-tech, modern subdivision. The farther he went, though, the distinct street signs, tropical foliage in front of mostly Mediterranean homes, and narrow streets reminded him of an older, slower time when Miami was more stately, more elegant.

Caine drove the Hummer through the time tunnel of a neighborhood, sticking to Granada Boulevard until he pulled into the driveway of a two-story antebellum mansion that looked out of place among all the Mediterranean homes. White, with an attached two-car garage, the house looked gray in the half-light of the yard shaded by two large banyans.

Sevilla got out of the passenger seat; Calleigh came from the backseat, her light blue lab coat now replaced by the jacket of her navy blue suit. A soft breeze carried the promise of a surprisingly cool evening to come.

After leading the way to the door, Sevilla rang the bell. No answer. After a minute, she rang it again.

"Nobody home, you think?" she asked Caine, who was trying to look through the small windows that framed the double oak doors.

"Maybe they're out to dinner," Calleigh offered.

"Looks quiet in there," Caine said, still peering inside. He trotted over to the double garage, but the windows were opaque. Returning, he checked his watch.

"You know these seniors and their early bird specials," Caine said. "Let's try Rosselli. Then we'll stop back."

"It's a plan," Sevilla said.

Caine drove to the next corner and turned onto Palermo. He pulled to a stop in front of the two-story stucco home of Anthony and Rebecca Rosselli. Tangerine-colored, with an orange tile roof and two-car garage, the house looked like an oversize Orange Crush stand dropped onto a massive green yard. The sun was setting and lights were on in the house as Caine, Calleigh, and Sevilla walked up the driveway to a sidewalk that curved to mahogany double front doors.

Sevilla rang the doorbell, badge already in hand. They heard movement almost immediately and the door opened to reveal a slender woman, five four or five five, with the slightly exaggerated look of an actress or showgirl after too many years and too much plastic surgery.

Nonetheless, this woman—all in black, a long-sleeved silk blouse and flared slacks—was still attractive. Her short, curly red hair was an obvious dye job, latterday Lucille Ball, and her bright brown eyes were large and heavily mascaraed. Those eyes were filigreed red, however, and some smear in the mascara told Caine she'd been crying. He didn't have to be a CSI to figure that out.

"May I help you?" she asked. Her smile was friendly, if forced, and she held the door only half-open.

Sevilla displayed her badge. "Rebecca Rosselli?"

The friendly smile vanished. "Doesn't it ever end?" their hostess asked rhetorically. "Cops," she added, with a headshake, the single word coming out like an epithet. "What do you want?"

Sevilla continued to press. "Are you Rebecca Rosselli?"

"Yes. Now, I've answered your question. Answer mine: what do you want?"

"Is your husband home?"

"He is not. He'd have slammed the door in your face by now."

Not convinced, Sevilla tried to look past the woman, and Mrs. Rosselli pulled the door closed a little more. Caine glanced at Calleigh, who shrugged a little.

"Where is your husband, Mrs. Rosselli?" the detective asked.

"Why?"

Sevilla's face was stone, and an edge was in her voice. "Mrs. Rosselli, if you keep answering my questions with questions, we're never going to get anywhere."

"You think so?" A hint of a smile returned to the woman's lips.

Finally, Caine stepped forward and offered his own smile, as warm and charming a one as he could muster.

"Good afternoon, Mrs. Rosselli. I'm Horatio Caine with Miami-Dade Criminalistics and this is Calleigh Duquesne from my office. Please don't get the wrong impression. We'd just like to talk to your husband."

Mrs. Rosselli shrugged. "Well, that may be, but he's not here . . . and I don't expect him for quite a while."

Nodding, Caine asked, "Might we come in and talk to you, then?"

"Certainly, young man." Then Mrs. Rosselli glared

at Sevilla in the fading light. "A little civility goes a long way, Detective."

"I apologize if I seemed rude, Mrs. Rosselli," Sevilla said.

The woman held the door open for them, her attention now on Caine and Calleigh, Sevilla all but dismissed.

Mrs. Rosselli showed them into a good-sized family room with a green leather sofa and two matching loungers arranged in a loose semicircle facing a thirty-two-inch flat-screen Sony television. The cream carpeting was plush, and maple tables and shelves scattered around the outside of the room held various cat sculptures that had a Beatnik-era feel to them. Family photos and two impressionist paintings of cats adorned the cream-colored walls.

Mrs. Rosselli gestured with a hand for Caine and Calleigh to take the couch while she sat in the nearest chair, leaving Sevilla to walk to the far end to the other chair.

"All right, then," Mrs. Rosselli said, businesslike. "What is it you think my husband can help you with?"

Caine said, "We're investigating a murder."

She frowned. "Here in the neighorbood?"

"No."

"Because things are getting terrible, you know. A decent person can't walk down the street anymore. We've had break-ins right on this block—in broad daylight!"

"Yes, Mrs. Rosselli, but that's not, uh—"

"But I'm a trusting person. You saw how I opened the door for you. You might have been thieves—murderers!"

"Well . . . we're not. We're police investigating a murder."

"I wish you'd get to the point, then."

Caine felt like he was on the wrong end of an Abbott and Costello routine. He said, "Our murder victim was shot with bullets that match a murder in Trenton."

Mrs. Rosselli frowned in confusion. "Trenton? Why, we haven't lived there for . . . I don't know how long."

"Fifteen years," Caine said.

"Well—yes. That sounds about right."

"This particular murder took place prior to your husband leaving the Trenton area. His friend and, I believe, business associate—Vincent Ciccolini?—was the major suspect in that crime."

She seemed to shrink in on herself; her voice was still confident, but smaller than before. "I suppose you think that because Vincent and Anthony are friends, Anthony was mixed up in that."

"The Trenton authorities, at the time—"

"There was no arrest, was there? No, Vincent wasn't arrested, and neither was Anthony, or for that matter . . . Abraham." Her voice had choked, right before the last word, and she paused to withdraw a tissue from her sleeve and dab at her nose.

Did Abraham Lipnick have something to do with why Mrs. Rosselli had been crying today?

She was saying, "I'm sorry, Mr., uh, Caine, was it? But I don't see why something we weren't even involved in fifteen years ago has anything to do with us in Coral Gables today."

Caine said, "I'm not sure it does, Mrs. Rosselli. It's

likely a coincidence. But we have to follow up. Procedure."

"Well, I'm sure you're required to do these things, I do understand, but you shouldn't really bother my husband and me. If Vinnie was the—suspect—then, I suggest you talk to Vinnie."

"We tried." Caine nodded in the direction of the Ciccolini home. "He's not home, either. Perhaps he and your husband are together. . . . What about Abraham Lipnick, Mrs. Rosselli? Do you know where he and Mr. Ciccolini are? Are they with your husband . . . ?"

A tear trickled down Rebecca Rosselli's cheek.

Caine exchanged glances with Calleigh and Sevilla. What was this woman upset about?

"Oh they're together, all right," Mrs. Rosselli said. "At least as much as they can be. You see . . . Abraham has passed away. Anthony and Vinnie are at the funeral home. They were the only family he had left."

Another round of glances was exchanged between the CSIs and the detective—understanding, now.

"I'm sorry for your loss," Caine said softly. "Can you tell us which funeral home, please?"

The dark eyes flashed at him. "Why? So you can intrude on their grief, and make a scene in front of God and everybody?"

Caine shook his head. "No, so we can straighten this out, and leave all of you alone . . . to your grief, and your privacy."

"You sound sincere, young man. Are you?"

"You have my word, Mrs. Rosselli—we'll be discreet. But the bottom line, ma'am, is a man was murdered recently with the same gun as in that long-ago Trenton case. And I have to find out what if any significance there is to that."

Sounding defeated, Mrs. Rosselli said, "They're at Longo's Eternal Rest in Coconut Grove. Visitation's on right now."

Not hiding her irritation, Sevilla said, "You might have told us that sooner."

Mrs. Rosselli shot her a look. "I might have . . . but cops like you have been trying to pin things on Anthony for the last fifty years. Why? Because our name ended in 'i' and we lived in a nice home? In Trenton, we came to expect it. But not here. Here, things have been different. Fifteen years, and this is the first time you cops have come around."

"We're aware that your husband has been an upstanding citizen," Caine said, noting to himself that earlier she'd reacted to their presence here as all too typical.

"Oh really? Then why are you turning up on my doorstep?"

"Because the evidence led there, ma'am. And as I say, it's probably just a coincidence."

She stared at nothing. Suddenly Caine realized the woman had been drinking before they got there. The lack of a tumbler in her hand or anything had fooled him.

She was saying, to no one in particular, "I don't deny that Anthony had his share of trouble when he was younger, but not anymore. We're retired. Retired!"

"Yes, Mrs. Rosselli," Caine said.

"We moved here because it was impossible to live in New Jersey anymore. Every time someone got shot, you cops came nosing around us. We couldn't take it anymore. We're old, we're tired." Another tear ran down her cheek. "My children, my grandchildren all back there . . . my home? Gone. This is a nice house"—she gestured around her—"but Trenton was my home. I grew up there, we all did, and now we can't even go back there for a visit, 'cept under a cloud of suspicion."

The speech seemed to use her up and she folded in on herself.

All three officers were on their feet now.

"Thank you for your time, Mrs. Rosselli," Caine said. "And again, we're sorry for your loss."

Mrs. Rosselli nodded without looking up from her tissue.

Calleigh—who'd been silent through all this, just watching, weighing the woman's words—hung back. "May I ask you one more question, ma'am?"

The calm voice with the southern accent seemed to soften Mrs. Rosselli, who said, "Of course."

"Why aren't you at the funeral home as well?"

Mrs. Rosselli shook her head slowly. "I was there all morning, helping make arrangements . . . but I couldn't take it anymore. Abraham looked so small, so powerless, I couldn't stand to see him that way. So—so—shriveled. Every time I looked at him, I started to see . . . to see my Anthony." She sniffed a little. "I don't know what I'll do if I ever lose him."

Stepping forward now, Calleigh laid a comforting

hand on the woman's shoulder. "Hopefully that won't happen soon," she said.

Mrs. Rosselli returned Calleigh's sympathetic smile and showed them out; but as they were leaving, the woman's eyes tightened, as if something ominous in Calleigh's words had finally occurred to her.

7

Simple Send-off

LONGO'S FUNERAL HOME was a long, low-slung, one-story brick building just off the South Dixie Highway in Coconut Grove. Horatio Caine figured it for a smaller business—formerly a little dry cleaner's, maybe, or restaurant—that had undergone some renovation, the two wings on either side of the main section looking added on, some time in the last twenty years perhaps, the mortar a significantly lighter gray than the older part.

Such observations on Caine's part were automatic by now—he'd been a detective too long to think any other way.

The generous parking lot on the west side of the building—had another business building been torn down to make way?—was full, accommodating both visitors' cars and a small fleet of hearses.

Adele Sevilla found a spot for her Lexus, and the redheaded CSI, the blonde CSI and the dark-haired detective clip-clopped across an asphalt lot even as several older people in non-funereal-looking pastels were wending toward various vehicles, many of which were big-as-a-boat Cadillacs and Buicks.

As the law enforcement trio rounded the corner onto the sidewalk, they almost bumped into another old couple; the man going bald, wearing a blue blazer with gold buttons over a crisp white shirt and equally crisp white slacks—striking Caine as a geriatric purser from some cruise ship—and the man's apparent wife, only a few years his junior, wearing a floral print dress and brassy blonde hair of a color unknown to God but familiar to beauty parlors. The couple nodded to them as the officers moved off the sidewalk to let them pass.

"Coral Gables all the way," Sevilla said, once the pair was out of earshot.

Two wide-shouldered guys in dark suits lumbered toward them, each in their late thirties, both looking like anger-management-class flunkees, one of them giving Caine a sideways glance when the CSI refused to surrender an inch of the sidewalk this time. They reluctantly paused and allowed Caine and the two women to pass.

After the duo was well away, Calleigh quietly inquired of Caine, "Emissaries from Don Venici?"

"Could be," Caine said.

Calleigh meant, of course, Peter Venici—the Don of Miami, the local Mafia crime boss who'd succeeded his retired father and was now left on his own to deal with the waves of competition who looked upon Miami as an open city ripe for the taking.

Caine felt sure that some time in the not too distant future he and his team would find themselves working the crime scenes of one of the biggest gang wars the United States would ever see; but today he had simpler crimes on his mind—like a double murder in Miami Beach comprising a torsoless corpse and a duct-taped chauffeur.

For now that would hold Horatio's attention just fine.

He held the door open for his two associates and then they were inside, where the floral scent was immediate and almost overwhelming. The muzak was nondenominational organ, a shade too loud; and the anonymous lobby—cream-color indoor-outdoor carpet and lighter cream wallpaper with framed floral studies—was home to a few knots of older people chatting, most of them not even bothering to look up as new blood entered.

One of the ancient greeters habitually hired by Miami funeral homes approached them, a reed-thin old man in a dark suit that had started to outgrow him. His hair dangled in limp white wisps around ears that extended from his head as if trying to jump ship, his glasses seemed determined to slide to the very tip of his nose, and his brown eyes were dim behind a milky haze. Only the smiling dentures were of a recent vintage.

Sevilla had her hand in her jacket pocket to pull out her badge, but she changed her mind and simply said, "Abraham Lipnick visitation?"

"Room H," the old boy said softly, and gestured to their right, like the Ghost of Christmas Past pointing out Scrooge's own gravestone.

"Thank you," Sevilla said civilly.

With Sevilla in the lead, they moved off down a

wide hallway that led into one of the wings. The rooms on either side had placards next to their door-less entries, each designated with a letter—F on the right, G on the left, then H back on the right side. The room itself was long and narrow, twenty by ten, Caine estimated.

A surprisingly—even shockingly—simple wooden coffin lay open at the far end of the room, two older men standing to one side, greeting the mourners in a line of twenty or so. Overstuffed chairs and sofas lurked on the periphery, while several shallow rows of folding chairs faced the floral arrangements. Perhaps a dozen mourners—all elderly—sat talking quietly among themselves.

Calleigh leaned in close to Caine. "Why the wooden coffin? These Coral Gables residents all look like they could afford more."

Caine replied, softly, "Jewish law—nothing that impedes a return to the earth. No embalming—hence the rush to burial. 'For dust art thou and to the dust thou shalt return.' Genesis."

Sevilla gave him a look, and Caine, feeling a little embarrassed, shrugged. He half-expected the detec-tive to charge up to the old men and start popping questions; but Sevilla got into the receiving line, Calleigh and Caine dropping in behind her. The line moved quickly enough, but still provided Caine time to study the two men they had come to interview.

Their New Jersey cop contact, Irv Brady, had fur-nished a photo of Ciccolini, who Caine made as the man on the left. Tall, his back rigidly straight despite his age, Vincent Ciccolini stood next to the coffin, at the moment shaking hands with a stubby man in an ill-fitting suit.

The reputed assassin's own suit was black with a light gray pinstripe, his shirt gray, tie black, shoes shiny and black and expensive-looking. He still had a full head of straight gray hair, parted on the left and swept right. His wide, bright brown eyes came up from the man in front of him, surveyed the room, paused for a second on Caine, then moved on until he was looking at the next person in line.

On Ciccolini's left stood a shorter, balding man with a brown goatee and a wreath of short brown hair around the back of his head. Caine took the goateed man to be Anthony Rosselli. He had bigger ears, a slightly smaller nose, fuller lips, and kinder brown eyes than Ciccolini. Rosselli also wore a dark suit, with a white shirt and striped tie; his black wingtips looked far less comfortable than Ciccolini's Italian loafers. Rosselli shook the hand of the man in the ill-fitting suit and where Ciccolini had used just one hand, Rosselli used both, making the gesture seem warmer, more personal.

Only two people remained now between Sevilla and Ciccolini, and Caine gave the two head mourners a hard study. He had little doubt that they had been the assassins the police authorities back east believed them to be. Or that is, to have been—fifteen years ago. Had they forgotten their trade, left business behind, for a world of shuffleboard, bargain matinées and early bird specials? Or, like some retirees, could they not let go of their trade?

Caine wondered.

Sevilla stepped forward and discreetly showed Ciccolini her badge. "We're sorry to intrude and have no desire to embarrass you."

In the somber mourning mask, Ciccolini's eyes sparkled. "How could an attractive young girl like you ever embarrass an old man like me?"

Sevilla frowned. "Is there somewhere we can talk?"

Ciccolini whispered to Rosselli, they exchanged nods, and Ciccolini excused himself to those nearest him, after which he ushered the trio of cops through a door behind them. For a second they were in the wide hallway again, but Ciccolini took the lead and, walking briskly for a man of any age, moved up a short corridor on the other side. In less than a minute, they were standing outside the back of the funeral home in the diminishing sun of late afternoon.

"I'm Detective Sevilla. This is Lieutenant Caine and CSI Duquesne."

Ciccolini smirked. "And I guess I don't need to introduce myself," he said as he withdrew a pack of Camel cigarettes from the pocket of his jacket. "Hey, no problem—I been dyin' for a coffin-nail."

"You seem to be holding up well," Caine said dryly, "where the death of your friend is concerned."

Smoke dragoned from Ciccolini's nose and his smile was tobacco yellow, the only liability in the asset that was his still handsome face. "One thing I never share with cops is my feelings about my friends and family. That's private. I'm willin' to talk business with you guys . . . and gals. Comes with the territory."

"But you're retired," Caine said, with a droll smile.

Ciccolini took a long drag from the smoke. Then he said, "Fifteen years, straight and narrow—and yet still there's something so important that the Miami Police have to interrupt the middle of my friend's wake?"

"Is a wake part of Jewish burial rites?" Sevilla asked with a frown.

Ciccolini shrugged. "Hell, I don't know. Just tryin' to do right by Abe somehow. We did the wooden coffin routine, I know that much."

"But you didn't speak to any of his Jewish friends," he noted.

Ciccolini made a V with fore- and middle fingers. "Abe had two friends down here—me and Tony. But I figured he'd want a kosher burial. Gotta be quick too . . . the guy here says he's gotta be in the ground twenty-four hours after the fact."

Caine lifted an eyebrow, then nodded toward Calleigh, who stepped forward and handed Ciccolini a photocopy of the top page of the Trenton police report from her pocket.

"We'll see if this jogs your memory," Caine said.

Ciccolini scanned it for only a few seconds. "This? You interrupt our mournin' for this stale shit? That was last century, guys—I was cleared of that before Blondie here hit puberty."

Calleigh frowned—not offended, Caine didn't think; she was probably doing the math.

Caine said, "Bullets matching the ones from that case have shown up this century—in a murder here in Miami."

Ciccolini exhaled smoke, his expression giving them nothing. "No kiddin'. That is kinda out there, isn't it?"

"Way out," Caine said. "Quite a coincidence, gun from a Trenton murder turning up in Miami. It's also a coincidence that the man accused of the original crime—however long ago—now lives here too."

Ciccolini shrugged, and his manner was not hostile. "Hey, I can see your problem, and why you might think I was involved—guess in your place, I'd come around and rattle this old cage myself—but if you read that file closer, you'll notice the Trenton police never found the murder weapon."

"Which is how it was able to turn up years later," Caine pointed out.

Unimpressed, Ciccolini said, "They never traced it to me, never arrested me. Oh, yeah, they rousted my ass—talked my ear off, held me for questioning, only when push came to shove . . . they had nada."

"But we both know," Caine said, keeping his tone carefully good-humored, "not being charged doesn't make you innocent."

Ciccolini gave the CSI a tiny smile. "I got a pal who can rent you a boat, Lieutenant, if you wanna go fishing. Look, this is a coincidence. You had to follow it up. You did. I cooperated. Anything else?"

Offering up his own little smile, Caine said, "In my line of work, you have to look at all coincidences with a skeptical eye."

"It's part of your job. No offense taken."

"Mrs. Rosselli said there've been break-ins in your neighborhood. I was just thinking, one way that weapon could've gotten to Miami would be if you owned it, and somebody stole it."

"Which would get me off the hook for this new murder, right?"

"Right."

"But for the old murder, I'd suddenly be openin' up a whole new can of worms for you to go fishing with. Sorry to disappoint you: I didn't do either one of these crimes."

"Then I would imagine you can account for your whereabouts on Monday evening."

Ciccolini nodded, his face turning melancholy. "That was our last night out, the boys. Abe, Tony, and me, we were playin' poker in a little club we like. We kinda lost track of time—Abe was winnin' big, which he didn't usually. Anyway, normally we wouldn't stay out that late . . . after all, we ain't kids."

"How late?"

"After midnight. Not sure how far past, exactly."

"And then?"

Ciccolini shrugged, pitched his cigarette and sparks flew; but his words were calm if grave: "On the way home, Abe complained that his chest hurt. We went straight to the hospital . . . and were there, in the emergency-room waiting area, until he passed away last night."

"We are sorry for your loss, Mr. Ciccolini," Caine said. "But you've been down this road enough times to know we'll still need to check out your story."

Ciccolini looked mildly exasperated, his eyes cutting toward the back door of the funeral home, then back to Caine.

"Then what do you need?"

"Where were you playing cards?"

"Carrelli's Social Club in Miami Beach."

"Can't say I've heard of it."

"It's on Drexel near Espanola. No idea the street number—you'll have to look it up on your own time."

Caine gave him a quick nod. "And which hospital?"

"Mt. Sinai."

As he thought about that, something struck Caine as odd, but before he could comment, the back door opened and Anthony Rosselli stepped outside.

"Vinnie, please—people are asking for you." Rosselli's voice was steady, but Caine could hear the struggle for control in it. His grief was closer to the surface than Ciccolini's.

Who turned toward Caine and raised both eyebrows and gazed at the CSI like a man through a gunsight. "We through here?" A new coldness was in the voice.

"You can go, thank you," Caine said; then—as Ciccolini headed for the door—he turned his own hard gaze on the bald, goateed man, adding, "Mr. Rosselli, a moment of your time?"

Rosselli still held the door open with one hand and glanced back down the hallway toward the main corridor. "If it can wait . . ."

"It's okay, Tony," Ciccolini said. "Get it outa the way. It's no big deal. These officers just have a weird kinda coincidence they need to satisfy themselves about. Just talk to them for a minute and they'll be gone. . . . Right?"

Caine nodded.

"Sure," Rosselli said, with a shrug. "Whatever, Vinnie."

So, Caine thought, *Ciccolini is the boss.*

At the doorway, Ciccolini paused. "Should I tell Abe you'll be interrogatin' him next?"

Caine said nothing, but he could feel Sevilla tense up beside him.

Rosselli said, "That ain't funny, Vinnie."

Nonetheless Caine smiled and said, "Well, Abe wouldn't be the most uncooperative witness I've ever had."

Ciccolini's face softened. "I really do wish I could send the old bastard out here. Losin' a friend, a close friend . . . like the kids say . . . it sucks."

Calleigh said, "Please accept our condolences. And thank you for your time, Mr. Ciccolini."

He favored her with another of those tiny smiles, then disappeared inside, door closing of its own volition.

Under the same line of questioning, Rosselli seemed more nervous than Ciccolini, his hands fluttering as he spoke, diving into his jacket pockets, only to come flying out again as he told them pretty much the same story Ciccolini had.

A little too close maybe, Caine thought, almost rehearsed; but then again, the two men had been friends for most of their adult lives and Caine knew that sometimes friends did tend to parrot each other. If they hadn't been two parts of a suspected three-man hit squad, he'd have thought nothing of it.

This time, Caine asked the question that bothered him about both their stories.

"If you were at a club on Drexel, South Beach, Mr. Rosselli," Caine asked, "what made you take Mr. Lipnick to Mt. Sinai?"

Sevilla chimed in: "Yes, instead of South Shore—that's closer to where you were."

Rosselli shrugged and nodded and turned his hands upside down. "True, true, but Abe liked Mt. Sinai better. He thought they had better heart doctors."

"Did he have a history of cardiac trouble?"

"He'd had a bad ticker for maybe ten years. Had a stroke too, a while ago, though he bounced back good. The docs knew him at Mt. Sinai, and Abe was comfortable there. I hope to hell he didn't croak 'cause we didn't take him to the nearest hospital. But he had attacks before and always come out of it. We just didn't know how bad he was."

Caine nodded, turned to Sevilla. "Anything?"

Before the detective could come up with a question, Rosselli, still a bundle of tics, said, "Look, as far as this gun is concerned . . . I don't have to tell ya, these pieces float all over hell. It really ain't such a surprise that a piece from the East Coast winds up down here."

"Perhaps not," Caine said, "but we have to look into it."

"Sure. Can I, uh . . . get back to Abe?"

"Certainly."

They followed the man back inside, this time filing past the coffin too. Looking down at the body inside, Caine wondered if these men could possibly have committed a kidnapping and double murder.

Ciccolini looked to be in pretty good shape, but Rosselli stooped a little, and even in the coffin Lipnick looked like he would have had trouble lifting more than a cup of coffee. Frail, riddled by the trouble his heart had given him, Abraham Lipnick might have been one of a million other men who had come to die in the sun and shade of Miami Beach.

Odd to think that, only fifteen years ago, the man in this coffin had still been a professional killer. Only the prominent nose that might have been flattened from long-ago punches gave any hint that this was not your average shuffleboard player; the wide wrinkled forehead, the deflated jowls, the wisps of gray hair, all reminded Caine of the greeter in the lobby.

Caine stopped in front of Ciccolini and Rosselli again on his way out. "We apologize for the intrusion and, again, we're sorry for your loss."

Ciccolini extended a hand. "No hard feelings."

Caine shook the hand, the grip firm. Then he shook hands with Rosselli, whose grip was less firm and noticeably clammy.

"You know," Ciccolini said, patting his side sportcoat pocket, out of which a brown paperbag peeked, "I'm sending Abe off the same way as Sinatra—with a pack of smokes, a bottle of bourbon, and a roll of dimes."

"So he can always make a phone call," Caine said, half-smiling.

Ciccolini nodded.

As Caine turned to go, Ciccolini said, "I hope you find who you're looking for, Lieutenant. I'd just like to see this cleared up, so we can finally leave Trenton back in New Jersey where it belongs."

At the back of the room, they paused and watched awhile, as the pair continued to greet mourners.

Sevilla asked, "What do you think, Horatio?"

"I usually have a gut instinct about these things."

"I know you do."

"But . . . not this time."

Silently, Sevilla led Caine and Calleigh outside.

Calleigh said, "Those old boys don't look like they could kill time, let alone two healthy, much younger men."

"It looks like a ground ball," Caine agreed, "but you know what we do with them."

"Run 'em all out," Calleigh said.

Sevilla said, "Ciccolini seems pretty spry to me."

"You'll be checking their story," Caine said.

"Oh yes."

"All right. Calleigh, let's get you back to the lab. I want you to keep up with your workload, so if anything else comes in on this case, you're clear."

"I'm for that. What about you?"

Caine's eyes tightened. "I'm going to take another shot at Daniel Boyle."

"I don't suppose you're talking about with a gun," Calleigh said, almost wistfully.

"No . . . but I've got a few Boyle 'bullets' I haven't spent yet."

He took the women back to headquarters, then drove to Miami Beach, crossing on the southernmost road, the MacArthur Causeway.

Night had settled over the city and blue lights highlighted the bridge to the Port of Miami across the main channel of Biscayne Bay. Tiny stars out over the ocean looked like pinpricks in the sky, as if some bright light was on the other side of the night, seeping in; it gave Caine a feeling of being something small in the middle of something big. He did not mind the feeling; in fact, he took a certain comfort in it.

As he came off the causeway, Caine glanced left at South Shore Hospital, right there on Alton Road. He took the left on Alton and went north ten blocks to Fifteenth, then cut east seven more to Drexel. At the corner, he looked to his right and there, on the other side of the street, was the social club Vincent Ciccolini claimed he and his two cronies were at Monday night. Twenty-two blocks from South Shore Hospital.

Mt. Sinai was closer to fifty blocks north through the bumper-to-bumper traffic of Collins Avenue—the same Collins Avenue where Felipe Ortega's limo had been found in a parking lot.

A car behind him honked its horn and Caine eased through the intersection going on east to Collins Avenue before again turning north. Maybe the men were telling the truth; it was possible that Lipnick's condition had worsened once he got to the hospital, or that Ciccolini and Rosselli didn't recognize just how bad off Abe was. Until Sevilla spoke with the folks there, there was no way to know.

During rush hour, people on their way home tried to drive fast on Collins but with little success. Once night settled in, the traffic moved at roughly the speed of a glacier. And again Caine had to wonder: why had the old men come this way? Monday was lighter traffic, granted, the weekend's tourists having bugged out Sunday night, but still . . .

At Forty-first, he glanced west toward Mt. Sinai as if merely turning that way would afford him a glance at the hospital that was still blocks away down that street.

He shrugged to himself. No use getting ahead of the evidence; when your brain got too far out in front of the investigation, you could get seriously whiplashed.

Anyway, his best suspect was still Lessor's stepson—Daniel Boyle.

Normally, the wife would be a good suspect, possibly the prime one, especially if (as with Lessor) there were rumors of infidelity; but she had seemed so adamant in her defense of her late husband, even arguing with her own son over what seemed to everyone else on the planet to be blatant infidelity, that Caine could only wonder if Deborah Lessor could be that skilled an actress.

Of course, her late husband had been, by all accounts, one hell of a talent scout.

Pulling the Hummer into the driveway of the Conquistador, Caine eased up to a vacant spot normally reserved for taxis and parked. As he got out, a cabby slid up next to him, rolling down the power window on the passenger side.

"Hey, buddy! That's reserved."

Caine showed him the badge.

"What, and you think that gives you the right . . ."

Bending down, his left arm resting on the roof of the taxi, Caine looked inside at the driver, a guy in his late fifties who smelled like he hadn't showered since the Marlins won the series . . . in other words, 1997.

"And how many violations am I going to find this evening?" Caine asked cheerfully.

"Fine, fine! Fuck it." The cabby hit the button to roll up the window, already pulling away, probably hoping to catch Caine's toes under the wheels.

His cell phone trilled and he answered it. "Horatio."

"H." Tim Speedle.

"Got something for me, Speed?"

"Guy named Plummer stopped by."

"Daniel Boyle's driver."

"Good one, H. How do you stay on top of details like that?"

"Because I lead by example, Speed."

"Ah. Anyway, Plummer verified his boss's story and brought in security videotapes that clearly show Boyle in the hotel, right when he said he was there."

"Any way to verify these tapes?"

"Not really. They could be cooked, all right."

"So this would be worthless information. Anything that isn't?"

"Yeah, but I can't take credit. Sevilla told me to pass along to you that the club on Drexel checked out—your geriatric suspects, right?"

"Right," Caine said. "Did she get times?"

"Nope. The manager she talked to remembered your coots coming in, but didn't see them leave."

"What about Mt. Sinai?"

"She hasn't got to that yet—had to go out on another call. Said she'll check the hospital tomorrow."

"Thanks, Speed."

"Hey, we're full service around here, H. Later."

"Later."

So, the old men were at the club—Caine just didn't know how long, exactly. Maybe he would swing past the hospital on the way back. Sticking the phone in his pocket, he walked through the glass doors and into the lobby of the Conquistador, which was not terribly busy—couple checking in, few people heading down the hall toward the bar, a handful going the other direction toward the restaurant for a late supper.

When the couple left the front desk, Caine stepped up. The clerk was an attractive Hispanic woman in her early twenties. She had short black hair, close-set brown eyes, and a thin mouth too generously covered with bright red lipstick. Her name tag read LARA.

She gave him her professional smile; where the Hispanics were concerned, Caine had to take it back: they were more consistently friendly and seemed to value tourists. "May I help you?"

"Daniel Boyle, please." He didn't bother with a badge or intimidating "Miami-Dade Criminalistics" introduction.

"Just a moment." She turned and called to someone in the back office. "You know where Mr. Boyle is?"

A female voice answered, "Where is he always this time of night? In the lounge."

Caine nodded his thanks and turned in that direction. As he neared the Explorer Lounge, the throbbing bass of the band thudded into his chest. A young black man in a black suit with a black T-shirt underneath sat outside the door. Caine could tell the man had been watching him all the way down the corridor and didn't miss much. No money box out here, so Caine figured the guy was just checking IDs.

Caine drew back his jacket so the man could see the badge on his belt. The guy's eyes widened, just a trifle, then he nodded his approval, his eyes returning to the corridor, where a young couple headed this way as Caine opened the door and slipped inside.

The lounge was dark, the candles on the tables providing the only illumination other than stage lights. There seemed to be a pretty good-size crowd, at least as much as Caine could tell courtesy of the swirling spots that intermittently let him see different parts of the room.

On stage, the band blasted away, the brass fighting percussion for dominion, as Maria Chacon ruled over them all, hardly trying; she was in a much more revealing costume than last time, singing to the crowd. Probably not Cole Porter, he thought, or Paul Simon for that matter; but the song did have that compelling bass beat and Maria's strong sultry voice. The crowd was coming out of their seats, a few even dancing in the aisles, animal and bird sounds erupting from around the room. Either Maria was very, very good, or this audience was very, very drunk . . . maybe both.

Quick-scanning the room over the tops of the bobbing heads, he searched for Daniel Boyle with no luck. Then, suddenly, he realized the man was standing right next to him in the dark; he'd been tucked back beside the doorway—Caligula viewing all from his box.

"Amazing what sex, loud music, and no cover charge can accomplish," Boyle said, working his voice up, leaning in to Caine's near ear.

"Let's step outside," Caine said, in no mood to compete with the roar of the band and the whooping crowd.

Boyle pointed to his ears, signaling that he couldn't hear. Caine was considering grabbing the man by the lapels of his Armani suit and dragging him into the hallway when Boyle pointed toward the door.

Out in the hall, Boyle did not pause, rather kept walking, toward the lobby, Caine falling in alongside him, as they put some distance between themselves and the noise of the lounge.

Halfway down the hall, the boyishly handsome hotel manager turned to Caine and paused. "What can I do for you, Lieutenant?"

A couple, walking hand in hand, moved past them.

"Could we use your office?" Caine asked.

"Why not?"

Caine followed Boyle across the lobby, past the front desk, and through a door marked PRIVATE. Boyle let him inside the non-spacious office, then closed the door before circling the long way around his cherry desk, a wing extending from the left side with a computer monitor atop it.

Behind the desk, on the wall, hung a large color photo of the Conquistador circa 1955, a large neon conquistador head standing sentry, the name in red script arching around his helmet. Another disembodied head, Caine noted. The picture hung just a little crooked.

Boyle motioned for Caine to have a seat, which he did.

"I assume you're here to update me on the investigation," Boyle said. "Do you have a suspect yet?"

"Yes," Caine said.

"Really. Who?"

"You."

Boyle almost seemed to lose his balance in the chair; quickly recovering, he said, "Why would I be a suspect? You know that I have an airtight alibi—"

"Funny thing," Caine said, "just about the only people who use that phrase—kind of antiquated, B-movie phrase, don't you think, 'airtight alibi'?—are murderers."

"If you're going to charge me—"

"Oh no. I don't have a case against you. Yet."

"Then why do you suspect me, for God's sake?"

"Because, Daniel . . . may I call you Daniel? Because you insist on lying to me."

The hotel manager swallowed thickly; his expression took on a wounded quality. "I have—I did lie about my feelings about Tom. I was just trying to . . . keep family business, you know . . . private."

"Private. As in, private investigator?"

That caught Boyle by surprise; his mouth dropped open. "You know about that?"

"I heard secondhand. But you've finally confirmed it. You hired one to try to get the goods on your stepfather. His cheating on your mom."

"That's right. Not here—it was on the Vegas end."

"Did you share this with the Las Vegas authorities? They arrested your stepfather on a murder charge—they believed he'd murdered a woman he was sleeping with. Anything your investigator found—"

"But that's just it. My stepfather was discreet. The investigator didn't find anything."

"Just the same, I'll need his name and contact information." Caine would pass this along to Catherine Willows.

"No problem," Boyle said, rather contritely. He went to his Rolodex and found the name and was writing it down on a memo pad when Caine spoke again.

"What else have you held back, Mr. Boyle?"

Boyle looked up, deer in the headlights; thought about it, really seemed to be considering the answer. "I can't think of anything that would help you."

Caine had come here to rattle the man and shake something loose; Boyle seemed rattled enough, but nothing was falling out. The CSI decided to go a step further.

"Let's talk about Gino Forlani," Caine said, "and the Cappelletti brothers."

"Shit," Boyle said, his face whitening. "You're not going to drag my . . . my friends into this?"

"Your friends who have organized-crime connections, you mean? Your stepfather's murder has all the earmarks of a mob hit. Did you think we wouldn't notice your associations?"

"They're just . . . acquaintances, that's all. Friendly acquaintances. We, you know, play some golf together. Once in a while. Now and then."

"Once in a while." Caine crossed his arms. "Now and then. I thought you weren't going to lie to me anymore."

Boyle's head drooped. "All right. You caught me in another, uh . . ."

"Lie. Want to try again?"

Boyle rubbed his forehead with his fingertips, as if trying to scrape the flesh off his skull. Finally, he exhaled, endlessly. "I . . . I owe them some money."

Uncrossing his arms and leaning forward, Caine said, "See? Isn't it a relief to tell the truth?"

The hotel manager just glared at him.

"And why do you owe them money, Daniel?"

". . . Gambling debts."

"Be more specific?"

Shrugging, Boyle said, "Basketball, football, horses, whatever season it is, that's what I bet. . . . What can I say, I'm a sports fan."

"How much are you into them for?"

"Not that much."

"How much, Daniel?"

"Really—only ten g's. Nothing."

Caine frowned. "Why don't you just pay them off, then?"

Boyle sighed. "I really don't have that kind of money. My mother has cut me off, where gambling debts are concerned; and I'm on salary here. I get paid just like everybody else."

"I doubt that it's like everybody else."

"I make money commensurate with just about any hotel manager in Miami Beach."

Caine nodded. "And you live in the family home. Not much overhead, Daniel."

"Fine. The truth is, I piss most of it away. I've been gambling for years, since college, and always done all right; but this basketball season is killing me. My reserve's gone and I can only pay Gino and the Cappellettis a little at a time. I'm barely covering the vig as it is."

Caine looked hard at the man. "You understand, Daniel, this is not clearing you. It's only making you a better suspect."

Boyle held up surrendering hands. "I'm trying to be honest with you."

"And I'd just find out anyway."

"You'd just find out anyway."

Caine mulled. Then: "Gino going to back your story?"

Boyle snorted a laugh. "He's a fucking mob guy! You think he's going to tell you the truth?"

"Well then . . ."

His eyes painfully earnest, Boyle sat forward. "Honest to Christ, Lieutenant—I've got no idea who killed Tom. Yeah, I hated him . . . but for what he was doing to my mother. She loved him, still does. I would never have hurt him, not physically—his death's practically killing my mother. And I would never do anything to hurt her, if I could help it."

"You'd never hire a private detective, for example, to follow her husband around?"

Boyle looked stricken. "You wouldn't tell her about that, would you?"

Caine didn't answer, instead asking, "How is your mother doing?"

He sighed again. "I just put her on a plane back to Vegas—sedated to the gills. She's going to make funeral arrangements. When are you going to release the remains . . . such as they are?"

"Not for a while. Could be a week. Could be more."

"Well, would you have the coroner contact me, Lieutenant, so I can make arrangements to get the—whatever—back to Vegas? I'll need to go back for the funeral, myself. I mean, if I'm a suspect, can I . . . ?"

"We could allow that, I think."

"Thanks for that much, anyway." He laughed, bitterly. "I could always take Tom home in a duffel bag. I do get two carry-on's."

Caine rose. Smiled. "You might not want to share that one with your mom, Daniel."

And the CSI left the hotel manager there, to ponder that.

8

Minor Discovery

As Horatio Caine approached Biscayne Bay, Mt. Sinai Hospital rose out of the night like a contemporary Stonehenge; these modern megaliths, however, had windows, many of which had lights shining within, hundreds of beacons in the darkness.

He could use a beacon or two about now.

After weaving through the maze of South Beach campus buildings, Caine pulled up to the emergency-room entrance and parked in a spot reserved for the police.

Inside, his first stop was at the check-in nurse's desk next to the triage station in the emergency room. He showed his badge, ID, and a smile to the check-in nurse—a blunt-featured, blue-eyed blonde about twenty-five who exuded brusque competence—and sat in the chair across from her. A placard on her desk read: JENNIFER BLAIR.

"Sorry to have to bother you, Jennifer," Caine said, keeping the smile going, but not forcing it. "I'm looking for information on a patient brought in on Monday night. A heart attack—Abraham Lipnick."

A frown dug creases in her forehead and the blue eyes all but vanished into slits in her face. "You know better than that, Lieutenant. I can't give out information about patients."

He nodded. "It's a murder investigation, Jennifer, and it would be no problem getting court permission."

"Then I'm afraid you'd need to do that. I'm not trying to be difficult—"

"I know you're not." He drew a breath, took a slightly different tack. "I'm not after specific information about this patient; it has to do with the friends who brought him to the ER."

The check-in nurse thought that over; then she nodded.

He asked, "Do you happen to remember Mr. Lipnick?"

She was shaking her head even as she typed the man's name into her computer. She frowned at the screen. "Monday, did you say?"

"Monday night, yes."

Scrolling with her mouse, she said, "We were pretty busy for a Monday. They just kept coming, but that is an unusual name"—it must have popped up on the screen because the check-in nurse paused for a long moment before finally completing the thought—"yes."

"So you do remember him? Good."

She smiled. "I remember typing in 'Lipstick,' before I caught the mistake. . . . Yes, Mr. Lipnick was in quite a bit of pain and he coded right there where you're sitting."

"Paramedics didn't bring him in?"

She shook her head. "It was like you said—friends."

"How many?"

". . . Two."

"Do you remember them?"

"Well, one was a good-looking older man. Very well groomed, gray hair. Well preserved. Could he have had an East Coast accent?"

"Yes," Caine said. Ciccolini. "What did the other man look like?"

"Not so good-looking. Short, bald, with one of those funny beards."

"A goatee?"

"Yes. Not so well groomed as his friend. Or so well preserved."

Caine shifted in the seat and raised an eyebrow. "Jennifer, I'm impressed."

She smiled, and it was a nice smile; the professionalism remained, but some humanity was easing through.

"And they were both here, at all times? The well-preserved one and the not-so-well-preserved one?"

The check-in nurse thought about that for a long moment. "The nice-looking one checked in Mr. Lipnick. He mentioned his friend was parking the car. I did see him, in the waiting area . . . enough to get an impression of him."

"When exactly did you notice him?"

Jennifer shrugged elaborately. "Like I said, it was brutal that night and Mr. Lipnick coded, so he got taken back immediately."

"Can you tell me what time that was?"

She looked at the chart on the computer screen. "Almost one-thirty in the morning."

"And the name of the doctor that treated him?"

"Dr. Rina Sarkar. And to answer your next question, she's not here. She left to do a month-long tour with Doctors Without Borders."

Caine nodded. "What about nurses?"

Looking at Lipnick's chart one more time, she said, "Nancy Blanco. Now, she is on tonight."

"Could you . . . ?"

She made a call, arranging for Blanco to come down.

"Thanks, Jennifer."

"Just doing my job."

"Obviously, you do it well."

They exchanged smiles and Caine met the next nurse at the Plexiglas-enclosed bench outside, set up for staff members who smoked. A thin, rather haggard thirtysomething, Blanco settled down on the wooden bench, lighted up one of those very long, too thin cigarettes marketed exclusively to women, and looked his badge and ID over so carefully she might have been checking for symptoms.

"I don't understand why you're here," Nurse Blanco said.

"It's a murder investigation."

This did not seem to impress her. "Mr. Lipnick wasn't murdered," she said. "He had a heart attack."

Caine said, "We're aware of that—he's not the victim. What I'm interested in is whether you saw anyone with him—when he came in, for example?"

She considered that. "Yeah, there was a guy. Nice-looking older man came in with him."

"No one else?"

"There was a second one, but I believe he was out parking the car."

"Did you see the second man?"

"Sure. Bald guy with a little beard. Sitting there with the old tall smoothie."

"The bald guy—was he there the whole time?"

She sighed smoke. "I don't really know. I walked by once and he wasn't, and the tall guy grinned and said, just kidding, y'know, 'You got something for the trots? My buddy'—he used his friend's name, I think it was Tony—he said, 'My buddy Tony's doin' the Argentina two-step tonight.' Stuck with me. Thought it was kinda funny."

"But you did see the other man."

"Oh yeah! He was here."

"When, exactly?"

"I couldn't say, exactly—but Lipnick had coded, so I was pretty busy helping Dr. Sarkar try to save him."

"It might be important."

She took a tiny puff on her cigarette as she thought about it. "I saw the bald, bearded gent for sure, after my break at five. I saw the pair of 'em on my way back from the cafeteria. They were standing outside. Smoking."

"Did you see them both before that?"

She nodded. "Yeah, I've got no idea exactly when. Look, uh . . . Lieutenant Caine, right? We work on the sick ones, not the well ones. It's the sick ones that stick with you."

"Like Mr. Lipnick? Anything special about him?"

Another puff as she thought. "Just . . . he was pretty far gone when he came in. He'd had a massive heart attack and already had a checkered cardiac history. We did everything we could. Sometimes it's just not enough."

Caine left Mt. Sinai feeling that he had little more information than he had come in with. Perhaps more in-depth interviews with the staff might yield something, but there didn't seem to be much else at the moment to mine here.

Daniel Boyle still seemed a far more likely suspect, or even his mother Deborah of the cheating husband (despite her denials), than three old men with no apparent ties to the case . . .

. . . except that one of them had been accused of a shooting using a gun with bullets that matched this homicide. And that was a doozy, wasn't it?

He would tell Sevilla what he had learned and she could track down the doctor or some of the other nurses. *Stick with the evidence*, he thought. *Follow the evidence.*

The CSI got back into the Hummer and caught the Julia Tuttle Causeway back to the mainland. The night had chilled and Caine felt a little cool in only his sports coat, but he liked the sensation—it refreshed him after a long day. On the mainland, he got onto the Dolphin Expressway, heading west toward HQ.

Eric Delko was in the lab when Caine got back.

"What are you still doing here?" Caine asked.

"You're here, aren't you?"

Caine grunted. "I guess I am."

Delko gave him a slight grin. "I tracked the battery we found at the beach."

"Make me happy I came back in."

"Do my best. Y'know, I thought we were looking at a watch battery, but it turned out to be for a hearing aid."

Caine's eyes narrowed. "And we have three elderly suspects . . . or two, anyway."

"Well, I knew Calleigh went out with you to the funeral home, and I checked with her. She said she got a good look at the old boys, and none of them wore hearing aids."

"That's true. I gave them a careful look myself."

"You're sure? Those hearing aids can be pretty small, and sometimes they're built into the earpieces of glasses. . . ."

"Eric. Observing is what I do."

Delko patted the air in surrender. "Okay, okay . . . just being thorough. This includes the guy in the box, right?"

"Abraham Lipnick was not wearing a hearing aid."

Delko arched an eyebrow. "Maybe the mortician didn't think he needed to wear one, where he was going."

"We'll have Detective Sevilla check with the mortuary, and at the hospital—see if a hearing aid was among his effects."

"It's a lead. And we can use a few of those."

"Yes we can."

"And you don't have to be a geezer to wear a hearing aid, H. What about our other suspects?"

"Thomas Lessor didn't wear a hearing aid. Daniel Boyle, Deborah, no hearing aids either. What about Felipe, our late chauffeur?"

"Calleigh's ahead of you on that. Talked to the family again—they say no."

"Get any prints off the battery?"

"Just smudges. Pretty small object, to grab a decent print offa."

Caine's forehead tensed. "Could it have been just lying there, not part of the case?"

"Sure—it's a big beach . . . and there's a lot of old people in Miami."

"Any traces of blood on the battery?"

"No. If there had been, we could tie it better to the case. Otherwise, darn thing could've just been lying there waiting to screw us up."

Caine nodded. "Wouldn't be the first time. Won't be the last. Did we get any prints off the garbage bag?"

Delko shook his head. "Killers wore gloves—nothing but smears and smudges there, too."

"Lessor's cell phone?"

"Only prints on that were his own."

Caine drew in a deep breath, and let it out slow. "Okay, Eric—what say we go home, get some rest?"

"I could be talked into that."

"Everybody else gone?"

"Yeah—Calleigh and Speed stayed late, too, just so you know. Both took off a while ago, maybe half an hour 'fore you got here."

"All right," Caine said, "now it's our turn. Let's get some rest and look at all this with fresh eyes, tomorrow."

As they walked into the parking lot, Delko said, "No rest for the wicked, they say. But the good guys gotta sleep."

"Don't kid yourself, Eric—the wicked get plenty of sleep."

"Yeah?" Delko grinned. "What do you suppose they dream of?"

"They dream," Caine said, with a whimsical smile, "they're innocent."

And the two men went home.

The next morning, Caine was in his condo, dressed and about to step out the door to get to work early. He had just holstered his side arm when his cell phone rang.

He punched the button. "Horatio."

A warmly masculine voice was on the other line, laid-back and yet quietly intense: "Lieutenant Caine, this is Warrick Brown. Las Vegas crime lab."

"You must be wrapping up your shift, Mr. Brown. I don't believe we've spoken since you were down here with Catherine Willows, last year."

"That's right, sir, we haven't—and it's Warrick."

"And it's not 'sir,' Warrick—it's Horatio. What can I do for you?"

"Catherine's had me looking into Thomas Lessor from this end, trying to see if we could help your investigation."

"I appreciate that."

"Well, we have a kind of proprietary interest in the late Mr. Lessor—since he's the one who got away."

"Considering his head was found in a garbage bag, Warrick, it wasn't the best getaway a bad guy ever made."

"Yeah—that is kinda comforting. We've talked to the PI here in town, that Daniel Boyle hired to try and get the goods on stepdaddy? And the guy didn't have a thing. We looked at his field notes, and Lessor was slippery. I mean, we know he was having an affair with Erica Hardy, and a divorce detective didn't turn up diddly."

"There may be another PI on this end. We'll be checking that."

"Good. But I do have one odd thing that might pan out for you—a phone number that Lessor called repeatedly in Miami. We just can't find out who the number belongs to."

"Could I have that number, please?" Caine said.

The Vegas CSI gave it to him.

"Thanks, Warrick. I'll look into it and let you know what we find."

"Cool. . . . Any luck on your end?"

"Interesting ballistics match," Caine said, and filled him in on the New Jersey connection.

"Old mob guys," Warrick said, quietly amused. "I guess you can take an old guy outa the Mafia, but you can't take the Mafia out of the old guy."

"Could be the case. And it could be what we have is a weapon that just passed itself along from one nasty customer to another, over a lot of years."

"My supervisor could provide you with discouraging odds against a coincidence like that."

"Well, he's a smart man, your Dr. Grissom—but coincidences do happen."

"I don't suppose the rest of the body has turned up yet?"

"No. Still looking. . . . But we've got some other leads. We'll let you know when we've got some progress. Thanks, Warrick."

Warrick said, "Pleasure doing business with you, Horatio," and hung up.

Caine spent most of the day digging through records. The phone number belonged to a residence in the Art Deco district of the city. The address indicated this was an apartment, but the owner's name wasn't a person, as he'd expected; instead, the phone was registered in the name Tee-Minor, Inc.

A business?

He phoned the number himself and listened to it ring four times before an answering machine picked up. A metallic voice that came with the machine said simply: "Please leave a message."

Caine didn't.

Instead, he went to work on the company name. He searched the Better Business Bureau, the Chamber of Commerce, state, and even federal records, and could find no mention of Tee-Minor, Inc.

Finally, with the shift winding down—and Caine starting to feel like he'd wasted a whole day—he decided, what the hell, to just go to the apartment and see for himself.

But it wasn't the sort of call a CSI made alone.

He phoned Sevilla. "Adele—care to go for a ride?"

"Where to?"

He told her.

"An actual lead. I'm your girl. Meet you at the Hummer."

Little more than a half hour later, Caine parked in front of the apartment building—a two-story stucco four-plex on the corner of Tenth and Meridian, a block south of Flamingo Park. A flat roof gave it a squarish appearance and it had a gaudy facade, recently painted mint green with white trim. Other than its startling pastel makeover, the apartment building looked little different than any of the walk-up hotels that predominated in the Art Deco district.

Caine checked the mailboxes and found "Tee-Minor, Inc." on a tab stuffed into the box for number 3. He nodded to Sevilla, pointed up, and they climbed the narrow stairs to the second floor. With bare, off-white plaster walls and indoor-outdoor carpeting, the place had zero personality and a transient air, but it looked clean and smelled like Lysol.

They looked at the beige-painted wooden door on the right—bearing a brass "4" and a peephole. The other door, the one they were looking for, was at the other end and across the hall.

Stepping to one side, Caine knocked on the door of number 3.

Nothing.

Number 3's peephole stared at them and Caine wondered if anyone was on the other side. He glanced at Sevilla on the other side of the doorway; she shrugged.

He knocked again. Still nothing.

"Well," Sevilla said, "we can probably justify a warrant."

"Why don't we get one," Caine said.

But just as they were about to turn and walk away, the door cracked open, till a safety chain stopped it. Over the little metal link barrier, Caine saw the attractive if sleepy face of a familiar woman . . .

. . . the Conquistador's lounge singer, Maria Chacon.

"Lieutenant Caine," she said, eyes tight, as if she were summoning the name from memory as she spoke. "What are you doing here?"

Caine graced her with a tiny smile. "Tell you truth—I was wondering the same about you, Maria." He turned to Sevilla. "This is Maria Chacon—headlining in the Explorer Lounge." And to Maria: "Why not ask us in?"

She strained to see who was with him.

"This is Detective Sevilla," Caine said, as the detective moved next into Maria's line of sight. "She's investigating Thomas Lessor's murder."

"I thought you were investigating that."

"It's a group effort. Can we come in?"

Maria said, "Hold it a sec," and closed the door while she released the chain.

She opened the door and gestured for them to step in, which they did. Her black hair was a little wild and she wore only a Dan Marino Dolphins jersey and white underwear, mostly covered by the shirt. Even with the CSI and detective inside now, Maria made no effort to put on more clothes.

Though small and modestly furnished in a rent-to-own manner, the apartment had a homey feel. A tall floor lamp in the corner provided the only light; a red chenille sofa hugged the wall next to the door, a multicolored wing chair beyond that squatting under a picture window with the shades drawn tight. A twenty-five-inch TV sat on a cart across the living room from the sofa, a small boom box on a low table next to it, a few CDs scattered on the floor nearby. To the left of the front door, a small white dinette set with two chairs sat on a white tile floor that marked the end of the living room. Past the table was a galley kitchen that looked small but well scrubbed.

"Anyone else here, Maria?" he asked.

She shook her head; yawned. "Just me. Sorry . . . I was sleeping."

"Sorry we woke you," Sevilla said, not sounding terribly contrite, really.

"It's all right." Maria shrugged. "The alarm was set for a half hour from now anyway. I work tonight."

"You put in a lot of hours," Caine said.

"It's my choice," Maria said. "I'm aggressive about my career, and we rehearse our asses off." Another yawn. "You want some coffee or something?"

They both shook their heads.

"Mind if I do? . . . I gotta wake up."

"No," Caine said, "go right ahead."

She motioned to the dinette. "Sit. Please."

Caine and Sevilla took opposite ends of the tiny table as Maria moved into the kitchen, flipped on the overhead light, and started working on putting together a pot of coffee.

"Why did you come to see me?" the singer asked, perhaps too casually.

"Actually, we didn't," Caine said.

Their hostess turned from her coffee prep to arch a confused eyebrow.

Caine gave her a tight, meaningless smile. "This apartment isn't in your name."

She turned her back to him as she ran water into the pot. "You're right. Come to think of it, you wouldn't know to come look for me here."

"So, Maria," Caine said, "maybe you could explain that? Why an apartment we've tracked down has you living in it?"

"I'm apartment-sitting for a friend."

"A friend named Tee-Minor, Inc.?"

"Well, the person who owns Tee-Minor," she said, perhaps too offhandedly, offering no further explanation as she poured the water into the machine. She flipped the switch to ON and, with the pot running now, turned, leaning against the counter and facing them.

Caine bestowed another non-smile of a smile. "And who would that be, Maria?"

Her smile was just half a one. "Didn't you detectives figure that out yet?"

"No," Caine said, getting a little testy. "Why don't you help us skip a step?"

Shaking her head slowly, she began to say something, then her chin crinkled and her mouth quivered. Caine exchanged glances with an equally surprised Sevilla, and when they looked back at Maria, she was wiping a tear with the tip of her jersey.

"The big dummy," she was saying. "I told him no one would be fooled . . . but then, he was right, wasn't he? Nobody ever figured it out. Except for you, finding the place . . . and even you still haven't put two and two together."

Caine felt a snake slither through his stomach. "Thomas Lessor," he said.

Sevilla frowned at him, uncomprehending.

Caine went on: "This is his apartment . . . or anyway, it belonged to him."

"Bravo," Maria said, and another tear trickled and was dabbed away.

"Tee-Minor—Thomas Minor, Thomas Lessor . . . ?"

"Tee-Minor owns this building," Maria said, "and a few others."

Caine said, "You and Lessor were involved?"

She studied him for a long moment. "Yes . . . but maybe not the way you think."

"He was providing you an apartment, but it wasn't an intimate relationship?"

She made a face. "Did I say it wasn't intimate? It just wasn't one of those . . . intense things, where I loved him madly and wanted him to leave his wife and all that storybook b.s."

"What did you want?"

"To have a little fun—and hang onto the lounge job at the Conquistador, maybe get a shot at the new hotel, Oasis, the lounge there . . . Vegas. We were grown-ups having a good time."

"He was using you," Sevilla said, "you were using him."

"And this is a bad thing," Maria asked archly, "why?"

Caine had just put something together. "The night Lessor arrived in Vegas—the night he was murdered— he was headed here, wasn't he?"

"You mean when he didn't show up at the hotel?" Maria asked. "Yes. Here."

"Weren't you upset when he didn't show up?"

"Upset? No. Maybe a little annoyed. See, with the kind of . . . arrangement we had, he might show up, or he might not."

"Didn't he usually call, if he was canceling?"

"Usually. But, what the hell—I just figured his wife decided to travel with him at the last minute or something. With her on his arm, he wouldn't be stopping by to say hi to me, now would he?"

Caine said nothing.

She went on: "It wasn't until I saw it on the news, that you'd found him on the beach, that I . . . I knew he was dead." Her chin crinkled again, but no more tears flowed.

"That wouldn't annoy you," Caine asked, "his wife coming along on a Miami visit with him?"

Maria rubbed at her forehead. "No! How many times I gotta tell you? I knew he was married and that he was going to stay married."

"Your relationship was serious enough," Sevilla said, "for him to pay for and maintain this apartment."

With a nod to the surroundings, Maria said, "Maybe so, but I make enough to keep it myself. He set me up here when I landed the job singing at the Conquistador. It was supposed to be a starter thing, help me get settled . . . but Tom just kept paying the rent, telling me to save my money."

"Is that when the sexual relationship started?" Sevilla asked.

"Was I trading sex for rent? You want to bust me for prostitution or something? Lady, I'm trying to help here."

Caine didn't point out that if she'd really been trying to help, Maria Chacon might have come forward with this information long ago. Instead, he said, "We're a little fuzzy on whether this is a personal relationship or a business one."

"Read my lips," Maria said. "Both. . . . Believe it or not, Tom was a nice guy, who liked to do nice things for people he liked."

Such as beautiful lounge singers who gave him sexual favors.

"Hey, sure, from jump, I could tell he wanted me." She turned her gaze on Sevilla. "You're attractive, Detective. You can read men. It's not hard to know what they want."

"So he came on to you?" Sevilla asked.

Maria thought about that. "Actually . . . I more came on to him. I mean, overtly came on, after I . . . got his number. Think what you want about me, but I was after a longer engagement here and I wanted my Vegas shot. Show business is hard—having a 'friend' like Tom made a lot of my dreams look like their coming true was a possibility."

Caine jumped back in. "Why the elaborate ruse? Why is 'Tee-Minor' your landlord?"

"The hotel actually paid the first month's rent—it was part of the deal. Tom gave me a six-month contract for the lounge, and helped me find an apartment. I didn't realize till later that he had the hotel rent something from a company he secretly set up himself."

Shifting gears, Caine said, "You aren't from here," more statement than question.

"That's right—I'm a New York girl. Parents are still there." She shrugged. "I did some singing in little clubs on the East Coast, and thought there had to be an easier place to break in. So I came to Miami."

"And you got the job at the Conquistador."

"Yeah, after like a hundred auditions at every rat hole along the beach and every dive between here and the 'Glades. But I knew it would happen."

"Knew?"

"With my looks, and Cuban heritage, I'm a natural for this market. Hey, damn straight, I got the job at the

Conquistador. On my talent. Later on, okay, so I feathered my nest a little."

"Ms. Chacon," Caine said, "if we've seemed judgmental . . ."

"I got a thick skin, Lieutenant. Show business is a hard road. And I'm making it, too—I drew the people in, almost from the start. Got some good reviews, and audiences came, and I blew through the first six-month contract and now I'm into my second. Tom booked me into Vegas, supposed to be coming up, but I don't know if it'll be honored now . . ."

"Why wouldn't it?"

With half a shrug, she said, "Daniel might be a prick about it. Might insist I stay put. What the hell . . . I've got mucho talent, mister, and every day I work at the Conquistador gives me the chance to polish the act a little more."

Caine changed course again. "Did you know Lessor had a similar relationship with another singer, in Vegas?"

She drew in a breath, almost like she'd taken a punch. "I found out," she finally said, letting out the air with the words. "I overheard him bragging about Erica to one of his buddies one night, when he thought I wasn't listening."

"And how did you feel about that?"

"Not all warm and fuzzy inside . . . but I wasn't jealous."

"Right," Caine said dryly. "It wasn't that kind of relationship."

"Now you get it." She shrugged. Her coffee was ready and she turned to it. "All it meant to me was that maybe there was someone between me and the Oasis gig . . . but there's a hell of a lot more than one hotel in Las Vegas."

"You figured if Tom didn't book you into the Oasis, he could pull some strings and get you in someplace else?"

"Exactly." Pouring herself a cup of coffee, she asked, "You sure you don't want one?"

The aroma filled the small room, but Caine said he was sure. Sevilla, however, relented and accepted a cup.

"Cream and sugar?" Maria asked.

"Black's fine," Sevilla said.

She served Sevilla, saying, "I mean, Tom knew every booker in Vegas. After Vegas, I figure LA, and a record deal. So what if the guy had a big libido—a wife and girls in every port. Who gives a shit? Me making it—that's all that matters."

Sevilla couldn't let go of it. "So it was strictly business, then, sleeping with him?"

Maria's sad smile appeared over the rim of her cup. "And for the fun, lady—Tom Lessor could be a lot of fun. Is it okay if I don't go into detail?"

"It's fine," Caine said. "But there must have been more to it than just the physical. There were a lot of calls from his cell phone to here."

She nodded. "Sure. We liked each other. We were pals. We talked a lot, after him and his wife moved to Vegas. Just to stay in touch, y'know, and keep 'love' alive between his visits."

Caine frowned. "You told me Daniel Boyle was using a private investigator to try to catch his stepfather fooling around. You said Daniel told you himself."

She looked sheepish. "That was a . . . little white lie. It was Tom who told me about the PI—he knew what Daniel was up to, trying to expose him to Deborah Lessor. That's why we had this place—why the place is in the Tee-Minor name."

"Lessor put the place in that name because of you?"

"I don't really know," she said, and sipped her coffee again. "I'm sure I wasn't the first singer he ever 'helped' and I'm pretty sure Tee-Minor figured into the thing with the girl in Vegas too."

"What makes you say that?"

She shrugged. "He was paying my way—why not hers?"

Caine had to admit the singer had a point. He would pass that on to the CSIs in Las Vegas.

"Daniel admitted to using a private eye in Vegas," Caine said. "You mentioned a PI in Miami, too."

"Tom thought there was one—thought he was being followed. But that's all I know. A guy cheating around like Tom, he's going to be paranoid."

Caine studied her as she casually sipped her coffee. Then he said, "Sometimes a woman in a relationship like this starts out wanting nothing from a man except what he can do for her—for her career, in this case."

"That's right."

"Only sometimes a woman in that kind of relationship can fall for the guy. Are you sure you didn't want more from him than a career boost?"

Maria shook her head. "What more could he have given me? Christ, I sure as hell didn't want him around all the time. I've got my own goals. Tom could help me achieve them, but I never saw him as the man of my dreams that I would share it with. Why would I want a tomcat like that in my life, for real?"

Caine frowned. "And you weren't worried that he would shut you out in favor of the singer in Vegas?"

Her smile turned lascivious. "Singing isn't my only talent, Lieutenant. And in our relationship, I wasn't the only one having fun. Tom was never going to shut me out completely. Besides, he knew that I knew Daniel was trying to bring him down."

Surprised, Caine said, "Are you implying you'd have blackmailed him, to get what you wanted?"

"No. But Tom had to respect the possibility. Hey . . . Daniel wanted him out of the picture, big time."

"And Daniel never really suspected that you and his stepfather were . . . secretly an item?"

She smirked. "You've met Daniel—does he strike you as a Rhodes scholar? He's a silver-spoon baby. And he never suspected anything. Trust me."

"How deep would you say Daniel's hatred for his stepfather runs?"

"How deep ya got? So much so that Daniel followed Tom to Vegas. What's that do for you?"

Caine leaned forward. "Daniel followed his stepfather to Las Vegas?"

"Oh yeah—hoping to catch him out there." She snapped her fingers. "He was out there a buncha times . . . including when that other singer was killed."

Silence draped the little apartment, as that sank in for all concerned.

Tentatively, Maria said, "You . . . you don't think Daniel could have killed her . . . and tried to frame Tom?"

Now Caine shrugged. "It is a possibility."

Another reason to call the Las Vegas crime lab.

Maria sat in silence for several long seconds, seemingly mulling her theory.

Finally, she said, "But why kill Tom when he got here . . . if he was going to frame him back there?"

" 'He' who?" Sevilla asked, frowning.

"Daniel Boyle," Caine explained, following Maria's line of thought. "If Boyle killed the singer in Vegas and was going to frame Lessor for it, why kill the man, especially in Miami, in Boyle's own backyard."

Maria nodded. "So—you do think Daniel killed Tom?"

Caine held up a hand in a stop motion. "I never said that. You laid out a theory, and I clarified it."

"Okay, okay . . ." Compelling and dark, her eyes locked onto his. "Who do you think did it?"

Caine only smiled, vaguely. "Maria—I'm a crime scene investigator. I don't think anyone is a better suspect than anyone else . . . until the evidence points me in that direction."

Maria took a long drink from her coffee, then twitched a little smile. "I didn't mean to pry, Lieutenant—I was just wondering if you thought it was safe for me to go to work. With a murderer on the loose and all."

This was said lightly, but with underlying seriousness, enough so that Sevilla gave Caine a look that said, "Oh, brother."

"Sure," Caine said, "it's safe for you to go to work. We just have to find out who the person behind the killing is . . . and why he or she wanted to have Tom killed."

"And you think you'll succeed?"

Rising, Caine said, "Maria, how convinced are you that you're going to make a name for yourself?"

She smiled. "Completely. Utterly. Ab-so-lute-ly."

"That's how sure I am," he said.

And he rose. So did Sevilla. Maria kept her chair, though.

"That's reassuring," the singer said. Whether there was irony in her tone, Caine couldn't say. "I'll sleep better."

Sevilla thanked the woman for the coffee and they found their own way to the door.

Back in the Hummer, the CSI and the detective stayed quiet as Caine pulled away from the curb and started east toward Collins Avenue.

"Well," Sevilla said. "What do you think?"

"She's a woman who knows what she wants."

"Yes indeed. . . . Do you think one of the things she wanted was Tom Lessor dead?"

Caine lifted one shoulder in a halfhearted shrug. "If she's telling the truth—and she wasn't jealous of either the wife or the other singer—then what's her motive?"

Arms folded, Sevilla smirked and looked out the window. "If she wasn't jealous, she's a lot more liberated than I'm ever going to be."

He laughed lightly and pulled up to a stoplight as it turned red.

"I will tell you one thing," Caine said.

"Which is?"

"I would not get between Maria Chacon and anything that she wants."

The detective thought about that. "I wouldn't disagree . . . but my money's still on the stepson."

"Well, then," Caine said, cheerily, "let's go find out why he never told us about being in Las Vegas at the time of the murder of Erica Hardy."

"Why don't we?" Sevilla said.

The light turned green. Caine swung the Hummer left and drove toward the Conquistador to have one more chat with Daniel Boyle.

9

Hard-Boyled

STUCK IN TRAFFIC with Detective Sevilla as his passenger, Horatio Caine used his cell phone to check in with Catherine Willows, or anyway try to—she wasn't picking up and he ended up leaving a voice mail asking her to call him ASAP. Then he called HQ and none of the team had anything new to report.

"You better wrap it up, then," he advised Speedle. "All this overtime is gonna bite us where we sit."

"We were just getting ready to call it a day here, H. You need anything before I head out?"

Caine momentarily mulled that over, then said, "Yeah, Speed—see if Detective Bernstein's still around and check on whether Gino Forlani or the Cappelletti brothers—or more to the point, any of their flunkies— were in Las Vegas in the last six months."

"Why Vegas, H?"

"The Forlanis and the Caps are acquaintances of Daniel Boyle. If he hired this done . . ."

"Gotcha, boss. Anything else?"

"Can't think of anything. Sevilla and I have to follow up on Boyle . . ."

"Jeez, how many times you gotta talk to that dipstick?"

"Until he stops lying and withholding information, I guess. After that, we'll pack it in too."

Good-byes were said, and Caine clicked off.

Tracking the mobsters might be a long shot, but this was looking like a contract job, and an organized-crime link made sense.

This reminded him of his geriatric Murder, Inc. trio, and he asked Sevilla, "Did you check on Lipnick's hearing aid?"

"Oh! Yes . . . sorry. Neither the mortuary nor the hospital logged that in among his effects."

Another dead end.

Still . . .

Caine said, "Probably should check with Lipnick's doctor."

"First thing tomorrow okay, Horatio?"

"Sure."

The Hummer pulled into the Conquistador and—as he parked, then climbed down—Caine noticed that the valet parking attendants didn't even look up when he drove in anymore.

They strode into the lobby, the early evening wave of businessmen rushing in for happy hour already in the bar. The tourists were either heading for the pool—even though it was pretty cool already—or trooping out the front door to their waiting cars and whatever dinner attraction awaited them.

As he strolled toward the front desk, Caine took off

his sunglasses and placed them around his neck inside the open throat of his black dress shirt. He saw no sign of Daniel Boyle as he quickly scanned the area behind the check-in counter front. Three clerks were on duty back there—one helping a customer confused by a map, the other two chatting.

With Sevilla at his side, Caine approached the pair, who were standing off to one side, and discreetly showed them his badge. "Daniel Boyle, please?"

The young woman, whose name tag said JUANITA, froze. Both she and her male companion—neither of whom Caine had dealt with before—had clearly heard about the police coming around.

Uneasily, Juanita said, "Mr. Boyle, he's in his office."

The second clerk, turning toward the door marked PRIVATE, said, "I'll announce you."

Caine shook his head. "Let's keep it spontaneous."

The two wide-eyed hotel employees nodded and hustled off to do something they had suddenly remembered needed tending. If Caine didn't miss his guess, their chores would take them away from the front desk by the time Boyle came out of that door.

Sevilla followed Caine around the desk to the private office, and the two walked in without knocking, to find Boyle on the phone.

The slender, boyishly handsome hotel manager wore an expensive gray suit with a blue dress shirt and a blue-and-red-striped tie. His cherry desk—so neatly organized on Caine's last visit—was piled with papers and open folders. When Boyle looked up and saw who the intruders were, his face registered surprise and then irritation.

"Let me get back to you," Boyle said to the phone. "I've just had something unpleasant turn up." He slammed the receiver in the hook, seemingly without waiting for a reply. "You don't just burst into my office unannounced!"

Caine put on mock surprise. "Actually, I think I just did, Daniel."

Politely, Caine held out one of the chairs opposite Boyle's desk for Sevilla to sit, which she did. Then he sat himself, crossed a leg casually, folded his arms, and beamed at Daniel Boyle.

"Jesus!" Boyle said. "What the hell do you want now?"

"Well . . . just as a change of pace . . . I was thinking maybe—the truth?"

"I haven't lied to you!" The hotel manager sounded injured. Then he thought for a moment, and added, lamely, "Except for . . . about my relationship with Tom. And I explained that."

Caine nodded, conceding that. "This is more a . . . sin of omission."

The wing of Boyle's desk curved around its owner giving him access to the computer monitor, which was humming—something on screen this time, though Caine couldn't see what. Boyle reached over and touched the power button, the monitor going immediately black.

"Really," Boyle said. "I've tried to cooperate, but if this harassment continues, I may have to call my attorney."

"Why?" Caine said, with mock amazement. "Do you need one?"

"You're accusing me of lying in a murder investigation! What . . . what do you mean, anyway? What 'sin of omission'?"

"I was thinking about your trip to Las Vegas."

Boyle's eyes tightened in confusion, and he leaned back in his chair as if doing his best to distance himself from the officers. "I've made a lot of Vegas trips. It's part of my job with the company."

"I was thinking specifically of you being in Vegas at the time of Erica Hardy's murder."

He made a face and shrugged. "Why is that important?"

Caine sat forward. "You didn't think a woman's murder was important?"

"I didn't say that! Hell . . . how was I supposed to know it was important in this matter—to you? That's a Vegas case. It's a thousand miles from here."

Sevilla said, "You know very well, Mr. Boyle, that we're exploring whether or not the Erica Hardy slaying had a bearing on your stepfather's murder."

He snorted. "Do I? My world doesn't revolve around you people."

Caine was watching Boyle carefully—were these natural reactions, or rehearsed ones? He asked, "Did you talk to the Las Vegas Police, while you were there?"

Sitting forward again, on safer ground, Boyle let his hands drop onto the desktop. "Of course I talked to them. They questioned me the night it happened, but it didn't take them long, at all, to determine my innocence."

Now Caine really wished he'd gotten through to

Catherine Willows. "Did they ask who you were traveling with?"

"Sure they did."

"Who were you traveling with?"

"Me, myself, and I."

"Were either Gino Forlani or the Cappelletti brothers in Vegas that week? Or their people?"

Boyle's palms flew wide and so did his eyes. "Jesus Christ, Caine! How the fuck should I know?"

"You might be interested to learn that we're checking on that now."

"Well, aren't you the thorough little Eagle Scout."

Caine notched his voice up. "And if your mob pals were in Vegas, you won't just be talking to me. It'll be the organized-crime task force, and probably the FBI. That won't be good for your reputation as a hotel man—particularly in Vegas. The gaming commission will take real interest."

"Why are you hounding me?" Boyle's voice was almost a whine. "I didn't do anything wrong. I didn't kill my stepfather and I sure as hell didn't murder that conniving little whore!"

"What did you say?" Sevilla asked sharply, rising in her chair; her voice was as cold and cutting as a well-honed knife blade.

Boyle whitened. "I . . . I'm sorry. I mean, what would you call a woman who was stealing your mother's husband?"

Caine's smile was icy. "Choice of words aside, Daniel . . . this all sounds suspiciously like a motive."

Boyle pounded his desk with his fist. "I . . . did . . . not . . . do it."

An awkward silence just hung there, for several seconds.

Then Caine said, "You didn't do it. . . . Even though with Thomas Lessor's death, you're in line for a promotion—both here at the hotel, and in your bank account, should anything happen to your mother."

Boyle leaned on both elbows, his face largely covered with his hands. "Please, Lieutenant Caine . . . just get off my back, will you? I've been over this, endlessly, with the Las Vegas cops."

"Go over it just once, for us."

Boyle lowered his hands; sat up; tasted his tongue; gathered himself. Then, calmly, he said, "When Erica Hardy was murdered, I was at the craps table at the Romanov. I was making out like a bandit, and there were a hundred witnesses . . . not to mention the hotel's videotape. Ask Las Vegas: I haven't killed anyone."

Caine shrugged. "Well, maybe not personally . . ."

". . . Not personally? What are you saying? . . . You think I hired it done?"

Caine leaned forward and raised three fingers; it was not an Eagle Scout salute. "Three men were involved in arranging the abduction and murder of your stepfather. It has all the earmarks of a mob-related assassination. You are a known associate of organized crime."

"What complete and utter bullshit!"

Ever since Boyle's unfortunate outburst, Sevilla had been staring at him coldly. She said, "You're a mama's boy, aren't you, Daniel?"

Caine glanced at the detective, keeping himself outwardly blank, if inwardly amused.

Boyle's eyes popped. "What did you say?"

Calmly, Sevilla said, "Two people were doing your mother wrong—your stepfather and his . . . woman. Maybe Mama would love you even more, if you took them out of the picture?"

Boyle was clearly unnerved; his lower lip trembling, he said, looking from the detective to the CSI and back again, "You better leave. Both of you. You better just leave. I want you—"

Caine's phone rang, interrupting the hotel manager in mid-rant. He held up a finger in "please wait" fashion, saying, "Hold that thought, Daniel."

Boyle's mouth dropped open and a breathy, you-gotta-be-kidding-me grunt emanated from down deep.

Punching the cell phone button, Caine said, "Horatio."

"It's Catherine Willows. You called?"

"Yeah, give me just a minute." He turned to Sevilla. "I need to take this—I'm gonna step out in the hall." He raised a finger and moved it from Boyle to Sevilla. "You two play nice while I'm away."

"Take your time," Sevilla said, and Boyle made the breathy grunt sound again.

In the hall, having closed the door, Caine said into the phone, "Sorry, Catherine. . . . I'm in the middle of an interview with a guy who just could be a suspect in your Erica Hardy case."

"All due respect, Horatio," she said. "I doubt you've got a new and valid suspect for us—DNA don't lie. And I've got Thomas Lessor's DNA under the victim's fingernails. Lessor murdered Erica Hardy, no question."

"The evidence couldn't have been cooked, by somebody who wanted to frame Lessor?"

"Highly unlikely. The CIA doesn't have the tools to fake that kind of crime scene evidence."

He sighed. "You better bring me up to speed."

"Scratches on his face, skin under her nails. The last DNA sample was from under her toenail. Scrappy little girl was really fighting. And our new evidence: her toenail matched the scratch in Lessor's chest."

With each tidbit, Caine became that much more disappointed. "Then I take it you did interview Daniel Boyle?"

"Oh yeah. Is he your new Erica Hardy suspect?"

Almost embarrassed, Caine said, "Afraid so."

"Well, Boyle's not much of a human being—and I wouldn't be surprised if he was dirty somehow. Maybe he did do your murder, his stepfather, I mean . . . but our murder—Erica Hardy? He's innocent. . . . How good is he looking for yours?"

"He just feels right, and there's some circumstantial stuff . . . but, really, Catherine, I've got no evidence that would catch any self-respecting DA's eye."

"Too bad. Wanna talk about it?"

Caine wondered if Willows was fishing, or actually trying to help. Either way, he just didn't have time.

"Maybe later. Right now, I have to get back to my interview. I left Boyle alone with a fairly pissed-off cop."

"Ha. Happy hunting, Horatio."

"Thanks, Catherine."

They rang off.

Back in Boyle's office, Sevilla was sitting in tense silence, her eyes boring into Boyle, whose nervousness was palpable.

To Sevilla, Caine said, "That was my contact in Las Vegas. Mr. Boyle is in the clear there."

"What did I tell you?" Boyle said.

Caine twitched a non-smile and sat back down. "That doesn't clear you in Miami, Daniel. Not hardly."

Boyle's face fell. "What in the hell do I have to do to convince you that I had nothing to do with Tom's death?"

"Be truthful, Daniel. Don't withhold key information." Caine settled. "For example—did you know about your stepfather and Erica Hardy?"

The hotel manager shook his head. "No. . . . That is, not until after she turned up dead."

Caine's eyes frowned. "But you had a detective following Lessor."

Boyle shrugged open-handedly. "I suspected Tom was screwing around, only I couldn't catch him at it. . . . Neither could the private eye I hired." His smile was tired, defeated. "But no matter what I thought of Tom, he was a clever son of a bitch. I really had no idea about Erica."

"Were there other women?"

With a little shrug, Boyle said, "Not that I could prove. I thought there were a couple of possibilities—showgirls—out there, rumors . . . but, end of the day . . . a handful of air."

Caine shifted in his chair. "Did you know about Lessor and Maria Chacon?"

Boyle laughed. "What? Are you high, Lieutenant?"

"I get a natural high whenever I put a murderer

away, Daniel. Lessor and Maria. Did you know they were having an affair? Simple question."

Now Boyle crossed his arms, his manner suddenly smug. "Let's just say I knew she was having an affair."

"But not who she was having it with, you mean."

"Lieutenant, I knew who she was having it with. Let me assure you"—he chuckled—"I knew."

Caine had the thought first, but it was Sevilla who blurted it: "You're having an affair with Maria Chacon?"

He gave a little shrug, smiled smugly, and lifted his eyebrows up and down; it was just a little less subtle than Groucho Marx making a suggestive remark.

"If that is what you mean," the detective said, her voice glacial, "then say it, Mr. Boyle—out loud."

He shrugged, and said, lightly, "I am having an affair with Maria Chacon. And—not that it's any of your business—I'm having a wonderful time."

Boyle glanced at Caine, in an I'm-a-luckier-guy-than-you-aren't-I manner; but the CSI supervisor was not impressed.

"Well, then," Caine said, in apparent good humor, "I guess this is one of those rare cases . . ."

"What rare cases?" Boyle asked.

"Like stepfather," Caine said, "like stepson."

"What . . . ?"

"Think about it, Daniel."

Boyle's eyes went wide and empty; and then those eyes began to fill up with realization. He sat back as if Caine had slapped him, his chin dropping to his chest. "You're . . . you're shitting me."

"Not a bit," Caine said.

"No way. Maria—she and Tom—no fucking way!"

"Way," Sevilla said quietly.

Boyle lurched forward in his chair. "Who the hell told you?"

"She did," Caine said.

The hotel man froze. Then he flopped back in his chair. His mouth hung open like a trapdoor he'd just fallen through.

"Let me ask you a question, Daniel," Caine said, filling the stunned silence. "Have you ever been to Maria's apartment?"

"No. We always go to the house, or . . . just use a room here."

"Never to her apartment. Why is that?"

He swallowed; shrugged halfheartedly. "She has a roommate."

"That's right, Daniel," Caine said. "And her roommate's name is—or was—Thomas Lessor."

Shaking his head slowly, Boyle said, "I can't believe it."

"He was paying for the apartment, Daniel . . . or anyway, a holding company was."

"I just . . . can't."

"I don't know what to tell you, Daniel—she admitted it."

His face reddened, his eyes flared. "That lying bitch! The dirty little—"

"Don't say it, Daniel," Sevilla said.

He was raving, though. "I asked her! Asked her point-blank if she'd done Tom to get this gig, and she swore up and down she didn't!"

Caine couldn't stop the smile. "And you really thought she'd give you a straight answer?"

Boyle began to pull on his dark hair and Caine wondered if he was getting some insight into how the hotel manager had developed the several cowlicks that plagued him.

"What a fool I am . . . I should have known—God! What a fucking fool!" Boyle's voice was raspy. He was holding back tears. "And you call me a liar! That little bitch—she lies about everything. Lies through her teeth!"

Interested, Caine asked, "For example?"

"Well, hell—about Tom! About me being the only man in her life—Jesus, every damn thing!"

Caine cut in between rants. "Do you think your stepfather knew about you and Maria?"

Boyle blanched. "Oh, my God!"

"That wasn't a statement, Daniel," Caine said coolly, "it was a question. Do you think he knew?"

The man's eyes were wild. "And if he did, what then? You'll have me killing Tom to have her to myself, or to keep him from telling my mother that I was screwing my own lounge singer! Maria was probably lying to him the way she was lying to me."

"Then, you don't think he knew?"

Boyle threw his hands in the air. "Christ, how the hell should I know? Ask the lying bitch yourself!" He stole a look at Sevilla, who was glaring at him. "Ask Maria!"

"Oh we will," Caine said.

Pulling at his hair again, Boyle said, "I should have known! Should've figured it out—I mean, after all, she lied from day one!"

Caine cocked his head. "Did she? How so?"

"Well, for starters—she lied to get the job."

"In what way?"

"The Latina thing! Oh, sure, we go along with it, it's good business."

"I'm not following you, Daniel."

"Oh yeah, sure, we advertise her as Maria Chacon, play up the Cubano angle . . . have her do lots of salsa music—the tourists go batty for that meringue shit."

Caine raised a palm; the guy was ranting again. "Daniel, I still am not following you."

Boyle grunted a laugh. "She's no more Cuban than you are, Lieutenant. Or Puerto Rican or even Mexican, for that matter."

"She mentioned being Cuban to us," Caine said, with a glance at Sevilla.

"Well, more lies." Boyle grinned rather crazily. "I didn't find out till we signed the contract, with her legal name. Hell—she's from Jersey! She's a goddamn wop!"

Sevilla leapt half out of the chair in outrage but visibly held herself in check.

Caine asked, softly, "Chacon—it's not her real name?"

Shaking his head, Boyle said, "No, it's . . . I don't know, I don't remember . . . it's Chiaverini or Chicanini or some such shit."

A wave of adrenaline swept through Caine, immediately replaced by the numbing calm that allowed him to control the situation, no matter what his emotions wanted him to do.

"Would it be . . . Ciccolini?" he asked.

"Yeah, yeah, that's it," Boyle said, nodding vigorously. "Ciccolini. It only came up at contract time, and then we had a little chat about it—she laughed and said, hey, it's just show biz. Cary Grant was really Archie Leach, she says. Hey, she's even got a bank account as Maria Chacon now—that's how she wants to be paid." Another shrug. "Latin thing's workin' for her."

Caine threw Sevilla a look and they stood.

"No trips to Vegas or anywhere else, Daniel," Caine said, "without checking in with us, first."

"No problem. So you're gonna go see Maria again?"

Sevilla said, "What we do next really doesn't have a thing to do with you, Mr. Boyle."

This was meant to be a put-down, obviously, but Boyle's reply only sounded relieved: "Good. That is good to hear."

As they drove to Vincent Ciccolini's home in Coral Gables, Sevilla said, "So Maria Chacon shares a last name with one of our elderly hit men . . . so what do we have? A family thing, or a contract kill?"

"Yes," Caine said.

As before, there was no answer when they rang Ciccolini's doorbell; and—once again—they drove around the corner to the Rosselli home.

Rebecca Rosselli answered the door, wearing jeans and a light blue Polo shirt, a little big for her, her husband's maybe. She had a smile that vanished quickly enough to indicate she'd been waiting for someone else.

"Oh—it's you," she said. "I suppose you want to know if Anthony can come out to play."

"Something like that," Caine said. "Is he home?"

"No—and I'm expecting a friend, and would rather not be embarrassed by you people being around."

"I can understand that. We'll make it brief."

She shook her head. "This is starting to feel like harassment."

Sevilla said, "You'll know when it's harassment, Mrs. Rosselli."

Caine shot the detective a look, then said to Mrs. Rosselli, "I'm sure this is an inconvenience . . . but two men have suffered the larger inconvenience of being murdered."

Mrs. Rosselli just looked at him, her big brown showgirl eyes cold as the big diamond on her wedding-ring finger.

Caine continued: "We have some new information that makes it necessary for us to talk to your husband again."

Worry tightened her eyes, just a little. "I said Anthony wasn't here."

"Then we'll talk to you. May we come in?"

Reluctantly, she moved aside so Caine and Sevilla could enter.

The home had a comfortable, lived-in feel, the living room spacious—a matching floral sofa and loveseat making a pit group in the corner to Caine's right. An end table squatted on either side, with a low, square coffee table in the middle; a dark green leather recliner perched at the other end, all of them facing a big-screen television on the wall to his left. A large oil painting of some venerable Italian city hung on the wall over the sofa. Family photos filled the space between the door and the picture window, immediately to his right, with more framed photos scattered on the tables and atop the TV.

"Won't you sit down," Mrs. Rosselli asked flatly—
no politeness in the words but no sarcasm, either—as
she moved to the far end of the sofa and perched on it,
seeming to barely touch the fabric. Sevilla and Caine
shared the loveseat.

Caine got right to it. "Do you know if Vincent
Ciccolini has any relatives in the city?"

She shrugged. "Sure."

"Such as?"

"His niece."

"Maria?" he prodded.

"Yes, Maria—she's a singer. Doing very well. We
went to one of her shows but left early—much too
loud. Why must modern music be so loud?" Another
shrug. "I've only met her once or twice."

"Are Maria and Vincent close?"

"Far as it goes. I mean, they're generations apart.
Guess they see more of each other than the average
uncle and niece, 'cause each other is all the family
they got down here."

"That's understandable."

"Of course you know how these young kids are—
not much time for us dinosaurs. She's got her career
and everything."

"You know much about her?"

"Just what I gather from Vinnie. She come down
here from Jersey, what—maybe a year, year and a half
ago?" Mrs. Rosselli's eyes narrowed. "Why so curious
about Maria?"

Figuring he had to trade something to get something, Caine said, "Maria was acquainted with one of
the men who was murdered."

Mrs. Rosselli frowned and she made a *tsk-tsk* sound that seemed more perfunctory than caring. "That's a shame for her. Is she doing all right with it? She was close to this man?"

"They dated." Treading carefully now, he said, "She's upset, naturally."

"Just a shame. You know, we've seen crime down here get worse and worse, over these fifteen years. Drugs and murder and perversion on every street corner—and then you police come bother harmless retirees like us."

"Don't you think Vinnie would be interested in helping his niece get through this painful experience?"

She didn't know how to respond to that; finally she said, "Wanna know that, you should talk to Vinnie. Anthony and I have nothing to do with Maria whatever-her-new-name-is."

"I'm sure. But I do need to ask him—and of course Mr. Ciccolini—a few more questions."

She glared at Caine and Sevilla. "Wasn't nagging them at the funeral home bad enough? Disgraceful. You people should be ashamed."

"We have to ask questions based on new information that's come up since we first spoke to your husband and his friend."

"What new information?"

"It's really nothing that concerns you, Mrs. Rosselli. As you rightly said, you have nothing to do with it."

She frowned, deep, her lip curling a tiny sneer. "You're trying to pin this thing on the fellas, aren't you? What a crock!"

Caine took in a breath and let it out slowly. "Mrs.

Rosselli, I don't pin anything on anyone. My job is following evidence. Evidence led me here. Once I've spoken to your husband again, it may lead me away, down some other avenue."

Now she seemed pouty. "Just the same," she said, "I can't think of why you should bother Anthony with this."

"Please tell us where we can find him."

Slowly, she shook her head. "We have a right to our privacy. To our own law-abiding lives."

Caine turned casually to Sevilla. "Call in a squad car, would you?"

The detective said, "Certainly. . . . Shall I have them approach with the siren on?"

"That's a fine idea. Then we'll know right when they get here."

Sevilla withdrew her cell phone and punched in dispatch. She identified herself, continuing, "I'm with Lieutenant Caine—we need a squad car at our location. Lights and siren."

She listened for a moment, then gave the person on the other end her badge number and the address. After another few seconds of listening, she said, "Thanks," and hung up. To Caine she said, "Ten minutes, tops."

"Fine." He returned his gaze to their wide-eyed hostess, giving her a blandly benign smile. "Now, Mrs. Rosselli, here's what's going to happen. We're going to keep that squad car right in front of your house, and the moment your husband comes home, the officers will let me know, and we'll be back—with our siren on."

"Why would you—"

"And in the meantime, that police car will sit right outside and I only hope you have a good relationship with your neighbors, that they're nice people who think well of you. We'd hate for them to get the wrong idea, in an upstanding neighborhood like this."

Rebecca Rosselli began to wring her hands. "You're bluffing. You wouldn't do that. You can't do that."

"I can and we just did."

"I'll file a complaint!"

"You can do that. And Detective Sevilla and I might receive a mild reprimand. But any damage to your reputation, here in Coral Gables, well . . . that will be done, won't it?"

She looked stricken. "Our neighbors . . . they'll never talk to us again."

"Very shallow of them," Caine said.

"Coral Gables can be a little snooty," Sevilla said.

Mrs. Rosselli sat forward. "I'm telling you the truth, Lieutenant—my Anthony left all that behind in New Jersey, Vincent and Abraham too. How can you be so cruel? Isn't it enough that we buried our best friend yesterday?"

"There's another option," Caine said.

"What?"

"Tell us where Anthony and Vinnie are. Where we can find them right this minute. . . . We only want to talk to them."

"Will you call off the car?"

"No."

"How about . . . just the siren?"

"Yes."

She swallowed, stiffened, chin out. "Do it, then."

Caine nodded to Sevilla, who made the call.

Struggling to keep her composure, Mrs. Rosselli finally said, "They've gone fishing."

"Where?"

"They have a place they always go on the river—the parks on the south side between Seventh and Twelfth."

"That's a good-size area."

She nodded. "Sorry I can't be more specific. They'll be along there somewhere, though."

"I can find them."

Through the picture window they could see a patrol car pulling up to park behind Caine's Hummer.

Mrs. Rosselli looked pleadingly at the CSI. "Would you make them go away now?"

"Glad to," he said. "But if this is a wild-goose chase, Mrs. Rosselli—we'll be back. Siren and all."

Caine and Sevilla rose to leave, the CSI taking the sunglasses from around his neck to stick in his pocket, now that night was falling. As he did, he turned to see the wall of photos next to the door.

One of them, right at eye-level, showed the three old friends—Anthony Rosselli, Vincent Ciccolini, and Abraham Lipnick. It was a portrait of the trio from the chest up, standing in front of the Rosselli home.

"Did you take this photo, Mrs. Rosselli?" he asked, pointing to the photo with the stem of his sunglasses.

"Yes." She swallowed and her voice turned melodramatic. "That was the last picture of the fellas together."

"Taken when?"

"Maybe . . . two months ago."

Caine studied the photo and Sevilla studied him, wondering what the fascination was.

All of the men were smiling, Rosselli and Ciccolini framing their late friend in the center, just three old men enjoying the good life in South Florida; casually dressed, Vinnie in a Dolphins Polo shirt, Tony in a red cardigan, and Abe wearing a brown V-necked pullover sweater over a tan shirt. Nothing special, really . . .

. . . except that Abraham Lipnick had a hearing aid in his right ear.

Looking at the photo, not Mrs. Rosselli, Caine asked her, "Mr. Lipnick—did he always wear a hearing aid?"

She didn't hesitate. "For as long as I knew him, he did."

"It wasn't an old-age malady?"

"Oh no, not at all! Abe had a bomb go off near him in Korea—screwed up his right ear real good. Never seemed to give him any problem, though—I mean, that the hearing aid didn't make up for."

Sevilla said, "When I saw him in the casket, he didn't have it in."

Mrs. Rosselli gave the detective an acid smile. "He doesn't need it, dear, where he's going."

"Thank you, Mrs. Rosselli," Caine said.

"Hurry back," Mrs. Rosselli said, at the door, and her sarcasm wasn't buried deep at all—not even as deep as Thomas Lessor's head.

The CSI and the detective were halfway down the sidewalk when the woman called out, "And would you please get that goddamn squad car out of here before someone sees it?"

"My pleasure," Caine said.

He and Sevilla stopped at the curb by the Hummer. Caine said, "Adele, catch a ride back with the squad, would you?"

"Why—where are you going?"

"To the river."

"After our fishermen?"

"That's right."

"And where, pray tell, am I going?"

"To find a judge who will issue an exhumation order for Abraham Lipnick."

"On what grounds?"

"I think I know where our murder weapon is."

She narrowed her eyes at him. "And how do I convince a judge to do that?"

"Remember the funeral home?"

"I'm not likely to forget."

"Jewish law states that Lipnick had to be buried within twenty-four hours. His friends were trying to see that he got his wish, in their own inept way."

"Right."

"Which means that as soon as they were finished at the funeral home, they went straight to the cemetery."

"Oh-kaay," Sevilla said.

"And what were they going to do?"

"Put keepsakes in with him." Then her eyes widened. "They put the gun in the coffin!"

Caine nodded. "Along with the Sinatra stuff—smokes and roll of dimes and bottle of booze. Can you sell a judge?"

"I know just the one," she said.

As Sevilla climbed into the squad car, Caine got into

the Hummer and started the vehicle with one hand and got out his cell phone with the other.

With Speedle and Bernstein already busy, he called Calleigh and told her what he needed; then he called Eric Delko, dropped the Hummer into gear and drove off . . .

. . . to do a little fishing, himself.

10

Gone Fishin'

THE FIVE-AND-A-HALF-MILE run of the Miami River was as diverse as the inhabitants of the city it bisected. Flowing roughly from Miami International Airport to the sea, the river was home not only to major shipping industry but recreational boaters, houseboats, and even the odd fishermen—like Anthony Rosselli and Vincent Ciccolini, if the former's wife could be believed about their current whereabouts.

Though night had touched the city like a cool, calming hand, few places in Miami were truly dark after sunset. From the brightly illuminated skyscrapers to the colored deco lighting along Miami Beach's Ocean Drive, the city glowed after dark—a glimmer that settled over the whole area, making it at once exotic and accessible.

Aiding Caine tonight were the parking lot lights where he left the Hummer and met up with Eric Delko.

"What's up, H?" Delko wore a light tan jacket over a cream-colored T-shirt with chinos; he might have been club-hopping.

"Our two surviving elderly hit men," Caine said, "are trying to make a catch along here, somewhere. . . . So are we."

"What's my job?"

"Back me up."

Delko grinned his boyish grin. "You think you need help, handling a coupla geezers?"

Caine looked at Delko sharply. "You might ask Thomas Lessor that question . . . just be prepared to divine the answer from his non-response."

"Uh, yeah. I get you."

"Good."

Streetlamps bordered the sidewalk that ran along the high ground, providing a yellowish glow. Once the two CSIs got down closer to the bank, Caine noticed that the lights of the city seemed to ride downriver with the current—it was a beautiful, slightly otherwordly shimmer.

As he and Delko walked along the grassy bank, Caine had more light than he'd hoped for; it was almost like dusk, though the sun had long since set. Every now and then they would pass a fisherman or two sitting in a lawn chair, maybe with a small Coleman lantern next to him, a line tossed casually into the water.

They had traveled nearly a mile, stopping by three different pairs of fishermen, and Caine was just starting to think Rebecca Rosselli had outfoxed him when they came upon the two men.

The suspected contract killers were sitting in lawn chairs, lines in the water, enjoying the peaceful evening, looking about as deadly as Felix and Oscar or maybe Ralph Kramden and Ed Norton.

Both men wore nylon warm-up jackets—Ciccolini's with a Dolphins logo, Rosselli's with a Marlins logo—and Ciccolini wore a matching Dolphins baseball cap while Rosselli had on a shapeless cotton hat with the brim turned down all the way around.

Ciccolini, in the far chair, saw him first. The yellow-tinged smile seemed amused, but the eyes were hard and cold and glittered in the night.

"Lieutenant Caine," Ciccolini said, as if tasting the words and not liking them. "What brings you out on the riverside on such a cool evening? I don't see any fishing gear."

Rosselli was frowning. "Who's the muscle?"

Delko seemed almost embarrassed by that, and Caine—genuinely amused—said, "This is one of my crew . . . Name's Delko. You know all about having a crew, don't you, fellas?"

Sounds of gentle laughter, possibly from a father and son they had passed up the bank, echoed off the rippling water. A peculiar combination of nature sounds and nearby traffic provided a unique sound-track to the tableau.

"Well, all due respect, boys," Ciccolini said, "we have this spot staked out. Find your piece of the river-bank."

Caine nodded, stared out on the water. "We're not going to interfere with your fishing. Caught anything yet?"

"No," Ciccolini said. "How about you?"

"I think so."

"You don't know?"

"I could use an opinion—an informed one. Mind if

I share my thoughts? I'll keep my voice down . . . try not to scare the fish."

Rosselli, shifting nervously in the lawn chair, said, "Free country."

Caine gazed at the lights of the city glistening on the river's mirror-like surface. He said, "It started with your niece, Mr. Ciccolini—Maria."

In the muted darkness, Caine could easily make out the discomfort registering on Vincent Ciccolini's face.

The CSI continued: "Maria Chacon, she calls herself now. She was jealous of Lessor's other women, or perhaps scared for her life, after Lessor killed that other singer in Vegas. We'll have a talk with her and nail that down. Either way, it was Maria's contract."

The two old men said nothing. Rosselli started fooling with his reel, probably just a pretense to cover his nervousness. Ciccolini might have been a statue of an old man fishing.

And Caine told the two men. Told them what they had done. . . .

Maria comes to her uncle Vinnie, needing help. The Trenton chapter of Murder, Inc. has come out of retirement already, in recent days . . . boredom, tight money, problems with Medicare. At least five hits in five months . . . Maria either knew of this return to homicidal form, or put the pieces together: Uncle Vinnie and his pals were back in business. And Vinnie and his two partners have a lifetime of experience—three lifetimes of experience—dealing with the kind of problem that Maria had.

And Maria's problem was called Thomas Lessor.

So the Trenton Social Club meets Lessor at the airport. Maria knows when her boyfriend's plane is getting in, and has tipped off Uncle Vinnie. It's late, middle of the night, fairly dead . . . which is good, because things would soon get deader. . . .

All three killers meet and greet Lessor and his chauffeur as the pair enter the parking garage. Two are wearing rubber masks, the other a disguise—a fake beard and mustache. One hustles Lessor into the car while the other two truss up the chauffeur with duct tape and toss him in the trunk. Lessor's bags are shoved inside with their owner, and the hijacked limo takes off.

"That much is on the airport videotape," Caine told them.

One man drives the limo, one rides in the back with Lessor, holding him at gunpoint, while the third brings up the rear in the trio's own car. The trip to Miami Beach doesn't take too long—traffic's light, and anyway, it's late, not too many people around, so they march Lessor right out onto the beach and pop him twice in the back of the head—an old technique which ain't broke so needs no fixing—using the same gun with which one of 'em shot Johnny "The Rat" Guzzoli, back in Trenton, in 1987.

"Now the gun I find particularly interesting," Caine said.

Delko was listening attentively, too, though the two elderly fishermen acknowledged no interest in anything but their lines.

"You like that .25, don't you, Vinnie? It's light, efficient, a good weapon in your line of work. I don't know which of you is the triggerman—maybe the late

Abe. Maybe it was his favorite piece. Maybe it's yours, Tony."

Delko said, "Being sentimental over a weapon . . . not a good idea."

"Not in this day and age," Caine said. "Of course, how could you know that when the case in Trenton got thrown out of court, the 'sentimental' CSI up there would hang onto his ballistics test results, and eventually enter them into a national bullet database?"

Ciccolini said, "No such thing. You're bluffing."

"It's called NIBIN," Delko said.

Up till now, everything's going fine. Only a distant security camera as witness to the kidnapping, and nobody was around when the trio popped the target. Looking like a piece-o'-cake hit for the Trenton three. That's when things start to go south.

The machete and garbage bags are in the trio's own vehicle, and the three old assassins—it's not as easy as in the old days, but it gets done—haul Lessor up onto a picnic table. Chop off the head and hands, the key identifiers; hack the torso into more easily disposable, portable chunks.

As Caine spun his scenario, Rosselli still fussed with his rod and fidgeted; Ciccolini, though, dropped all pretense of fishing and fired up a cigarette and turned toward Caine, sitting sideways on the lawn chair. He seemed to be enjoying the narrative.

"We found blood on the table," Caine was saying, "and cuts in the table matched those in Lessor's hands and feet—that's how we know you used a machete."

But somewhere in the midst of the butchery, Abraham

Lipnick—possessor of a bum ticker—goes and has a heart attack. Now things get complicated. Ciccolini and Rosselli have just killed and carved up a victim, have a kidnapped witness stuffed in the trunk of a stolen car, and suddenly their accomplice is threatening to flat-line on 'em.

Abe is on the ground, writhing in pain, perhaps semiconscious. The remaining two quickly confab. Ciccolini will drive Abe to the hospital, and do his best to make it seem as if Rosselli is also present . . . by mentioning him to nurses, "Tony's parking the car, Tony's got the trots. . . ."

But what Tony is really doing is finishing up with disposing of Lessor's body.

"Tell me, Tony," Caine said. "Did it bother you?"

Without looking at Caine, the old man, eyes on the river, said flatly, "Did what bother me?"

"That Vinnie left you alone, on the beach, to deal with a dismembered body? Did you always get the shit jobs?"

Ciccolini frowned at Caine. "Be polite."

"Didn't mean to step over the line," the CSI said. "But that's what happened, Vinnie—you took Abe to Mt. Sinai . . . not because that's where Abe wanted to go, but because it's the closest to where you were on the beach. If you'd been at the club on Drexel, where you're supposed to have been—and where you established a sort of alibi, earlier in the evening—you'd have taken him to South Shore. It's a no-brainer—much closer. Your pal's in trouble, after all—big trouble."

"I was at the hospital too," Rosselli said, eyes still on his line and the water.

"Sure—several of the staff at Mt. Sinai remember

seeing the both of you . . . but no one can nail down seeing you in the flesh, Tony, till much later. Maybe as late—or as early, depending on how you look at it—as five in the morning."

While Vince Ciccolini rushes Abe to the hospital, Anthony Rosselli cleans up the picnic area. The head, hands, and Lessor's personal items go into one garbage bag, the rest of the body into two or three or four more.

"You see," Caine said, "I'm not sure at what point in the process Abe had his heart attack. If it happened early on, Tony might've been left to do most of machete work himself."

"See?" Rosselli said, finally turning to look at Caine, with a sneering smile. "You're just guessing."

"That's how criminalistics works. We find evidence that provides puzzle pieces, then we extrapolate what the missing pieces are, or might be. For example, the bags that the torso went into. Maybe you buried them on the beach, too, Tony. Or maybe you just buried the bag with head and hands, and carted the other garbage bags off to pitch off a bridge or over the side of a fishing boat. We'll probably never know where the torso went, unless you fellas are nice enough to tell us."

Rosselli sneered some more. "You need a body to make anything stick."

"Oh, we have a body. Enough of one."

The old man on the beach, left alone to dispose of the dismembered corpse, is tired. It's been a hard night, he's beat, he's scared, so when he buries the head, hands, and personal effects, he doesn't go as deep as he might on a different occasion, on a different night, when he had two old friends to help him.

And as Rosselli is cleaning up after the murder, he finds Abe's hearing aid, where it fell when Abe's heart attacked him and the old boy had hit the ground. But Rosselli didn't realize that when Abe took his tumble, and the hearing aid popped free, the mechanism's battery slipped out . . . providing a tiny metal clue. . . .

"We found the battery on the beach, fellas," Caine told them. "But it didn't make its special meaning clear to me until about an hour ago . . . at your house, Anthony, where your charming wife was kind enough to invite us in."

"You'll need a warrant next time," Rosselli said.

Delko said, "We'll have one."

"The death of the chauffeur was an accident," Caine said. "You'll only do manslaughter on that death—plus kidnapping, of course. From what I've read of your file, you boys have never taken out a civilian—no innocent bystanders. But this time that policy, well . . . it kinda got away from you."

When Rosselli finishes burying the parts of Thomas Lessor, he still has one job left—he has to leave the limo where it will be found easily and Felipe Ortega . . .

"That's the chauffeur's name, by the way," Caine said, "in case you boys like to keep track of who you kill."

. . . and Felipe Ortega would be freed. After all, the hit is supposed to be on Lessor, not some innocent driver. Only Rosselli—perhaps a little flustered, a little frazzled, working on his own, in a hurry to get to Mt. Sinai and improve his alibi—never thinks to remove the duct tape gag . . . so when Felipe starts throwing up, the foul stuff has nowhere to go except his lungs.

"When I saw a photo of the three of you good fellas," Caine said, "I noticed that Abe was wearing a hearing aid. Mrs. Rosselli told me that Abe had worn a hearing aid since Korea, but I hadn't noticed, because the only time I'd seen him, in his casket, he hadn't been wearing it."

Ciccolini stood, tossing his fishing pole to the bank. He strode up to Caine. Hands on his hips, he said, "You don't have enough, Lieutenant. A hearing aid battery found on a beach frequented by hordes of seniors like us? Forget about it."

Caine smiled gently. "We will have something . . . very soon. Remember when we dropped by, the evening of Abe's visitation?"

"I'm not likely to forget you guys spoiling that sad occasion, no."

"Again, I'm not sure which of you carried the .25. Maybe it was Abe's gun, and you decided to bury his 'sword' with the fallen samurai. Or maybe it was just a good place to make a murder weapon go away. Maybe it's your favorite piece, Vinnie, and you were packing it, and when you saw us cops at the party, you panicked and decided to stuff it in Abe's coffin."

"Guesses. Just a buncha stupid guesses."

"Well, right now I'm guessing the gun's in the Sinatra sack you arranged to slip into the box."

Delko stepped forward, cuffs in hand, and Ciccolini lurched toward the young CSI, shoving him into Caine, knocking Caine back even as Delko tumbled into the river with a yell and a splash.

Ciccolini was running now, sprinting down the path into the darkness.

Caine scrambled to his feet and ran after the suspect. He did not draw his weapon—he didn't take the time. The old man was quick, his long legs striding, his arms pumping. It seemed to take forever to close the distance, and as Caine came up he yelled, "Stop, Vinnie! Stop before I stop you!"

But Ciccolini only kept running, and got out in front again, and Caine—breathing hard—gave it all he had, charging up behind the man and throwing a tackle into him, bringing him down in a rolling pile on the grass.

Ciccolini twisted around, throwing Caine off, and the CSI grabbed onto the man's nylon jacket, yanking on it, stopping him from fleeing. But the old hit man slipped out of the jacket and ran free from it, and Caine was left just holding the garment.

So he flung the thing and it whipped around and caught Ciccolini at the ankles, tripping him. The man went down and then Caine was looming over him, hand on the butt of his pistol, about to draw the weapon. . . .

Ciccolini kicked Caine in the stomach. Doubled over, all the air out of him, Caine made a perfect target for Ciccolini, who swung a hard right fist into the CSI's jaw.

But now Caine had his pistol in hand, trained on the suspect, whose yellow teeth were bared in a savage grimace that made the CSI think he was getting a glimpse of the real man.

Ciccolini—his face a contemptuous mask—put his hands in the air. He was breathing hard, but then, they both were.

"Don't have a heart attack, Lieutenant," Ciccolini said.

Caine wiped blood from the corner of his mouth with his free hand. "Hands in front, Vinnie."

Ciccolini lowered his hands. "You arresting us, then? Next stop, jail?"

"That's right."

"Then can I get something out of my pocket?" And the hit man began to slip his right hand into his jacket pocket.

"Don't!"

"Oh, for Christ's sake," the old man said. "It's not a gun—I'm reaching for my cell phone to call my lawyer!"

Caine leaned in and patted the pocket—it was a cell phone.

After examining the phone, Caine allowed Ciccolini to call his attorney ("I just want him to be able to meet us over at lockup") and then cuffed the man and walked him back down the beach to where Eric Delko—dripping wet—had taken Rosselli into custody. Rosselli's fishing rod was draped across the nearby lawn chair.

Delko had already called for uniformed backup, who within minutes had arrived and deposited the two suspects in separate squad cars, where Caine presented each of them with a search warrant for their homes and cars. The concession he had made to their age—allowing them to be handcuffed in front—also allowed Caine to hand each man his warrant.

"Vinnie," Caine said, "you want to turn over the keys for your car and house?"

The old man sneered and grunted a that'll-be-the-day response.

"Your choice," Caine said. "I'll just have to break into your car and house, then. We're not responsible for any loss or damage, by the way. Your call."

"Fuck it," Ciccolini said. "Left jacket pocket."

Caine reached in and came back with a ring of keys—five, only one of which was a car key, for a Chrysler. Caine pointed to a silver Intrepid a few spaces down and Ciccolini nodded sourly.

"Nice ride," Caine said.

"I'm fuckin' thrilled you approve," Ciccolini said.

Caine went over and fitted the key into the lock, opening the trunk just as the squad cars were rolling off into the night.

Delko ambled up. "Anything good?"

"Not at first glance."

Caine had hoped to find something here—the machete, a roll of garbage bags, the masks, something; but the trunk was so clean, the car might have come off the showroom floor this morning.

Shortly thereafter, Delko reported: "Passenger compartment looks scrubbed, too, H."

Caine stood with hands on hips. "Car's just not gonna help us, Eric. Oh, we'll give it the full process, but . . . let's just hope the rest of the team's having better luck."

A devilish grin was crinkling Delko's lips. "Okay, H. And I promise not to tell them."

"Tell them what?"

"That you were dukin' it out with a retirement home escapee. That he almost outrun ya."

Caine couldn't hold back the smile. He turned his gaze on Delko, still damp from his trip into the river. "That's thoughtful of you, Eric. And I won't tell them how you got wet."

"Uh, yeah . . . thanks."

Caine put a hand on Delko's shoulder. "Look at it this way—you finally got to go diving on this case."

And they headed back to HQ.

Detective Sevilla snugged her leather coat around her.

A chill hung in the night air like a persistent ghost and—although she was hardly superstitious—Sevilla was not overjoyed to be standing in the middle of a cemetery, next to a backhoe, as it grunted away under the harsh glare of halogen work lights.

She respected Caine's dedication, but . . . wouldn't the damned gun still be there tomorrow?

That is if it's even there to begin with.

The backhoe roared again as it pawed at the freshly turned earth packed on top of Abraham Lipnick's coffin. The diggers had to be careful—the wooden coffin would be no match for the backhoe, if the operator dug a little too deep in his haste . . . after all, the guy was probably just as anxious as Sevilla to get the hell out of here.

The only one here who was not in a hurry was Abraham Lipnick.

The cemetery crew was working their second night in a row—first to bury Lipnick in the timely fashion his friends demanded; and now to dig him back up. To them this was probably starting to feel like a futile exercise.

"We're used to makin' deposits," the operator had told Sevilla. "Not withdrawals."

"Shouldn't be much longer," Calleigh Duquesne said, coming up behind the detective, yelling to be heard over the noise of the tractor motor.

Sevilla nodded.

Calleigh held out a steaming Styrofoam cup of coffee to the detective, who gratefully accepted it in both hands. "You're a lifesaver."

"Don't sip it yet—it'll scald you." Calleigh was also bundled up, a heavy CSI jacket zipped to the neck, her hands already encased in latex gloves, ready to get at it.

Sevilla said, "Smells like heaven."

"Eric's cafe cubano recipe. It's got some bite to it."

"I don't mind."

Calleigh's pretty, infectious smile flashed. "The good news is there's enough caffeine we won't have to worry about fallin' asleep out here . . . or probably anywhere else, for the next two days."

Sevilla chuckled, the laugh feeling good. They stood awhile and finally Sevilla braved taking a sip, and the warmth flooded through her. "Thanks, Calleigh—I needed this."

The tractor's motor cut off in the middle of "thanks." The rest of it came out way too loud in the sudden silence, but the three-man work crew was concentrating on their task. One still sat in the seat of the backhoe while the other two jumped down into the newly excavated hole and started digging more carefully, precision work with smallish shovels.

The two women moved closer, peering down inside the grave.

"See anything?" Sevilla asked.

"Mud and men's boots—that's it."

They stood in silence at the grave's edge, drinking their coffee for a couple of minutes. Sevilla wondered if Calleigh was at all spooked by the eerie circumstances and surroundings; she seemed unflappable in almost any situation.

One of the men down in the hole said, "I think we hit paydirt, fellas."

The one on the backhoe came down and shone a flashlight in: they could all clearly see the wood that one of the shovels had unearthed.

Sevilla said, "Getting close now."

"I'll get my camera," Calleigh said, as peppy as a tourist at Sea World preparing to snap dolphins.

Sevilla knew, however, that this was an important investigative and procedural step. The CSI would record the exhumation from here on with her 35 millimeter, so they would have documentation when it came time to lay all this out in front of a jury.

Perhaps Abraham Lipnick was in heaven or hell facing eternal judgment right now; but his friends, Sevilla hoped, would be facing judgment here on earth, very soon . . .

. . . thanks to what they hoped to find in the dirt.

Two hours later, Calleigh Duquesne found herself alone in the lab with Abraham Lipnick's spare wooden coffin, the heavy wooden box poised atop a heavy metal worktable.

The temperature of the room was turned down in order to keep the body as cool as possible; Calleigh had ditched her coat, accordingly, and now wore a blue lab coat over her sleeveless green blouse. Working carefully with a short crowbar, she jimmied loose one corner at a time and then slowly pried up the sides.

Caine wandered in just as she finished.

"Are the old fellas in custody, Horatio?" she asked.

"Yes. We had enough to bring them in. Not enough to prove we're right about them."

"Well, I'll see what I can do," she said, her voice cheerful. "That is, I will if you can give me a hand gettin' the lid off this cigar box."

She moved to the far end of the coffin and together they lifted the lid off and set it on the floor, leaning it against the legs of the table, nails facing in. Per Jewish custom, the body inside hadn't been embalmed, and twenty-four hours in the ground—if a relatively short tenure for a corpse in a cemetery plot—hadn't done any favors for the still-ripening body.

They took time to put on painters' masks. Then, with Caine looking on, Calleigh reached over the side of the coffin and began feeling around the edge of the shroud. She began at the head and worked her way toward the feet—she wasn't quite tall enough to see straight down the side, so her impressions were mostly tactile.

"You want me to do that?" Caine asked.

"No thanks," she said, "I'm fine."

She worked a little further, the cotton of the shroud stiff and chilly to her touch, the wood of the coffin cool against her bare wrist where the sleeve of the lab coat rode up and her latex glove didn't quite reach.

She was almost to the midway point when she touched something metallic. . . .

A chill ran through her that had nothing to do with the temperature.

A nice chill, though—a satisfying one; not surprisingly, a gun was involved.

Wrapping her hand around the object, she pulled it up and brought it out . . .

. . . a silver-plated .25-caliber automatic pistol.

"Nice work," Caine said.

"I'm just getting started," Calleigh said, on the move. "I'll get it through the lab as fast as I can."

Only when a firearm showed itself did Calleigh Duquesne truly spring into inspired action.

Tim Speedle and Eric Delko took the Rosselli residence.

The two CSIs thoroughly searched the house, while brawny Detective Bernstein sat on the sofa with a tearful Rebecca Rosselli.

They found no guns, but confiscated two different pairs of shoes to be checked against footprints on the limo's brake pedal; also, a black suit that looked vaguely like a chauffeur's uniform and would be compared to fibers lifted from the driver's seat.

As they walked out, Mrs. Rosselli got up and walked them to the door. Speedle, touched by her politeness, turned to apologize for the intrusion, but before he got out a word, the door slammed in his face.

A uniformed officer—who had possession of the key Caine had gotten from Ciccolini—met the CSIs and Bernstein outside the man's house. They entered, finding the house dark and silent, the living room feeling lonely and cold. Speedle found a wall switch and flipped on a light.

The room had an Old World feel—heavy, long swords crossed on the wall behind a dark Mediterranean sofa, a large leather globe on its perch between the sofa and matching chair, which faced a television only slightly smaller than the monster monitor at the Rossellis. A painting on the wall to Speedle's left showed three wooden ships sailing toward the setting sun—the ships of Christopher Columbus on their way to the New World.

"Upstairs or downstairs?" Speedle asked.

"Upstairs," Delko said.

The two CSIs separated, Delko heading up to the second floor, Speedle staying down. Moving to the back of the house, Speed decided to start in the kitchen and work his way forward.

In the kitchen's junk drawer, he found a blister pack containing several small, flat hearing aid batteries identical to the one Delko had picked up on the beach. With a smug smile, he put them in an evidence bag and marked it.

Under the sink, he discovered a roll of garbage bags, the same green-black as the one Lessor's head and hands (and cell phone) had been buried in on the beach. With any luck, he could match up the perforations and prove the bags came off the same roll; but that would be a long shot.

Rest of the first floor yielded little, though of course Speedle went through everything painstakingly. He was just finishing up when Delko came downstairs lugging two more black suits, two more pairs of shoes, and an evidence bag.

"What's in the goodie bag?" Speedle asked optimistically.

Delko held up the evidence pouch for him to see: inside, a hearing aid. Most likely belonging to the late Abraham Lipnick.

Nodding his appreciation, Speedle showed Delko the batteries he had found.

"What's left?" Delko asked.

They had a decent pile of stuff already, but they both knew there was one more item well worth finding . . . if it was here, and hadn't been flung off the side of a road or into the ocean.

Speedle said, "We still got the garage."

"Let's do it, then."

They took what they'd gathered out to the Hummer and stowed it in the back. The two-car garage seemed to have been cobbled onto the house as an afterthought, its masonry a slightly different shade of gray. Going back through the house to the connecting door, the pair of CSIs strolled into the empty garage and looked around.

A small oil stain in the center of the cement floor told Speedle that only one car had been parked in here. A homemade workbench crafted from two-by-fours and plywood ran along the far wall, a small window centered over it, two toolboxes on the floor below the bench.

The right-hand wall was the double overhead door, the left-hand wall the back of the garage along which stood the lawn mower, a small wheelbarrow, and a grass seed spreader. Various tools could be seen: a leaf blower, a hedge trimmer, shears, and two rakes, hung from nails. The wall with the access door had two garbage cans and a recycling container along it.

"It's a garage, all right," Delko said.

"I'll take the far side," Speedle said.

"Why not."

Even though the night was chilly, the lack of ventilation in the garage had them sweating heavily after an hour of going through everything, taking the tools off the wall, going over the workbench, sifting the trash. Speedle had even gone through the toolboxes twice and come up with the same thing both times— nothing pertinent.

A little exasperated, Speed called out, "Any luck, Eric?"

Delko shook his head. "If that machete's here, it's duct-taped to the rafters."

They locked eyes, shrugged simultaneously, and shone their flashlights upward for a moment . . . no. They looked at each other in frustration.

Shrugging, Delko said, "They knew we were on their tail, since that funeral home visit. It's probably in a canal somewhere."

"Damn," Speedle said, pounding the workbench. "Would be nice to have that sucker!"

Delko stared at him, kind of goofily.

"What? It would be nice!"

"No, Speed . . . do that again."

"Do what again?"

"Hit it."

"The workbench?"

"The workbench."

Speedle frowned. "Is this some sort of sado-masochistic trip? Because if it is, well, Speedy don't play that."

Delko's expression was thoughtful. "Just hit the bench again, like you did the last time. Same place and everything. . . ."

Speedle tapped the bench with his fist.

The heavens did not part.

"Don't be a wimp, Speed! Hit that baby—pissed, like you did before."

Still not getting it, Speedle smacked the bench. This time, he heard it too . . .

. . . a faint bump.

Like something on the underside of the bench, re-verberating when he banged the wood. He hit it again, harder this time, and the bump was easy to hear.

Bending down, Speedle looked under the work-bench for the third time, and still saw nothing.

"Shit," he said.

Then he sat on the floor and turned to face the front as he leaned back under the bench. Shining his Mini-Mag Lite up under the bench, he finally saw what he had been looking for all along.

There, on the underside of the bench, Tim Speedle saw the black handle of an object.

A machete.

The blade was wedged between the two-by-four frame and the plywood bench top.

This time, Delko pounded the bench, and the ma-chete's handle bounced off the plywood. Dust flew.

"What's the idea!" Speedle said, waving a hand in front of his eyes and nose, coughing.

"What can I say?" Delko said. "I'm a cut-up."

They took pictures of the machete before dislodging and bagging it. They were pleased, and they knew Horatio Caine would be pleased with them.

11

"Girl Named Maria"

WITH MARIA CHACON finishing her last show for the night, Horatio Caine positioned himself on a chair outside her dressing room, which was off stage right, in the wings. From where he sat he had a good view of her, a blur of energy out in front of the band, a Latin whirlwind of high hair and flashing eyes and white teeth and endless legs, swinging her hips and pumping her arms like a bandito firing off six-guns.

Right now she was doing her signature "shake your bon bon" number, an encore she'd been in the midst of when he arrived. The CSI had been sent with no hassle whatsoever to the backstage area of the Conquistador's Explorer Lounge by a most cooperative Daniel Boyle, who had then made himself singularly scarce.

Back here, the music didn't seem so loud; off to the side, where Caine waited, the effect was hollow, like a muffled explosion. As for Maria Chacon, she sang well enough—a husky alto—and she stayed on pitch; but mostly it was flash. Style over substance, energy over heart . . . or at least that was Caine's admittedly biased view. Right now, he didn't like this woman much. Well, that wasn't entirely true, was it?

He liked her for Thomas Lessor's murder. Liked her a lot.

The backstage area lacked the glamour of the lounge and even the upkeep of the rest of the hotel. Here you could see that this facility had been around awhile—concrete walls, worn wooden floors. A tattered glittery cardboard star rode the closed dressing-room door, and a placard with Maria's name was cardboard as well and held up with duct tape, written in black marker by a careless hand.

Even though he hadn't slept in twenty-four hours, Caine was none the worse for wear. He had worked long hours before—the pace never bothered him; he seemed to derive energy from the chase, and as he closed in on his man—or woman—the promise of closure fueled him further.

And, frankly, an undercurrent of nervousness spiked his energy, right now—because the truth was, he didn't have any evidence against Maria Chacon except the circumstantial variety. And it was Horatio Caine's job, his team's mission, to find and interpret physical evidence.

Right now he was left with the psychological warfare of taking her downtown, showing her what they had, implying she was seeing the tip of the iceberg when she was seeing the whole damn cube, and hoping she would crack . . . or that one of those two old boys would roll over on her.

But the latter didn't seem likely—especially with Ciccolini, who was after all her uncle. This was much more likely a family favor than straight murder-for-hire.

It would be hard—it always was, in a matter of contract murder. If a hit man didn't give up his employer, what physical evidence could there be? At the time Lessor was picked up from the airport, Maria was on stage at the Conquistador—singing to a roomful of corporate types putting their martinis on the company expense account.

When the "bon bon" tune finally ended, the explosion of applause peppered with whistles and cheers told Caine how well Maria had gone over. He found her act rather contrived, but perhaps she did have star power; she had a certain charisma, and obvious sex appeal.

And some said that successful stars needed a ruthless streak. Caine was sure she had that.

The crowd was still yelling for more as the musicians in the band paraded past the dressing-room door on their way to their own quarters farther down.

He didn't see her immediately—she was hidden by the musicians, most of whom were taller than her, and was walking among them, just one of the guys, albeit a very unlikely one in her long, silvery gown with a slit that opened thigh-high whenever she took a step. Her black hair, in a pile on top of her head, was sweat-beaded, and her face, bare shoulders and chest gleamed with moisture.

Her eyes narrowed a fraction when she noticed Caine.

"Isn't it past your bedtime?" she asked, as he rose from the chair and faced her.

"I caught a nap while you were onstage. Spare a moment, Maria?"

She shrugged, opened the dressing-room door, and went in. She didn't exactly invite him in, but since the door hadn't been slammed on him, Caine took the liberty of entering.

Small and spare, the room was little more than a concrete closet with a lighted makeup table (bordered with taped-on clippings of favorable reviews), two chairs, and a flimsy metal rack that held various costume changes.

Already seated, she read his expression in the mirror and said, "Disappointed? . . . I thought you'd been around Miami long enough to know that show business is mostly illusion."

He took a seat in the straightback chair, positioned behind her and to the right. "I don't get backstage much."

She was dabbing at her face with a towel she picked up from the makeup table. "What can I do for you, Lieutenant? Somehow I don't think you're here for an autograph."

"I'm here to request that you come with me for questioning."

This only seemed to amuse her and she continued to study him, looking past herself in the mirror. "Why—am I a suspect now?" She pulled something on top of her head and her ebony hair tumbled down to cascade over her shoulders.

"You are. I'd like you to come with me for an interview, and we'll present you with what we have."

Underneath the amused expression, a suggestion

of apprehension revealed itself. "You're not arresting me?"

"No. But there are indications that we need to look in your direction. I thought you might like to have the opportunity to convince us otherwise. To show us where we're mistaken."

"But you can't require me to come?"

"No."

"And if I did, I could bring an attorney?"

"You could. What I have in mind is rather more informal . . . give you the chance to straighten this out."

She swiveled in the chair, looking over her shoulder at him with a mocking smile. "Aren't you the thoughtful one, Lieutenant. . . . I'll need a few minutes to change into my street clothes."

"Of course."

"And I'll need you to step outside."

"Of course."

Her smile widened. "Unless you feel you need to stay . . . and make sure I don't slip out a window or something? Make my getaway?"

Caine surveyed the dank, windowless room. "Oh, I think you can be trusted. Remember, this is purely voluntary on your part."

"Right. So we can clear this up."

"Right," he said, and stepped into the hall and shut the door. Twenty minutes later, when he checked his watch for the tenth time, the closed door still separated them, and Caine was starting to wonder—there wasn't really a way out of that dressing room, was there? She couldn't be a suicide risk, could she? Did he need to break that door down?

He was about to knock when the door swung open.

Maria walked out, wearing a silk shirt buttoned only about halfway up, tight blue jeans, and a denim jacket left open. Her black hair flew loose and free and she carried a large leather bag over her left shoulder.

"You'll have to take me as I am," she said, moving into the hall and closing the door. Her stage makeup was gone, replaced by a smidge of lipstick and little else.

He just looked at her.

"I don't have a shower here," she explained. "If you want a fresher me, we'll have to stop by my apartment first."

"No. Let's just rough it."

"Your choice."

As they exited out through the lounge, toward the door into the hall leading to the lobby, Caine had a feeling that something had changed, however subtly. There was something about Maria's attitude, her demeanor, that bothered him. Her apprehension seemed to have evaporated, and she might have been looking forward to spending the next few hours under interrogation.

They weren't even to the lobby when the first reporter approached. One of the TV guys, a tall, skinny guy with brown hair and a navy blue suit—Jackson, Caine thought the man's name was—was accompanied by a cameraman with a WFOR 4 decal on his camera. The CBS affiliate.

"Lieutenant Caine," the reporter said, shoving his microphone toward the CSI. "Are you arresting Ms. Chacon?"

So that's what Maria had been doing all that time in her showerless dressing room: calling the media, hoping to fire up the free publicity machine! That also meant that she figured she had nothing to fear from Caine, which troubled him far more than the presence of the press.

His knee-jerk reaction was to spoil Maria's shabby little media blitz by revealing her real name and that her uncle was in custody for murdering the Conquistador chain's own Thomas Lessor. She wanted publicity? Then how about making sure every media outlet in the South Florida area knew that the Miami-Dade PD had Maria Chacon's uncle cold.

Instead, he remained superficially cordial to the press of press.

"No," Caine said, "Ms. Chacon is not under arrest. She is a material witness in a case currently under investigation."

Another reporter blurted: "Ms. Chacon is a very popular entertainer!"

"That's not a question. If you'll excuse us . . . ladies . . . gentlemen. . . ."

The CBS reporter walked right along with them now, the cameraman backing up in front of them, trying to keep all three of them in the shot. The other media people pushed and shoved each other, as they tagged along.

"Lieutenant Caine, would the case in question happen to be the Thomas Lessor murder?"

Caine did not intend to perform in the center ring of this circus, not any longer, and as they neared the doors of the lobby, he saw more reporters, both TV and newspaper, making their way inside—and among the logos were CNN and MSNBC. He went into shutdown mode.

"No further comment," he said.

"Is Ms. Chacon a suspect?"

"Which part of 'no comment' isn't clear to you, Mr. Jackson?"

"Maria! What do you have to say? Are you worried?"

Her smile seemed to illuminate the whole lobby, even more than the TV lights. "I'm just a good citizen, cooperating with law enforcement—and you'll see me back on stage tomorrow night! Right here at the Conquistador!"

Their progress ground to a halt as the other reporters pressed around them and Caine cursed himself for allowing her that much time alone in that dressing room. Leave it to her to turn a murder into a career move.

He took her by the elbow and steered her through the crowd that had now grown to nearly a dozen media piranhas, and they smelled blood. He got her out the front doors, into the cool night air, but more media were waiting, and the rest were on their heels.

"Thomas Lessor was a dear friend," Maria said into one camera, a microphone bobbing in front of her, even as Caine struggled to get the woman past the hungry media eyes and ears, and to the Hummer.

"Tom Lessor will be missed," she said sorrowfully to another reporter.

Caine finally maneuvered the Hummer's door open and deposited Maria into the backseat. The reporters split into two groups, half staying to either yell questions through the closed window or get a video shot through the glass, while the others hounded Caine as he moved around to the driver's side and got in. He locked the doors, fired the engine, and rolled slowly forward until they had put the reporters behind them; then, with a relieved sigh, he gunned it down Collins Avenue.

Watching her in the rearview mirror, he said, "Quite the stunt, Maria."

"Thanks."

"It wasn't a compliment. Somehow I don't think I'm the first man you've made a chump out of."

Her self-satisfied smile said, *Or the last.* Then, as she looked out the window, she said almost absently, "You know what they say—it doesn't matter what they're saying as long as they're talking about you."

"Doesn't matter what they print, as long as they spell your name right?"

"Exactly."

"Do you think they really know how to spell your name?"

He saw her, in the rearview mirror, look pointedly at him. "What do you mean?"

But it wasn't time to play the Ciccolini card, not just yet.

"Nothing," he said.

". . . I am grateful to you, Lieutenant. You were the one that made all this possible. I'll get more free airtime for the next twenty-four hours than I could possibly afford even with a major record company behind me."

"You really think being linked to two murders is good PR?"

"As long as I'm an innocent victim in all of this, sure. And I'm helping the police, right?"

Caine shook his head. "Innocent or not, you're exploiting two dead men."

She frowned. "You think it's better if they died for nothing?"

He threw her a sharp look. "Is that why they died? To better the career of Maria Chacon?"

"Lieutenant—I have no idea why they died. I wish Thomas Lessor were alive right now—not just because he was my . . . friend . . . but because that would be good for my career. Don't make me rethink helping you people out on this thing."

They made the rest of the trip in silence. When they got to headquarters, Caine deposited her in an interview room.

"I'll be with you shortly," Caine said. "Can I have someone get you some coffee?"

"No. I'm fine. Will you be long?"

"Just gathering some material to discuss with you."

"Good. I don't want to have to go through this indignity more than once."

"I couldn't agree more."

In truth, Caine needed to check in with his team and see if they'd come up with anything new, particularly relating to Maria herself.

First on his list was Speedle and Delko. They were in the DNA lab taking blood samples from a machete.

"This the murder weapon?" Caine asked as he came through the double glass doors.

"Well, it's a machete that was hidden under Vincent Ciccolini's workbench," Speedle said. "We're testing it now."

"Prints?"

Delko said, "Some real beauties on the handle—Rosselli and Lipnick."

"Good job," Caine said. "Keep at it. Anything else?"

"Fiber is working on the clothes," Delko said. "We might be able to match one of their suits to the driver's seat in the limo."

"That would be nice."

"And," Speedle added, "we've already matched footprints from all three to dust in the parking lot."

"Excellent. What about the beach?"

"Nope—can't make that happen. Sand was too messed up. But we used the electrostatic print-lifter in the parking lot, also the car. We should be able to match one of their shoes to a really sweet print we got off the brake pedal."

"So," Caine said, eyes tight as he summed up, "we can put them in the car and with the machete."

"Dead bang," Delko said. "And the composition of the garbage bags Speed got from Ciccolini's house matches the one we found on the beach, though the perforations are off."

"Which means . . ." Caine began.

Delko, nodding, finished: "There was definitely more than one bag."

"And," Speedle put in, "the hearing aid and batteries matched. Those old boys were on that beach."

"Actually, we can only put Lipnick there . . . but it's good. Very good." And now the big question. "Anything to tie Maria to this?"

Delko and Speedle glanced at each other, then looked sheepishly at Caine, and shook their heads.

"Not to brag about, anyway," Speedle said. "But we did run her phone records. There's one interesting, possibly significant call . . ."

"Shall I guess or will you tell me?"

"Maria got a call from Vegas the night before Erica Hardy died."

Caine frowned. "Who from?"

Speed said, "This is the interesting—and weird—part: it was Erica Hardy's number . . . and the call lasted three-quarters of an hour."

That threw Caine. "Maria said she didn't know Hardy—she only had a vague sense of the affair from something she'd overheard."

"Been an epidemic of lying in this case," Delko pointed out.

"Erica calling Maria is an interesting new wrinkle," Caine said, frowning. "Very likely helpful. We just have to think it through. Solid work, fellas."

His next stop was the morgue, where he found Alexx Woods bending over her latest client, talking to the corpse in a soft, soothing voice. "Who did this bad thing to you, baby?"

The corpse—a young Hispanic man in his late teens to early twenties—did not respond.

"Who's your new friend?" Caine asked.

"Graveyard shift brought him in from Little Havana. GSW to the chest."

Gunshot wound—far too many of those in this city; all Caine could do was shake his head. Another young man who would never marry, never have a family, never buy a house.

Alexx bestowed a sultry smile. "You want to know if I have anything new for you on your double murder, right?"

"I do," he admitted.

"I don't." She shook her head. "I wish I did, Horatio—but the bullets from Lessor were it."

"I had to check."

"Yes, you did. . . . All right now, baby . . . this won't hurt at all. . . ."

Caine hadn't expected much, which was exactly what he'd gotten. The mention of bullets, though, sent him next to Calleigh Duquesne—who was in her lab, lowered over a microscope.

"Please say you have something for me," he said.

"You sound in a hurry."

"I have Maria Chacon cooling her heels."

"We have enough to arrest her?"

"I wish. She's just being 'cooperative.' "

"She's just yanking your chain, you mean. And you're doing a quick tour of your troops to see what we've come up with. Well, how about a perfect match on the gun that killed Thomas Lessor and Johnny 'The Rat' Guzzoli?"

"Sweet. We can't be lucky enough to have fingerprints on the gun, old pros like them?"

"Yes, we can. Two sets—Vincent Ciccolini and Abraham Lipnick."

"No kidding."

"Abe's heart attack must've really thrown a wrench in the works. The .25 didn't even get wiped down."

Nodding in thought, Caine said, "It would be nice to know which one fired the shots."

"It would," Calleigh said, "but it's way too late to check for gunshot residue on their hands. Of course, their clothes might tip us."

"If we knew what each of them was wearing and assuming that they haven't gotten rid of it."

"Well, yeah," Calleigh said. "But we have what looks like chauffeurs' uniforms, confiscated from their homes. And if they were off their game enough to leave prints, maybe . . . ?"

"Maybe. What about your Trenton friend—Irv Brady? Does he have enough evidence up there on the original crime to make an arrest, if we give him the gun?"

Her expression turned doubtful. "So much time has passed, the case would have to be mostly circumstantial. Irv's got no concrete tie between them and the gun back then. It would be a heckuva coincidence, though, the boys just happenin' to have that weapon now. I think a jury would side with the state . . . but the point may be moot. We're gonna nail these vintage torpedoes on Lessor."

That expression made him smile a little. "All right, Calleigh. Thanks. Did I mention you're the best?"

"Not often enough."

Caine picked up Detective Sevilla from her desk and went to the observation booth next to the interview room where Maria Ciccolini aka Chacon sat at the table, her pack of cigarettes and lighter in front of her as she puffed away. Glancing at the interview-room floor, he could see two squashed butts, meaning that in the brief time he'd left her here, she was already on her third smoke.

Maybe she wasn't as calm, cool and collected as she wanted him to think. He studied her a short time longer, as he assembled his strategy in his thoughts.

Then he asked Sevilla, "You don't mind me taking the lead on this?"

"Not at all."

"Join me in there?"

Her eyes narrowed as she too studied their prime suspect. "I'm leaning against it," she said, her eyes riveted. "I think Maria'll try to manipulate you . . . just like she has every other man in her life. If I'm there, the mix'll be wrong—she might feel hampered."

"You're saying she'll come on to me?"

"Not exactly. But her sexuality, her femininity—that's her favorite weapon, Horatio. She doesn't use a gun or a knife."

"She uses men," Caine said, nodding. "Think I can make the songbird sing?"

Sevilla studied the woman for a long moment. "Truth?"

"Truth, Adele."

"Probably not. I think she's too smart."

"But I have to give it my best shot."

"You do. Try to trip her up, use her emotions against her. See if you can't find a way to get her worked up, and maybe she'll let something slip. Otherwise, I think it's gonna be a real cold day in hell before she cops."

"Or a real cold day in Miami, at least."

"There's a difference?"

They exchanged somber, fatalistic smiles.

When he walked into the interview room, Maria raised her eyes to him, flashed a smile, and shifted in her seat; her silk blouse opened a little more, which was perhaps her intent. She took a drag on her cigarette and let it out slowly through her nose.

Caine pulled up a chair. "And here I thought you only smoked when you were nervous."

Gesturing with the cigarette, she said, "Maybe you make me nervous, Lieutenant."

"I kinda doubt that, Maria. But I'm afraid there's no smoking in here."

"I noticed the lack of ashtrays," she admitted, dropping the cigarette to the concrete floor and stubbing it out with the toe of her open-toed shoe. "Maybe you really will arrest me—for smoking . . . or littering?"

"If I arrest you," he said, in a light, friendly tone, "it'll have to do with your real name being Maria Ciccolini."

She jerked up straight, her eyes flashing, her smile dropping. Unconsciously, she reached for the pack of cigarettes, but when she saw her hand moving, she stopped.

"You changed it, legally, recently," Caine said. "But not before you signed your contract at the Conquistador."

"Oh," she said, disgusted, recovering quickly. "You got this from Daniel. He's so afraid you're going to get him on Tom's murder, he's throwing mud at anything that moves."

"Revealing to us that your real name is Ciccolini— that's mudslinging?"

"No, but . . . what's the big deal? It's no huge secret. If you'd asked me, I'da told you."

"You might've thought to tell us. I'm sure you knew we'd questioned your uncle Vincent in the matter. He must've told you."

She shrugged.

"Of course, he may not have had a chance to let

you know that both he and his friend Tony have been arrested for the murder of Thomas Lessor. He used his one phone call to contact his lawyer. Or did the lawyer contact you?"

"No. First I've heard. But if you've arrested Uncle Vin, how am I a suspect?"

"We'll get to that. No defense for your beloved uncle?"

"He doesn't need one. It's silly. Ridiculous. I don't know what ever made you go in that direction. I mean, how can you possibly believe that two sweet old-timers like that—"

Caine pointed to the bruise by his mouth. "Your uncle Vin gave me this, earlier tonight, when he tried to flee from custody."

She arched an amused eyebrow. "Fighting it out with the elderly, Lieutenant? And now you're taking on a woman—coming up in the world."

"Let me tell you how I can believe 'two sweet old-timers'—and actually it was three—could have done this. It's because of overwhelming physical evidence, from the murder gun to the machete they chopped your boyfriend up with."

The reference to her boyfriend's dismemberment didn't cause a twinge.

"They left more evidence behind than they would have in their prime, back in Jersey. But they had a bump in the road—seems Abe Lipnick wasn't as fit a senior as your uncle Vin. He had the bad manners to up and have a heart attack in the middle of the murder slash dismemberment . . . and wound up dying in the wee hours."

She was frowning now. "Honestly, Lieutenant . . . I know my uncle had a reputation, back in New Jersey, for being some kind of mobster. But everybody with an Italian last name got stereotyped that way. Why do you think I changed my name?"

"To take advantage of another stereotype."

"Well, it's absurd. He was a retired businessman and so is Tony and so was Abe. Why in God's name would they do such a thing to Tom?"

"Well, it wasn't in God's name, Maria . . . it was in yours."

She tried to look shocked but it didn't quite play. "My name? They did this for me? Why would they kill Tom for me?"

"That's one of the things I was hoping you might clear up."

She thought about that, his frankness throwing her off a little. Then she said, disingenuously, "I'm afraid I don't follow you, Lieutenant—how in the world are you going to convict Uncle Vin and Tony of murder, if you don't have a motive?"

He smiled and laughed a silent laugh. "I didn't say I didn't have a motive. Actually, I have two, either of which work just fine for me. Would you like to hear them?"

Any sense of playfulness, much less flirtatiousness, was gone now; her eyes were cold and yet they burned.

"Both motives begin with a phone call you received from Erica Hardy."

She smirked, disgusted. "I told you before! I never knew her, and only learned about her from something

I overheard. I wasn't in love with him! He could chippie around all he wanted!"

"Maria, don't embarrass yourself. We checked your phone records—Erica called you the day before her death."

"A wrong number."

"A forty-five-minute wrong number?"

Her eyes narrowed. "Wait a minute. Let me think. I might have heard from Tom that night. Maybe he was using her phone. How would I know where he was calling me from?"

"With the pressure he was under, stepson undermining him, private eye dogging his tracks, I doubt he'd just hang around his girlfriend's pad making phone calls. He certainly wouldn't call mistress number two with mistress number one around. And he certainly wouldn't risk putting your phone number on her phone bill. Can I continue?"

"Do what you want. It's your show."

But she was glancing at the cigarettes again; he'd struck a nerve.

"Well, stick with me," he said. "This is where my performance gets a little complicated . . . and I hate it when I'm too hip for the room."

Her glare said drop dead. At least.

"Let's assume," he said, "that the phone call was from Erica, and not from Tom using her phone. Somehow Erica found out about you—after all, you'd found out about her, not even trying—and she called you, and told you what was going on between her and Lessor. She was planning to confront Lessor about you—and she wanted you to leave her fella alone."

"That's a motive for her to kill Tom."

"Well, she's in the clear, Maria." Caine couldn't keep the archness out of his voice: "Tom had already killed her, prior to his own murder."

"So she called me, and I was, what—jealous?"

"Yes. And had your uncle pop your faithless lover."

She chuckled, shook her head. "You know better than that, Lieutenant."

"I didn't think you'd like that one. I don't really like that one myself . . . but it fits the facts, so in fairness, I had to air it."

"Fairness. You'd know about fairness?"

"I don't think you get jealous, Maria—oh, you might have been jealous of Erica for being in the way of your career; she was a singer, too, doing well in Vegas. If you were going to take some action against that couple, Erica would have been your target."

"Gee—where was I the night she got killed? Oh yeah, I remember—over half a continent away."

"You didn't kill Erica. The Vegas crime lab has proven beyond a shadow of a doubt that Thomas Lessor was responsible for that brutal crime. And it was a brutal crime—a frightening crime."

She gave in and lighted up another cigarette.

"Which is where theory number two comes in."

She looked exasperated, smoke streaming from her mouth. "And what is behind door number two?"

Calmly, he said, "Erica Hardy called you when she found out about you and Tom . . . only instead of being jealous, you two career girls—both feeling a bit used by a man, for a change—decided to blackmail Lessor."

"Blackmail Tom? You're losing it, Lieutenant. You're not too hip for the room. You're a hick. And you're flopping."

"What a ripe blackmail target this guy was—he had money; he could build both of your careers."

"Blackmail him how?"

"By threatening to go to his wife. That's what he feared more than anything; that's what he valued more than any . . . frolic with a lounge singer, here or in Vegas."

She shifted in her chair. "This is stupid. Tom Lessor wouldn't allow himself to be blackmailed."

"Exactly. He didn't want to play—he killed Erica, over it. And when you realized that he was heading your way, maybe coming after you, you got your uncle and his old Murder, Incorporated crew to add you to their client list. You knew they'd gotten back in the killing business. So you asked Uncle Vin for a favor. This is your opportunity to convince me otherwise, Maria. Show me that I'm wrong."

She blew a long plume of smoke toward him. "Just start talking, you mean? . . . I think you should arrest me, first. Only—you don't really have anything, do you?"

"We have so much on your uncle, I hardly know where to start. And as for you, the phone call from Erica—"

"Is all you have. Are you going to bust me? No? Yes? Well, if you are, you didn't inform me of my rights before this little interview, did you? And you as much as told me I didn't need a lawyer."

"You can call one if you like."

She took another long drag on the cigarette. "Why should I? I haven't done anything wrong."

Caine's words came out slow. And cold. "Just because you didn't pull the trigger, Maria, that doesn't make you innocent of murder."

"If I am innocent, you're harassing me . . ."

"Maybe you should sue."

"Then I guess I *would* need a lawyer," she said, her voice now as cold as his. "And if I was guilty—if you had enough evidence to prove I'm guilty—you would have arrested me by now. In the meantime, I'm getting tired of this little cat-and-mouse nonsense, Lieutenant. Are you going to arrest me?"

He said nothing.

She shrugged. Sighed smoke. Rose. "Then I'm outa here."

Seething, but not showing it, Caine watched the beautiful singer pack up her smokes and walk out of the room as if she owned the place. When the door closed, and he knew she was past the first turn in the hall, Caine pounded his fist on top of the table.

Sevilla strolled in, her expression a wry cocktail of amusement and disgust. "Didn't that go well?" she said.

"There's got to be something we missed."

She sat next to him. Her voice was gentle. "You know, Horatio—sometimes we have to face it. Sometimes bad guys get away."

"Not on my watch."

"Well, this isn't your watch. We're on graveshift's time, now. We need to go home. All of us."

"I want everyone in the layout room."

Sevilla's eyes widened and then rolled. "You're

joshin' me, right? Your kids are all about a hundred miles past exhausted. So are you. We're at the far end of a double shift already. The overtime taxi cab's meter is about to burst."

"Help me round them up, will you?"

". . . All right."

Ten minutes later, a bleary-eyed Speedle was the last to stumble in. Alexx Woods was absent—the coroner had finally gone home to spend some time with her family. Looking around the room, Caine saw the truth in what Sevilla had told him: the exhaustion on his team was palpable; and he knew that they were giving two hundred percent on this one. Three hundred.

Delko's eyes were bloodshot and his shoulders drooped, and Speedle—who frequently looked like the end of the day when he first came in—resembled a train wreck survivor who'd wandered away from the accident site. Even the perennially chipper Calleigh—who always seemed to have an extra cache of energy even Caine didn't have access to—looked like a whipped pup.

For all their effort, all their time, somehow it still hadn't been enough: the real killer was about to walk.

Caine said, "We're missing something, people."

They all groaned in unison.

"H, we've been all over this," Speedle said, the class spokesman. "If Uncle Vin decides to take the wrap for his niece, we're finished."

"We're not finished. We've just missed something."

"H, how can you say that?" Delko asked.

"My gut says so," Caine said.

"Well, that's scientific," Speedle said, eye-rolling.

"What do you want us to do?" Calleigh asked, worn out but always game.

"What I want you to do . . . is go home."

They looked at him in astonishment.

"Go home. Get some rest. And most important—sleep in."

A small spark of life snapped among them.

He raised a lecturing forefinger. "And if I see any of you here before nine—I swear I'll dock your ass, a full day's pay."

They laughed. They all laughed. It was music to Caine's ears.

"Tomorrow we start over with fresh eyes." Their tired eyes were locked on him. "This evil woman will not walk away from this. From us. She set this up. We're going to prove it. I'll see you all tomorrow."

12

Showstopper

As MUCH AS HE hated budget meetings, Horatio Caine knew it was his fate to attend an ungodly number of them—that was the personal price he paid for having one of the premier crime labs in the United States. So, after spending the entire morning having his every decision questioned by the county's accounting department, Caine greeted the lunch hour by grabbing some fast food and eating in the car, as he headed back to the office.

Maybe he was crazy—but he couldn't wait to get back to work.

Caine had intended to swing right into checking in with his team to see how they'd done after a good night's sleep; but out of habit he played his messages first, and found that an agitated Daniel Boyle had phoned this morning—no message other than, "Call me ASA-fucking-P, Lieutenant!"

Rather than get caught behind his desk, Caine made the call on the move, on his cell phone, as he headed for the ballistics lab to see what Calleigh had come up with.

The operator at the Conquistador transferred Caine to Boyle's office.

"About fucking time!" Boyle said.

"And a pleasant good afternoon to you, too, Mr. Boyle. How may I be of help?"

"You can tell me just what the hell you said to Maria last night!"

As he walked down the hall, techs weaving around him, Caine smiled to himself, and said, disingenuously, "Nothing pertaining to you, in particular."

"Yeah, right! And it's my imagination that she came in here this morning yelling like a goddamn crazy woman and broke it off with me!"

"And that's a bad thing?"

"You may find this difficult to believe, Lieutenant Caine, but Maria means . . . she means a lot to me."

Caine didn't bother to keep the amusement out of his voice. "Mr. Boyle—the last time we spoke about Maria Chacon—Ciccolini—you called her a 'lying bitch' and worse. Furthermore, you seemed delighted we were looking at her for your stepfather's murder, and not you."

"Well . . . I was hurt. Wounded by finding out she and Tom were lovers."

"Why exactly was Maria mad at you, Mr. Boyle?"

"Because you learned what her real name was! And the only place you could have gotten that information was from yours truly. She said I betrayed her . . . that she couldn't trust me anymore!"

"And you pointed out that you couldn't trust her, either—that she'd betrayed you with Tom Lessor . . . right?"

". . . Right."

"So," Caine said slowly, "you can't really lay this breakup at my feet. Listen, Mr. Boyle, I'm in the middle of a very complicated murder investigation. This is the crime lab, not the lonely hearts helpline."

"All right . . . I'll admit to you that the personal relationship . . . the personal relationship isn't the biggest problem you've caused me."

Barely following Boyle's ramblings, if at all, Caine paused outside the ballistics lab long enough to ask one more question; he was that curious, anyway. "Sir—what are you talking about?"

"Maria was so bothered by what you told her last night, so furious with me, that she called my mother this morning and demanded to be released from her contract here at the Conquistador. Told her that I'd made 'inappropriate sexual advances' and wanted out."

Calleigh looked up from her microscope, smiled at Caine, and he waved a little, but stayed out in the hall, moving away from the lab door.

"How exactly did this go down, Daniel? Were you present during the phone conversation between your mother and Maria?"

"No. Maria called Mother, before she came around to see me."

"And your mother called you?"

"Later, yes . . . but first I heard about it from Maria. She burst into my office and tore me a new one and *gloated* about how she'd played my mother."

"Played her how?"

"Maria convinced my mother to honor that upcoming Oasis contract."

"You mean, Maria's playing Vegas, after all?"

"Yes—and sooner than you'd think."

"How so, Daniel?"

"There was a cancellation in the Oasis lounge, an act got caught in a double-booking situation, and, anyway, Mother told Maria that if she could get herself on a plane today, with her entire band, they could open tomorrow night at the Oasis."

"Is that even possible?"

"Absolutely. Maria and her boys will be rehearsing this evening. Things move fast in this business."

"I should say." Caine tried to quickly process this new information and all its ramifications. "Does your mother know about your stepfather's relationship with Maria?"

"Not to my knowledge."

"What about the arrest of Maria's uncle?"

"I didn't tell her. Why would I? I can't see hitting her with that, at a time like this . . . my stepfather isn't even in the ground yet."

Caine recalled how "concerned" Boyle had been on that score—the man's remark about toting Lessor's remains home in a carry-on bag.

"Daniel, surely your mother asked you about Maria's claims of sexual misconduct on your part."

"She did, and I told her I did have a consensual relationship with Ms. Chacon. But we both felt the possible legal ramifications—sexual harassment lawsuits can be a bitch, Lieutenant—were worth avoiding.

Maria is a fine performer, and she'll do well at the Oasis."

Caine understood part of Boyle's initial anger, suddenly. "You're not upset about losing your little girlfriend, are you, Daniel? The real problem I caused you is you've lost your star attraction at the Explorer Lounge."

"I'm a businessman at heart . . . and my mother is, too. Otherwise, why would she book that little bitch into the Oasis?"

Caine frowned. "Do you know when Maria's leaving for Vegas?"

"Sure. Her flight's scheduled to leave at two-thirty."

The CSI checked his watch—it was past noon.

And in this day and age, people got to the airport early. If he left now, he could probably find her at MIA.

"I appreciate the information," Caine said. "And Daniel—you're better off without Maria Chacon in your personal life and your professional one. The woman is a killer."

"I figured that," he said hollowly. "Why did she do it, Lieutenant Caine? Why did Maria have Tom killed?"

"I can't really discuss that, Daniel," he said. "But let's just say she and Tom Lessor were well matched."

A slight pause. "I hear that," Boyle said. "Is my mother in any danger?"

"To Maria, your mother is just a means to an end."

"That's what everyone is to Maria," Boyle said.

And the two men said their good-byes. Caine had

already been on the move and was in the parking lot now, having left a slightly bewildered Calleigh behind in her lab.

Half an hour later, after winding through traffic with his siren screaming (for whatever good it did in a city that no longer seemed to notice such things), Caine found himself striding through the main concourse of Miami International Airport, looking for Maria Chacon aka Ciccolini.

Traffic was as heavy in here as on the expressway, people all around him dragging wheeled suitcases, all scouring signs to find their gates, gazing at monitors with anticipation and dread. Occasionally, the din of the crowd would fade slightly as an intercom voice made a canned announcement in English, Spanish, and Japanese, leaving a good share of passengers out in the linguistic cold.

Maria Chacon probably spoke at least Spanish and Italian, in addition to English; but her native tongue, Caine knew, was the language of deceit.

He had been looking for her for the better part of a half hour—and was thinking that either she wasn't here yet, or somehow he'd missed her—when he got the idea to go back outside.

Caine spotted her maybe twenty yards away, sitting on a bench with a couple guys he recognized from her band, all puffing cigarettes. MIA had unwittingly done him a small favor years ago, when they forced smokers to congregate in only a couple of spots just outside the airport.

In black slacks, black silk blouse and denim jacket, an oversized leather purse over one shoulder, her long hair in a ponytail, Maria looked like one of those people you thought might be a celebrity, but couldn't quite place. From a distance she might appear to be a normal human; but even the most cursory closer inspection revealed that she was somehow special . . . and knew it.

He sat down next to her, several other smokers huddling around them, an ashtray at each end of the bench and one out front in the middle, three oases for the smokers to drop their ashes and stub out their butts so they could keep the place neat and tidy as they poisoned themselves.

At first she didn't notice him, not enough to recognize him, anyway. Then he said, "Nervous?"

Maria turned toward him, eyes wide, nostrils flaring. "What the hell . . . ?"

"Must be. I remember how you said you burn through the cigarettes . . . when you're nervous."

She sighed smoke, gazed at him with half-lidded contempt. "Are you here to arrest me, Lieutenant?"

"No. Just . . . seeing you off. Saying good-bye—for now."

"Oh, I'm not coming back to Miami. I have no desire to work this sleazy town again."

"You never know when a command performance might come along."

A half-sneer. "You don't have anything on me, Lieutenant."

"Tell me—does it give you even a twinge? I'm curious."

She said nothing.

"Letting your old uncle take the rap for you. Doesn't bother you at all?"

She stared out at the cars and taxis and buses, their fumes mirroring the smoker's own exhaust. "Let's suppose I did what you say I did . . . which I didn't. Let's say my uncle did this because I asked him to. Which I didn't."

"Let's."

She turned toward him again, showing him eyes so cold he knew he'd never forget their chill. "Uncle Vinnie still committed the murder. My joining him in lockup doesn't help him in the least."

"And an old mob guy like him isn't likely to sell you out for a shorter sentence. He wouldn't fink on his boys, and certainly not his niece."

She gave him the definitive what-the-hell shrug. "What's a 'short' sentence to a guy his age? . . . He's had a great ride. So he closes out his act playing a small room. Way it goes."

"You'll play a small room yourself, Maria—the room where they give the lethal injections, it's not the Flamingo."

"Big talk from a little cop." She took a deep drag on the cigarette, and rose, standing over him now, as if the high ground would give her the advantage.

From below, he said, calmly, "You won't be hard for me to find, Maria—your name'll be in lights. And when I have evidence proving that you sent the geriatric hit squad that took down Tom Lessor and Felipe Ortega, I'll be in your audience. Look for me—I'll be the one who isn't clapping. And I will bring you back to Miami . . . and you will stand trial for murder."

She leaned past him, provocatively, and stubbed the cigarette out in the ashtray, looking sideways at him as she did. "You know why you're in Miami, Lieutenant? Because you aren't ready for the big time. Strictly road company."

Then she rose and, with a dismissive wave, walked away and through the automatic double doors into the airport, leaving Caine sitting in a cloud of blue smoke.

She turned back once and blew him a kiss, and laughed. He tried to hold her eyes, but Maria Chacon turned and disappeared into the crowd . . . still a free woman.

After the solitary ride back to headquarters Caine was in no mood to see Speedle standing in his office doorway, a goofy grin on the young CSI's face, one hand behind his back.

"You're smiling, Speed."

"I sure am."

"Make me smile too."

"Okay."

Speedle brought out a plastic bag for Caine to see.

"A cell phone," Caine said. "I'm not smiling."

"Anthony Rosselli's cell phone. I went back to the beginning—with fresh eyes, right?—and found this in the property room. Rosselli had it on him when he was arrested, and nobody ever bothered to have a look at it."

Caine's eyes tensed. "Tell me you got a search warrant before you did anything."

Speedle's face fell. "Jeez, H, gimme a little credit! 'Course I did."

Caine tried to restrain the smile but it escaped anyway. "Nice to know you've been paying attention."

"See—I did make you smile."

"Make me smile wider. Anything on it?"

Shrugging, Speedle said, "Don't know yet—waiting for Detective Sevilla to actually serve the warrant to Rosselli before I do anything."

"Keep me posted."

"You know it, H."

Speedle disappeared down the hall and Caine hunkered down in the office to start collecting the various documentation he would need to appease the accountants at a second budget meeting scheduled for tomorrow morning. He was glad that his supervisory position allowed him to still work crime scenes; if his duties were solely this bureaucratic nonsense, he'd have long ago found something more meaningful to do. Like working security at a dog food plant.

The day went away before Caine realized it; suddenly he was turning on his desk lamp as darkness seeped in and took over his office. He got up, stretched—the muscles in his back loosening—then his spine talked to him, making several cracks, and he decided to take a turn around the warren of labs to see if anyone from his team was still around.

He found Delko in front of a computer monitor, two shoeprints next to each other on the screen. "Talk to me," Caine said.

"Me or the screen?" Delko said, good-naturedly.

"At this point I'm not that choosy."

Delko gestured to the monitor. "Matched the shoeprint from the brake pedal to one of Rosselli's. He

was the driver. Fibers from his suit match some I got
from the driver's seat, too."

"All right," Caine said, nodding. He was just turning to leave when Calleigh came in, her arm raised to
keep the black suit she carried on a hanger from graz-
ing the floor.

"Presenting . . . Vincent Ciccolini's suit," she an-
nounced. "GSR on the right arm and breast."

Gunshot residue—music to Caine's ears. "Ciccolini's our shooter?" he asked.

"Yes, sir."

Caine clapped, once. "All right . . . this is coming
together. Either of you seen Speed?"

They both shook their heads, then went back to
their work.

Caine searched several rooms before finding Tim
Speedle in the sound lab, huddled with technician Peter
Ballard. Trim, his dirty brown hair starting to recede,
Ballard had skin the ghostly pallor of someone who
spent way too much time inside. Headphones on, he sat
in a chair in front of his massive mixing board, the oscil-
lations of whatever he was testing flooding past on the
screen in front of him like a bizarre vital-signs monitor.

Speedle sat in a chair next to the tech, his eyes
closed as he concentrated on whatever was coming
through his headphones. When Caine touched his
shoulder, Speed jumped out of the chair, his hands
tearing the headphones off as he spun to face his boss.

"Jesus, H! Christ . . ."

Caine twitched a smile. "Sorry, Speed—didn't mean
to startle you. How much caffeine have you had
today, anyway?"

The young man's rolled eyes were his only rejoinder, and he took a moment to gather himself, his heart obviously pumping hard. Ballard worked, with marginal success, at keeping his eyes on the monitor and biting his lip to keep from laughing.

"So, Speed—any luck with Rosselli's phone?"

"What's the most irritating thing about old people you can think of?"

Caine shook his head. "Don't think we're gonna play this game, Speed. Just give."

But Speedle pressed on, raising a declamatory forefinger. "Their inability to master even the most rudimentary technology. Do you know anybody over seventy who has mastered their VCR's timer?"

"I haven't mastered mine. Your point, Speed?"

"God bless him, Anthony Rosselli never learned how to erase his cell phone messages."

"Which means?"

"Which means there's a shitload of messages . . . if you'll pardon a technical term. Pete and me been runnin' through them for"—Speed glanced at the clock on the monitor—"going on three hours."

Caine tried to make that work. "Rosselli had three hours of messages?"

"No, H—the system will hold thirty messages, two minutes max, and Rosselli's been getting them hot and heavy for the last week."

"And this adds up to three hours how?"

"Well, ya see, most of 'em are from Abe Lipnick . . . and the late Mr. Lipnick had some sort of a speech impediment. We checked his medical records and he had a stroke a little over a year ago. He had no residual damage except for a problem with his speech. Which is why it's been so much fun trying to decipher his messages."

"Any luck?" Caine asked.

Peter finally spoke up. "I considered having you round up a close friend or two of the late Mr. Lipnick's—who would be able to translate fairly easily, being familiar with him and all."

"But you didn't."

"No. I thought that would complicate the courtroom process—add in a nasty human variable. We need to be able to play these tapes for a judge and jury."

"Agreed."

"So," Peter said, "I decided to stay in the domain of electronics—the kind that I know will hold up in court. After I figured out what filters to use, we were finally able to understand most of what Mr. Lipnick was saying."

"Just the same, H," Speedle said, "these are guys who probably had their phones back in Jersey wiretapped for decades. So they were pretty careful."

Peter played one of the original, unprocessed messages for Caine, who tried to listen closely; but when the message was done, he just shook his head. "Did he say something about Venetian chinook sorrow?"

Speedle grinned, grunted a laugh, and said, "Now you know the kinda hit parade we've been dancin' to all afternoon."

"It's evening."

"See?"

"Let me play it for you with the filters on," Ballard said. He twisted some knobs, punched two buttons, then pushed PLAY again.

Lipnick's gargle now sounded slightly metallic; but the words were clear: "Vinnie says we should know tomorrow."

"See what you mean," Caine said. "Any of them been helpful?"

"Some circumstantial stuff," Speedle said. "But pull up a chair—we've got one message left to check."

Caine leaned against the wall and Ballard played the last message with the filters on. Again, the vaguely metallic voice of Abe Lipnick came on. "Maria says we should collar the tomcat at the airport. She says he's usin' a limo. Oh yeah, and Vinnie says bring Nixon and the sex perv."

Tom Lessor, a limo, and the Nixon and Clinton masks.

Peter shut off the tape player and a stunned silence filled the room.

"It's not a smoking gun," Caine said. "But I'll take it."

"Yes!" Speedle smacked a fist into an open hand. "All because that old geezer never learned to use his cell phone."

"Funny," Caine said. "From Tom Lessor's cell phone ringing under the sand to the cell phone of one of his killers . . ."

"It's a trip," Speedle admitted.

Caine checked his watch; his Vegas contact, Catherine Willows, would not be in at work for at least two more hours. He could call this in to the LVMPD dayshift; but he would stick with Catherine and her crew. He'd call her tonight from home and ask her to pick up Maria Ciccolini.

"Okay, guys, hit SAVE on that baby, and call it a day. The accounting department's crawling all over me about overtime."

"We got her, H," Speedle said, grinning. "We've got her."

"I believe we do. Peter, can you make me a cassette copy of that last message and give me a small tape player?"

"No prob, Horatio. I'll drop it by your office on the way out."

"What next, H?" Speed asked. "You heading home, too?"

"No—I have one last stop tonight. . . ."

The interview room in the county lockup was even more spartan than the one at CSI HQ—gray concrete walls and simple metal table and chairs that gave the place a cold feeling during even the hottest of Florida summers.

Caine sat on one side of the table, the palm-size cassette player like a friendly brick in his jacket pocket.

He watched as a jailer brought Vincent Ciccolini— tall, with a movie-star presence his niece shared. The baby-faced guard uncuffed him and pointed to the chair opposite Caine.

"Vinnie," Caine said with a nod.

The eyes in the handsome face were bright and intelligent and something else . . . feral.

"Lieutenant Caine," Ciccolini said. "You'll have to ask the kid here to take off my cuffs, if you wanna go another round with me."

Caine smiled a little. "No thanks, Vinnie. I don't think I'd risk humiliating myself again. I don't imagine you've lost too many fights."

"No. But then, you'd be surprised how few I've ever really had."

Caine leaned back, folding his arms. "But a lot of fights have been fought for you, right, Vinnie? By guys like Abe Lipnick, and Tony Rosselli?"

"I'm a natural leader. What can I say?"

"And yet you're taking the fall this time . . . for a woman."

"I'm not taking any fall. And it's for family."

Caine counted—one finger. "We have you as the shooter." Two fingers. "We can place you at the scene." Three fingers. "We could convict you three times. You'll spend the rest of your life on death row, and maybe, just maybe, live long enough to die in the electric chair, or take lethal injection—pick one."

"Let me know when you get to where you want me to bust out crying."

"I can't offer you much, Vinnie. In fact, I can't offer you anything—but I can make a recommendation that will have weight. You can plea-bargain for a life sentence and do your time in the cushiest facility in the state—the country club where the white-collar crooks go."

Ciccolini grunted a laugh. "For which I give you what? Tony? Forget about it."

"Not Tony. I want Maria. She hired you to do this . . . or I should say, asked you to do this."

But Ciccolini was shaking his head before Caine

could even finish. "Lieutenant, if I did this thing—which I didn't—I woulda done it because some prick was a danger to my sweet little niece. She didn't put the thought in my head. She didn't have to fuckin' hint or nothin'. Nobody has to tell Vincent Ciccolini to whack a scumbag like Tommie Boy Lessor. If I whacked him. Which I didn't. . . . This visit's over."

And Ciccolini let the guard know that he was ready to go back to the lockup.

Soon Caine was watching as a jailer brought Anthony Rosselli in—slumped in his orange jumpsuit. The guard uncuffed the prisoner and indicated the chair opposite Caine.

The old man sat down across from the CSI; the mob hitter's goatee seemed more gray than Caine remembered it, and when Rosselli rubbed a hand over his bald head, he seemed very much like a tired old man, not some legendary hit man back in the game.

"Having trouble sleeping, Tony?"

Rosselli shrugged.

"Kinda surprising. What else is there to do in stir but rest?"

"What do you want, Caine?"

"Still, I can see it." Caine made a sympathetic click in one cheek. "Gotta be hard to be in here, your time of life."

The old man leveled his gaze at Caine, his eyes sharp and steady. "I got nothing to say to you. I'm here 'cause it gets me out of my cell."

"Fair enough," Caine said. He withdrew the cassette player out of his pocket and set it on the table between them. "I don't have anything to say to you, either. But Abe does."

Rosselli's eyes focused on the machine like he was staring down a cobra.

Caine pushed PLAY and Abraham Lipnick's (filtered) voice came through the small but clear speaker: "Maria says we should collar the tomcat at the airport. She says he's usin' a limo. Oh yeah, and Vinnie says bring Nixon and the sex perv."

"That . . . that's not Abe's voice. He was a marblemouth, since the stroke."

"Electronics can work magic. For instance, you can even erase your old cell phone messages, *if* you know how. Which you don't, right, Tony?"

Rosselli's eyes narrowed. "That . . . that's why the warrant, this afternoon."

"Bingo. Thanks to you and Abe, we can implicate Maria in this."

"Are you going to arrest her?"

"Yeah, we'll arrest her. That is, the Las Vegas cops'll do it for us."

"Vegas?"

"Ms. Chacon recently got her lucky break. Hadn't you heard? She says she has no intention of ever returning to Miami." Caine smiled thinly. "But we'll have a warrant that tells her otherwise."

"If you have her . . . why bother with me?"

"I think we can convict her on just that answer machine message. But if you were to spell out her role in this, chapter and verse . . . guaranteed, she'd be held over for an unlimited engagement. At the state pen."

A single tear trailed down the old man's cheek and his hands trembled on top of the table. His eyes went to his hands and he seemed to study them for a long time, almost as if he was trying to memorize them. Finally, Rosselli looked up at Caine. "I'm going to need a deal."

"I can recommend no death sentence."

That only made him smile, albeit sadly. "We're all under a sentence of death, young man—I'm just looking at a shorter one than you. That's not the kinda deal I need."

"I don't know what else I can say."

He swallowed thickly. "Maria was supposed to take care of Rebecca for me. You know—be there for her, help her through this. That was part of the deal—the little bitch wasn't supposed to run off to Vegas before we even went to trial."

"Deal," Caine said. "Tell me about the deal."

The old man shook his head. "Look, Lieutenant— Abe's dead, and at this age, a life sentence is short time for Vinnie and me. But I have a wife. I love her. How many years we got left together? I don't want to be without her. And she needs me."

"You should've thought of that before you came outa retirement."

"Wait and see how Medicare treats you, smart-ass. Here's how it's gotta lay: I cop to manslaughter, and you put me under house arrest. They put an ankle bracelet on me and I don't leave my home except to go to the doctor's and funerals and shit. You talk to the DA about that idea—and I'll give you chapter and verse. Soon as you bring me my deal."

"No guarantees."

The old man shrugged. "Guess it all comes down to how bad you want Maria. I might even throw in clearin' up all those old kills on the Jersey books, if I get immunity."

"See what I can do, Tony."

Rosselli nodded. "Hell of a thing, though."

"What is?"

"Goin' out of this life a fink. A guy in love'll do a lot of goddamn dumb things."

"I've met your wife. She's a lovely lady."

"You shoulda seen her in the Copa line. I still do—every time I look at her."

And Anthony Rosselli was led back to his cell.

By the time Caine was ready to call Catherine Willows, he was dressing to go into work bright and early the next morning. The team would be in, trying to wrap up the case in a big red bow for the DA's office, where the Rosselli plea bargain was already in the works.

He speed-dialed Catherine's number.

Casino sounds could be heard behind the familiar voice: "Catherine Willows."

"Horatio, Catherine. We're back where we started, only this time I need you to pick somebody up for me."

"Glad to, but I'm at a crime scene right now."

"No rush. I'll fax you the paperwork."

"Who's the pickup?"

"A singer named Maria Chacon. She was Thomas Lessor's other mistress."

". . . Someone put you up to this? Did Warrick—"

"No," Caine said. "This is straight up, Catherine. I

need you to get her for me; I'm not sure where she's staying, but it's likely the Oasis—"

"The Oasis is where I am now," Catherine said, her voice oddly measured. "In the lounge."

Caine hesitated. There was something in her tone. . . .

"And we are picking her up, Horatio . . . just not the way you mean."

Dread swept over Horatio Caine like a dry desert wind.

He gathered his team in the layout room. Calleigh looked wide awake, Delko and Speedle both clasped coffee cups like they were lifelines, and Alexx sat in the corner, a cup of tea in her hand.

Caine said, "Thanks for dropping everything and getting right here. I just wanted to let you know that the Maria Chacon aspect of the Lessor/Ortega case is closed."

"Why?" Calleigh asked, a frown creasing the brow of the perfect face. "There's nothing wrong with our evidence—"

Overlapping her, Speedle blurted, "But Vegas was gonna bust her for us!"

"Maria Chacon landed in Vegas, went straight to the Oasis Hotel and Casino, where a courtesy room awaited her. She changed and went down to the lounge to rehearse with her band for her new gig—opening tonight. She was in the middle of her rehearsal when Deborah Lessor walked onto the stage, said, 'Welcome to my husband's hotel,' and shot her three times in the chest."

Stunned silence draped the room.

"Maria died within minutes. Deborah Lessor sat at her feet, with a gun to her own head, crying. The band members did not have the courage to try to take the gun away from her . . ."

"Can't blame 'em," Speedle said.

". . . but the first officers on the scene were able to take the weapon away. Mrs. Lessor did not harm herself."

"She didn't do herself any favors," Calleigh said numbly.

"No, she didn't," Caine said. "Or us, either. I would have preferred to take Maria Chacon into custody to face whatever justice the system might offer her."

Reeling, Speedle said, "I didn't even think Mrs. Lessor knew about Maria and Tom Lessor."

"Nor did I. Daniel Boyle said he didn't tell his mother, but maybe he lied to me. Every other time he talked to us, he lied, after all. Or he may have called her after I spoke to him."

"She used to live here," Calleigh said, meaning Deborah Lessor. "A friend could have called."

"You taking Maria in for questioning," Delko said, "was all over the media, last night—including CNN."

"A mistake on my part," Caine said curtly. "Okay— we've cut a deal with Anthony Rosselli, but Vincent Ciccolini is still in line for Murder One. He's a bad man who's been waiting a long time for a real reckoning . . . so let's get all our ducks in a row, people."

Speedle, Delko, and Calleigh filed out, looking a little shell-shocked, and went their separate ways to finish their work. His plan was to cut them loose after lunch—they deserved and needed the break.

He turned to notice Alexx, still sitting in the corner, a Greek chorus that hadn't spoken yet, her white coat a striking contrast against her dark skin. She sipped her tea and waited for him to give her his full attention. After a long moment, she said, "It isn't really necessary, you know."

"What isn't?"

Slowly shaking her head, she said, "Horatio, who do you think you're talking to? You don't have to beat yourself up over Maria's murder."

He said nothing.

"Maria set this entire chain of events in motion by plotting to kill Thomas Lessor."

"Vigilante justice isn't justice. Revenge isn't justice."

She shrugged elaborately. "Not even close. Deborah Lessor committed murder, just like Maria Chacon did when she manipulated those old boys into killing her lover. Her actions also caused the death of a very innocent individual named Felipe Ortega."

"I could have prevented Maria Chacon's murder with a phone call."

Alexx laughed. "If Deborah Lessor wanted to murder Maria Chacon, do you really think your phone call would have stopped it?"

"There wouldn't have been an opportunity."

"Horatio. Truth is, if somebody is determined to murder somebody else . . . there's precious little any of us can do to stop it."

"We have to try."

"Of course we do. And when we can't stop it from

happening, the least we can do is make sure something like justice happens, afterward."

His eyes tensed. "Something like justice. . . ."

She came over and put a hand on his shoulder. "I'm just sayin', Horatio—you don't have to beat yourself up over this."

He nodded, managed a tiny smile for her, and she gave him a big warm smile as she walked out.

When she was gone, his smile vanished and he quietly said to no one but himself, "Yes I do."

Author's Note

I WOULD AGAIN LIKE to acknowledge the contribution of Matthew V. Clemens, my assistant on these novels.

Matt—who has collaborated with me on numerous published short stories—is an accomplished true crime writer; he helped me develop the plot of *Florida Getaway,* and worked up a lengthy story treatment, which included all of his considerable forensic research, from which I could work.

Matt also took a research trip to Miami, returning with extensive photographs and notes on locations and plot ideas for future *C.S.I.: Miami* stories.

Once again, criminalist Sergeant Chris Kaufman CLPE—the Gil Grissom of the Bettendorf Iowa Police Department—provided comments, insights and information that were invaluable to this project. A big thank you also to Victor Murillo, firearms section, Iowa DCI Criminalistics Laboratory.

Books consulted include two works by Vernon J. Gerberth: *Practical Homicide Investigation Checklist and Field Guide* (1997) and *Practical Homicide Investigation:*

Tactics, Procedures and Forensic Investigation (1996). Also helpful were *Scene of the Crime: A Writer's Guide to Crime-Scene Investigations* (1992), Anne Wingate, Ph.D, and *The Forensic Science of C.S.I.* (2001), Katherine Ramsland. Any inaccuracies, however, are my own.

Again, Jessica McGivney at Pocket Books provided support, suggestions and guidance. The producers of *C.S.I.: Miami* were gracious in providing scripts, background material and episode tapes, without which this novel would have been impossible.

Finally, Anthony E. Zuiker, Ann Donahue and Carol Mendelsohn are gratefully acknowledged as the creators of this concept and these characters. Thank you especially to Mr. Zuiker for allowing us to briefly incorporate characters from *C.S.I.: Crime Scene Investigation* into *Florida Getaway;* as the author of the C.S.I. novels, it was important to me to establish that these stories take place in one world. Our thanks to the other writers for *C.S.I.: Miami,* whose inventive and well-documented scripts inspired this novel and have done much toward making *C.S.I.: Miami* the rare spin-off worthy of its predecessor.

A MYSTERY WRITERS OF AMERICA "Edgar" nominee in both fiction and nonfiction categories, Collins has been hailed as "the Renaissance man of mystery fiction." His credits include five suspense-novel series, film criticism, short fiction, songwriting, trading-card sets and movie/TV tie-in novels, including *In the Line of Fire, Air Force One* and the *New York Times* bestselling *Saving Private Ryan*. His many books on popular culture include the award-winning *Elvgren: His Life and Art* and *The History of Mystery*, which was nominated for every major mystery award.

His graphic novel *Road to Perdition* is the basis of the acclaimed DreamWorks feature film starring Tom Hanks, Paul Newman and Jude Law, directed by Sam Mendes. He scripted the internationally syndicated comic strip *Dick Tracy* from 1977 to 1993, is cocreator of the comic-book features *Ms. Tree, Wild Dog,* and *Mike Danger,* has written the *Batman* comic book and newspaper strip, and several comics mini-series, including *Johnny Dynamite* and *CSI: Crime Scene Investigation,* based on the hit TV series for which he has also written a series of novels and a video game.

As an independent filmmaker in his native Iowa, he wrote and directed the suspense film *Mommy*, starring Patty McCormack, premiering on Lifetime in 1996, and a 1997 sequel, *Mommy's Day*. The recipient of a record six Iowa Motion Picture Awards for screenplays, he wrote *The Expert*, a 1995 HBO World Premiere; and wrote and directed the award-winning documentary *Mike Hammer's Mickey Spillane* (1999) and the innovative *Real Time: Siege at Lucas Street Market* (2000).

Collins lives in Muscatine, Iowa, with his wife, writer Barbara Collins; their son Nathan is a computer science major at the University of Iowa.

CSI:

CRIME SCENE INVESTIGATION™

THE COMPLETE FIRST SEASON ON DVD

**THIS SPECIAL EDITION
SET INCLUDES:**

·ALL 23 ORIGINAL,
UNCUT EPISODES FROM
THE FIRST SEASON.

·EXCITING
BONUS FEATURES:

·Character Profiles

·CSI Music Video
"Who Are You?"

·Featurette:
"People Lie... But The
Evidence Never Does"

OWN THE SEASON THAT STARTED IT ALL

IN STORES NOW

CRIME GOES GRAPHIC

CSI's unique visual approach is mirrored in the first CSI graphic novel by *New York Times* bestselling author Max Allan Collins with art by Gabriel Rodriguez and Ashley Wood. When a Jack the Ripper copycat terrorizes Las Vegas, it's all the CSI crew can do to keep up with the body count.

> *"Max Allan Collins, who wrote the graphic novel that inspired last summer's 'Road to Perdition,' brings a gritty feel to this IDW Publishing monthly miniseries."*
> – TV Guide

CSI: SERIAL GRAPHIC NOVEL
144 FULL COLOR PAGES • $19.99
ISBN: 1-932382-02-X

Also look for *CSI: Crime Scene Investigation— Thicker Than Blood* and *CSI: Crime Scene Investigation—Bad Rap*, on sale now, and *CSI Miami: Smoking Gun*, coming soon from IDW.

www.idwpublishing.com

CSI: Crime Scene Investigation is a trademark of CBS Worldwide, Inc and Alliance Atlantis Productions, Inc. The IDW logo is ™ 2003, Idea and Design Works, LLC.